Also by

FIONA BRAND

and MIRA BOOKS

KILLER FOCUS
DOUBLE VISION
BODY WORK
TOUCHING MIDNIGHT

BLIND
FIONA BRAND
INSTINCT

MIRA®

MIRA®

ISBN-13: 978-0-7783-2581-9
ISBN-10:   0-7783-2581-4

BLIND INSTINCT

Copyright © 2008 by Fiona Walker.

www.MIRABooks.com

Printed in U.S.A.

For Marion. The very best of friends.

Thank you to Jenny Haddon, a former bank regulator, for her invaluable advice about the world of international banking; Pauline Autet, for help with the French language; Claire Russell of the Kerikeri Medical Centre, for help with the medical details; Robyn Kingston, for lending me two wonderful books about spies and codes; and Tim and Simon Walker, for supplying ballistics and WWII military information. Thank you also to Miranda Stecyk for her professionalism and help with this trilogy.

Prologue

The drone of a Liberator B-24 bomber broke the silence of the forested hills and valleys that flowed like a dark blanket to the Langres Plateau. The plane dipped below ragged clouds that partially obscured the light of a full moon. Below, bonfires pinpointed the drop zone and a light flashed from the edge of the thick pine forest.

Morse code for "zero." The agreed signal.

The engine note deepened as the American aircraft banked and turned to make its drop. A pale shape bloomed against the night sky, growing larger as it floated to earth.

Icy air burned Marc Cavanaugh's lungs as he

stripped a leather glove from his right hand. Unfastening a flap pocket, he extracted a magazine for the Sten submachine gun that was slung across his chest and slotted it into place.

Fingers already numbed by the cold, he jerked on the parachute cords, steering himself toward the flashing pinpoint of light. He studied the thick swath of forest from which the signal had originated, the stretch of open country below—a plowed field bare of crops. As he lost altitude, detail rushed at him: a tree, wind-blasted and skeletal; a rock wall snaking across ground plowed into neat furrows; the glitter of frost.

Shadows flowed across the field. Jacques de Vallois's men—he hoped.

Marc jerked on the cords, slowing and controlling his descent then braced for landing. Seconds later, he unlatched the harness and shrugged out of the straps. Stepping away from the distracting brightness of the chute, he dropped into a crouch, the Sten pointed in the direction of a flickering shadow to his right.

"Benis soient les doux."

Blessed are the meek.

Cavanaugh let the muzzle of the gun drop, but only fractionally. *"Car ils hériteront de la terre."*

For they shall inherit the earth.

"De Vallois."

White teeth flashed and metal gleamed as de Vallois lowered a Schmeisser MP40. "At your service."

A brief handshake later, de Vallois barked orders at his men. A former attaché of de Gaulle, de Vallois was formidably skilled in clandestine operations. One of the architects of the French Resistance, he had worked tirelessly refining their systems and training recruits. It was unlikely that his efforts would be fully recognized during his lifetime, but de Vallois's determination was unshaken. He lived for *la France,* and he would die for her.

De Vallois said something in rapid French. With economical movements, two of his men gathered up the chute, which glowed with a ghostly incandescence. Within minutes the field was clear, the bonfires doused.

De Vallois jerked his head. *"Allons-y!"* Let's go.

Seconds later they were beneath the cover of the pines.

The parachute was buried in a hole that had been previously dug and the disturbed ground was covered over with a thick scattering of pine needles. As high a price as the silk would command in Lyon or Dijon, the risk of being searched while transporting the parachute was too high and de Vallois's men too valuable to risk. With the recent incarceration and execution of key Resistance figures, Himmler's SS and the Geheime Staats Polizei—the Gestapo—were actively hunting insurgents and traitors against the Nazi Regime.

Half an hour later, they walked free of the trees and stepped onto a stony track. De Vallois checked his watch, then signaled them off the road.

Lights swept across the bare fields. An armored truck rumbled past.

Long minutes passed. De Vallois grunted. "Come. That is the last patrol of the night. Even the SS have to sleep."

Marc stepped up onto the road. The cloud cover had broken up, leaving the night even colder and very clear. Moonlight illuminated the barren fields and a stark avenue of pines.

Jacques grinned at the exposure. "Don't worry—my information is exact. My people understand that many lives are at stake."

A truck, its headlights doused, cruised out of a side road and halted beside them. Jacques opened the passenger door and gestured for Marc to climb in. "The only thing I can't guard against is a traitor."

One

Mae Fischer flicked on her bedside lamp and shook her husband's shoulder, the pressure urgent.

Ben's eyes flipped open, instantly alert. "She's sleepwalking again."

"And talking."

"Damn." He thrust out of bed in time to see his seven-year-old daughter, Sara, dressed in pink flannel pajamas, her long, dark braid trailing down her spine, drift past his bedroom door. He walked out onto the landing as she came to a halt alongside the landing rail, staring fixedly at something only she could see.

Since the phenomenon had started several months ago, they had blocked off the stairs with the wooden gate they had used for her when she was tiny. There was no danger of her falling down the stairs, but he lived in fear that she would either climb the gate or fall over the landing rail. The drop to the hardwood floor below was a good twelve feet. At the very least, she would break bones.

She unlocked an invisible door, stepped "inside" and knelt down. He watched, resisting the urge to shake her awake or simply scoop her up and carry her back to bed.

Their family doctor had warned them against waking her suddenly. Apparently the shock could be dangerous. A specialist, Dr. Dolinski, had seconded the opinion. Ben wasn't certain what *dangerous* meant, exactly, but he had assumed Dolinski was talking about physical shock, maybe even a seizure of some kind.

Mae seemed to have even less understanding of her daughter's condition than Ben did. At times, she was actively frightened by Sara's episodes which was why, confused as he was by what was happening to his daughter, he had taken over dealing with the situation.

Soft lamplight poured from the bedroom as he crouched down beside her. The blank expression on her face and the intensity of her gaze sent a shaft of fear through him. "Sara, honey, you can wake up now. It's only a dream."

Talk softly, and keep talking. Bring her back slow, that had been Dolinski's advice. Don't do anything that might jolt her out of that state.

His heart squeezed tight as he watched her repeat actions he had seen her do a number of times. Her movements were smooth and precise as she reached into some invisible cupboard, pulled out an invisible book and leafed through to a page. When she was finished, she replaced the book, locked the cabinet, pushed to her feet, walked a few steps, then appeared to close another door and lock it. She placed the "keys" she had used on what he had decided was an imaginary shelf, a part of the landscape she had created on the landing that must be, to her, as solid and real as the walls and rooms of this house.

She paused and stared in the direction of her room, a sharp, adult expression on her face. For a split second he had the unnerving impression that he was looking at someone else, not his daughter. The notion made him go cold inside as she drifted back in the direction of her room.

But crazy as her actions seemed, he didn't think Sara was suffering from a personality disorder. He recognized what she was doing, and she repeated the same actions over and over again.

His theory, developed over months of observation, was even crazier than Dolinski's. To most people—civilians—what was happening to Sara was simply weird, but to Ben, an ex-Naval officer, the actions formed a familiar pattern. Sara's symptoms pointed to a particular diagnosis that shouldn't have affected a seven-year-old child.

His father had suffered battle fatigue after the Second World War, and Ben himself had seen and heard about enough cases firsthand. For the past few months he had done extensive research on the effects of posttraumatic stress syndrome. He had talked to old soldiers and visited veteran's hospitals. It wasn't unusual for soldiers to relive battles in their dreams, night after night, going over and over the same incident, as if the scene had been burned so deeply into their minds that they couldn't forget or move past it.

He'd had his own share of posttraumatic stress

syndrome after the Gulf War. Sleepwalking was rare, but there were documented cases.

He shadowed Sara as she made an invisible turn, his attention sharpening. This was something new.

He watched as she shrugged into an invisible coat and wound what seemed to be a scarf around her throat. Her head came up and the remote expression on her face turned to terror.

"Rouge."

He frowned. "Sara?"

She looked directly at him, her gaze once more sharply adult, but he had the distinct impression that she didn't register him; she was looking at another face.

She spoke clearly and precisely. The content and the language she used—German—chilled him. A name registered: Stein.

He watched as she unwound the invisible scarf. "Who is Stein?"

Her face went blank, and for a moment he thought she wasn't going to answer. The technique of trying to enter into the dream, to defuse the grip it held on his daughter, had so far proved spectacularly unsuccessful. It seemed that when she dreamed she was literally locked into another world and, short of physically intervening by shaking her awake, he couldn't reach her.

She fixed him with an eerie gaze. "Stein?" she said in a coldly accented voice that shook him to the core. *"Geheime Staats Polizei."*

All the fine hairs at the back of his neck lifted. Sara was his daughter; he loved her fiercely, and yet, in that moment she was not, by any stretch of the imagination, his cute, lovable little girl.

"Stein's dead," he said softly. "You don't have to worry about him anymore. The war's over. We won."

He kept talking, relating what his own father had told him about the Second World War, emphasizing several times that the Allies had won. It had hurt, it still hurt, but they were okay now. They would never let the mistakes that had led to the horror of the Second World War be repeated.

He didn't know if what he was saying was penetrating the world she was locked into, or if he was making any sense, because talking to Sara as if she had actually *been* there didn't make any kind of sense. But if even a fragment got through, it could help.

She blinked, and the terrible tension left her face. She stared at him, the dream Sara abruptly *there,* with him, her gaze incisive. For the first time, he had the impression that he was finally making headway, even if this uncanny "grown-up" Sara still shook him.

Dolinski had mentioned the possibility of multiple personalities, but Ben had never been prepared to believe that. His daughter was tall for her age, already strong willed and with a sharp intelligence. Today, she had spent most of the afternoon down at the swimming hole with her cousin, Steve, and the Bayard kid who had moved in next door. Sara had been calling the shots, and that was typical. She had a natural knack for organization and command. To him, the "sleep" personality was recognizably Sara.

"Did you hear what she *said?*"

"Not now, Mae," Ben said calmly, his gaze still locked on Sara's, but the high pitch of Mae's voice had shattered the fragile bridge he'd built. He had been so close—

Sara blinked at him, in an instant shifting from eerily self-possessed to sleepy and bewildered. "Did I walk again?"

The fear in her eyes tugged at his heart. He scooped her up, walked to her room and placed her in her bed. "Just a little, but it's okay. I got you, honey. It's over now."

Sara's gaze clung to his as he tucked her in, taking her through the comforting bedtime routine, even though it was after midnight. He didn't know how much of the experiences she retained. Before tonight he would have said none, but now he wasn't so sure. Something had changed in that moment he had made contact with her inner world. He had thought about the contact as a bridge. If that was the case, then he had finally made a start at crossing it and maybe neutralizing whatever it was that was upsetting her.

"What's *Geheime Staa*—" She frowned. "I said that, didn't I? When I was sleepwalking."

"It doesn't matter, honey. It was just a dream." He gripped her hand and gently squeezed it. "This is what matters, this is real."

But he was beginning to think they had a bigger problem than Dolinski had outlined in his reports. He was no longer certain the therapy sessions were helping. Building a bridge to the core of the stress that created the behavior was all very well, but he would prefer that Sara forgot whatever it was that was upsetting her.

Ben sat on the edge of the bed, keeping a

watch on his daughter to make sure it *was* over. Within minutes her eyelids drooped and she sank into an exhausted sleep.

Mae had gone back to bed. He should follow her, but even if he climbed between the sheets, he didn't know if he could sleep.

Sara was a highly intelligent, creative child. After extensive physical and mental testing, Dolinski was convinced she was suffering from some kind of mental stress that had been brought on by an event that had made a shocking and indelible impression. Perhaps a graphic scene witnessed on television at a time when she was feeling especially vulnerable, or even in real life. Unable to cope with what she had seen, her mind had sublimated the event and the sleepwalking occurred when fragments kept surfacing in dreams.

According to Dolinski, dreams were a "safe" level to process unpalatable information, or create an acceptable context for an event, so the mind could absorb the information and move on. In his opinion, as upsetting as Sara's symptoms were, they would fade with time. Young children were mentally tougher than most people gave them credit for—they bounced back when adults crumbled. He could see no reason why Sara should be the exception to the rule.

Ben had been happy to go along with Dolinski's optimism. His explanations had seemed logical and scientific, and they had been backed by several impressive diplomas on his office wall. Now he was forced to revise that opinion.

He was no authority on mental disorders—or, for that matter, psychic phenomena. But over the past few months, he had read exhaustively on both subjects. As difficult to understand as many of the mental conditions were, at least they seemed to have identifiable causes and were researched and presented in a logical, scientific manner. Most of the material in books on psychic phenomena had been presented with a distinct lack of methodology or any kind of scientific or logical grounding.

As open as he had tried to keep his mind, he'd had difficulty buying into theories that seemed as wild and crackpot as some of the psychic conditions described. But a certain category of "cases" had uncannily mirrored what was happening to Sara.

Past-life memories.

He hadn't mentioned the concept to Mae.

Getting his head around the idea that Sara could have lived a previous life, and that the memories of that life were filtering into this one, made *him* feel like a crackpot. But for her sake, he had to open his mind to possibilities that he would normally dismiss.

First fact: she was seven years old and she could speak French and German—two languages in which she had received no formal instruction. Ben knew a smattering of both of those languages from his time in the Navy, enough to conduct some basic conversation. But even allowing for the fact that Sara could have picked up a little of either language from other kids at school, she shouldn't be capable of the sophisticated syntax she had used while sleepwalking. And if she could speak a small amount of French and German, why hadn't they ever heard her doing so while she was awake?

Secondly, any normal American kid mentioning Germany's historic secret police would have used the popular term *Gestapo, if* they had known about it at all, not the full name, *Geheime Staats Polizei.*

Thirdly, when Sara was sleepwalking, Ben had the distinct impression that she was not a child. Her actions were smooth, controlled and precise, the expression on her face chillingly adult.

In his mind, those three facts added up to the kind of proof no one would believe—certainly not Dolinski.

Ben was convinced his seven-year-old daughter wasn't mentally unstable and that she hadn't witnessed a shocking event either at home or at school. However, he did believe she *was* suffering from posttraumatic stress syndrome—but from another place, and another time.

Specifically, occupied France in the Second World War.

Her eyes flipped open, disconcerting him. "I don't want to be like this, Daddy."

He let out a breath he hadn't been aware he was holding. Her voice was normal, her expression that of a child. The sharp, incipient Sara who had lifted all the hairs at his nape and upset Mae wasn't in evidence. "Then don't be, honey. Just tell yourself, 'I'm Sara Fischer, I'm seven years old, and the only place I have ever lived is Shreveport, Louisiana.' Repeat it after me, then when you go back to sleep it'll be true."

"What if it isn't?"

"*You* have to make it happen—inside your head. Remember what Dr. Dolinski said? Whenever you're frightened, just tell yourself not to have the dreams."

"I like the way you say it better. I'll do that."

The crispness of her decision was disconcertingly close to her sleepwalking voice. "Do you ever remember any of the dreams?"

She turned her head on the pillow, and he realized she was checking to make sure Mae wasn't in the room or lurking at the door. "Sometimes."

His chest tightened. This was the first time she had admitted that she remembered anything, and the reason was obvious. Mae's reaction, and probably the visits to Dolinski, had frightened her. "What are you doing when you kneel down and reach into the cupboard?"

"Getting the book. I have to get words, but only one word at a time."

"Can you remember what the book is?"

She shook her head.

So, okay, not too detailed. He didn't know whether that was a blessing or not. But like it or not, the "memories," if that was what they were, had already changed Sara, and he was very much afraid that they were here to stay.

Abruptly his mind was clear. He had tried

Dolinski's method for long enough and it wasn't easing the situation. In fact, he was certain the "bridging" tactic was making the dreams more acute. From now on he was going to do this his way. He would teach her a technique he had learned during his years of active service in the Gulf. The technique was straight-down-the-line-simple. He was going to teach Sara how to forget.

Two

Sara Fischer hooked her handbag over her shoulder, dried her hands and paused at the night-club's washroom counter to check her makeup and her hair.

She frowned at a face that was faintly exotic and sophisticated, and subtly *not* her, courtesy of the makeover her mother had given her as an eighteenth birthday gift.

Mae Fischer adored shopping, lunching and parties. The fact that Sara would rather take long solitary walks or bury her head in a book was incomprehensible to her mother. The harder Mae worked to break Sara out of what she called "her shell," the more Sara resisted. They were mother and daughter and they loved one another, but they were like chalk and cheese. Sara was far more comfortable with her father's company and his quiet acceptance of the way she was.

She made her way back to the table she occupied with her cousin Steve, his latest girlfriend, Cherie and Marc Bayard, Steve's best friend, who was back from Baton Rouge for the weekend. Steve and Cherie were absent from the table, which meant they were part of the raucous, gyrating crowd on the dance floor, leaving her alone with Bayard—alone as anyone could be in a nightclub packed to capacity.

Bayard got to his feet, towering over her as he pulled out her chair. A familiar tension locked her jaw as she sat down. She had known Bayard for years, although they didn't often cross paths now. He was two years older, from an old and extremely wealthy "cotton" family.

A law student at LSU, and on the college football team, by definition, he was popular. The fact that he was also tall and dark, with the signature Bayard good looks—dark eyes, chiseled cheekbones and tough jaw—and that she'd had a crush on him since he had moved next door when she was seven, didn't make him any easier to be with. Steve's idea of a blind date as a birthday gift couldn't have gone more horribly wrong.

"Would you like to dance?"

Her cheeks burned with embarrassment. She was certain Bayard had a steady girlfriend and that he should be with her rather than here on a mercy date. "To be honest, I'd like to go home."

"Stay here a minute, I'll tell Steve we're leaving."

"No, *wait*. I can get a cab."

But he had already gone. Seconds later he was back. Looping the strap of her bag over her shoulder, she rose to her feet. His fingers slid through hers, the contact unexpected and faintly shocking as he pulled her through the crowd. When they stepped outside, he didn't relinquish his hold. Instead of heading for the parking garage, he pulled her in the direction of the river. "Let's walk for a few minutes. I need to clear my head."

A cold breeze straight off the water sifted through her hair and sent a damp chill sliding over her skin. Mist swirled, curling up and over the bank to lie in drifts across the road, muting the syncopated flash of casino lights.

"Cold?" Seconds later, his leather jacket dropped around her shoulders.

A small shudder at the transition from cold to blazing warmth went through her. The old saying, *Someone is walking over my grave,* ran through her mind.

She pulled the lapels of the jacket together, both relieved and irrationally disappointed that Bayard was no longer holding her hand. That presupposed that she had *wanted* him to hold her hand, and there was no way she was going there. She wasn't big on setting herself up for a fall.

She'd had boyfriends, although no one she had wanted to get too up-close-and-personal with. Her mother worried that she was emotionally cold. Sara had another theory. When it came to men and relationships, she was naturally reserved, but she wasn't without feelings. She *liked* the men she dated; she just didn't love them. The people she did love—the members of her family—she loved fiercely and without reserve. One day she would fall in love and that would be it; she would have chosen her mate. Until that moment happened, if she couldn't drum up any enthusiasm for her dates, she wasn't going to worry about it.

Bayard slowed, then came to a halt on a small footbridge that led into a picnic area. When she stopped beside him, his long fingers curled into the lapels of the jacket. His dark eyes fastened on hers as he pulled her loosely against him. "If you don't want this, just say so."

As his head dipped, her stomach lurched. A kiss: she had not seen that coming.

She stared at his mouth and panic hit. If he kissed her they would cross a line, and she wasn't sure she wanted to go there. As frustrating as her crush on Bayard was, at least it was controllable, and safe. "Did Steve put you up to this?"

A high-pitched scream jerked his head around. He said something short and succinct. "Wait here."

Two youths—one with long, greasy blond hair, an iron bar held in a two-handed grip, the other shorter, with dark hair, holding a knife—had backed two young women up against a park bench.

Bayard grabbed the one with the iron bar, knocked the bar out of his hand and flung him to the ground. The guy with the knife wheeled, spitting abuse. The two young women scrabbled for their purses, which had fallen to the ground, and ran toward a lighted parking lot.

Sara watched, heart in her mouth, as the knife wove through the air. Another figure darted out of the cover of a clump of trees. Adrenaline pumped, Bayard was easily strong enough to take on two attackers, but not three, and the knife tilted the odds against him.

Without thinking, she darted forward, letting the jacket slide from her shoulders, and grabbed the iron bar. Bayard spun, his gaze locked with hers for a split second. A blow from the blond guy, who had pushed to his feet, caught him on the jaw, rocking his head back. The knife arced and for a dizzying moment time seemed to stop. Emotion roared through her. The iron bar chopped down on the knife-wielding thug's arm, the shock of the blow numbing her fingers. The bar spun away. Fingers closed in her hair, jerking her sideways. A split second later, her attacker was on the ground. Bayard had laid him out with one well-timed punch.

The short, dark guy had disappeared. The third youth, a carbon copy of the greasy blond, jerked his friend to his feet. Within seconds they had melted into the trees.

Bayard picked up the knife and tossed it into a nearby trash can, his dark eyes glittering. "You should have stayed out of it. You could have been hurt."

"What I did worked out." She massaged her

scalp, which was stinging. Her head felt weird, throbbing and heavy.

"You *are* hurt."

She glanced down, saw the dark stain on her side, and registered that she was bleeding.

Bayard dragged the flimsy silk top up. Reaction shivered through her as he probed the cut across her midriff. Now that she knew it was there, the stinging pain made her eyes water.

"It's long, but it's just a scratch. You won't need stitches, but you'll probably end up with a scar." He shrugged out of his shirt, and folded it into a pad. "Is your tetanus shot up to date?"

"I had one last year when I cut my foot swimming in the river."

The sweet scent of blood filled her nostrils. Bayard's warmth swamped her as he tied the makeshift bandage around her waist. Her eyes squeezed shut as the pressure in her head tightened another notch.

Icy water flowing. Rank upon rank of dark pines.

Cavanaugh…bandaging the deepest cuts. Then they were moving, skirting tracts of open land that glowed, stark and bare beneath the moon. Cavanaugh babying her along, his arm around her waist—

Not Cavanaugh...*Bayard.*

Her eyes popped open again. She stared at Bayard, the moment of recognition shocking in its intensity.

Bayard frowned. "Who?"

It registered that she must have said the name, Cavanaugh, out loud. She blinked, shaking off the weird, shifting sense of déjà vu, the clinging tendrils of that dreamworld.

"Damn. Steve said you weren't dating."

His hands closed on her hips, his mouth brushed hers, clung, and the memories evaporated in a raw surge of heat.

Sound burst from her throat, smothered and urgent. Her fingers dug into the smooth pliant muscle of his shoulders. Her breasts were flattened against his chest. She could feel the firm shape of his arousal pressing into her belly. One hand gripped her nape, the other cupped her bottom, uncomplicatedly carnal. He hauled her hard against him, and the concept that she was emotionally cold and incapable of feeling passion dissolved in a white-hot flash.

Her arms closed convulsively around his neck. A split second later she was off the ground, her feet dangling, the short skirt pushed up around her hips. A short, sharp shock went through her as she felt Bayard, hot and heavy, between her legs. The constraints of his jeans and her panties aside, if he got any closer they would be making love.

His mouth lifted, sank again, taking her under. She gasped for air, breathing in his heat, his scent. She felt as if she was drowning, *dying...*

Cold, pure air, burned her lungs. Harsh light bounced off towering peaks. Numbing pain, like a vise crushing her chest.

A detonation, echoing...

Shock spasmed through her. She jerked free, stumbling back a step. Bayard's fingers closed around her arms. If he hadn't grabbed her, she would have fallen.

"What's wrong? What is it? Was I hurting you?"

"No."

Yes.

She had *died.*

Her heart was pounding. On an intellectual level, she knew that if she had memories of a previous life, then of course she had to have died. How else could she be here now? But in all the time she had dreamed and remembered shadowy, insubstantial fragments of that past life she had never remembered the moment of her death.

Nausea rose at the back of her throat. She pushed free, needing the distance. With shaky fingers she smoothed her skirt down around her thighs. Her mouth felt swollen. She could still taste Bayard; her body was throbbing. But the emotion was somehow entwined with the memory of her death.

She couldn't say, "I remember you, but not from here, now."

The phenomenon had stopped, years ago, when she was twelve.

The year Bayard had gone away to boarding school.

Comprehension hit. The answer so simple she wondered she hadn't seen it before. The dreams had started when she was seven. The year the Bayard family had moved into the big house next door. In that first year, Steve, who lived less than a mile away, and Marc had become inseparable, and Marc Bayard had become a part of the Fischer family. *Until he had turned twelve and gone away to boarding school in Baton Rouge.*

Ever since then she had been *normal*. The memories, the visits to specialists, had become a part of her past. She had almost forgotten them, and she had needed to forget.

Now, Bayard had walked back into her life and suddenly she was remembering again. And more sharply, more distinctly.

She dragged her gaze from Bayard's jaw and the memory of that hot, crazy kiss. His face was shuttered; he probably thought she was insane. She had lost count of the number of times she had considered the possibility herself. There was no way he wouldn't have heard at least the basic details of her illness. Living in such close proximity, it was a cast-iron certainty that Mae Fischer had shared her worries with Mariel Bayard.

"Sara—" Bayard reached for her hand.

She evaded his grip on the pretext that she needed to retrieve his jacket. She bent and picked up the buttery soft leather, wincing as the cut throbbed. "You'd better have your jacket back."

She pressed her hand to her side where blood was leaking through the makeshift bandage.

Bayard draped the leather jacket over her shoulders. "You need it more than I do."

The fleeting pressure of his touch, his clean masculine scent enfolding her, was a reminder of what they had been doing just minutes ago, and how close she had come to more. A part of her still craved him, which was doubly crazy. She stepped away, pointedly avoiding any further contact.

His gaze was remote. "It's all right, I won't touch you."

That's right, don't touch me. Don't come within a mile of me.

It had taken her years to recover from the dreams, the horror that had pushed through into her life. She still had trouble with the night, and sleeping.

She wanted Bayard, but she couldn't allow him near her again. She couldn't afford him.

The trip home was awkward. The evening was mild, but she couldn't get warm despite the jacket and the heater switched on. Half an hour later, Bayard dropped her back at her house. He waited until she made it to the porch and stepped inside the front hall before reversing and heading down the drive.

Cavanaugh.

The stark moment of recognition shivered through her again.

She had remembered Bayard. That fact alone was stunning. If someone from that previous life was going to be in her life now, why wasn't it someone like her parents or Steve?

She watched until the sweep of Bayard's headlights disappeared. She didn't know anyone by the name of Cavanaugh, although she was sure that if she checked the phone book, she would find a long list. Not that she was going to do that. As far as she was concerned the past was the past and it could stay there; she didn't want it in either her present or her future.

She was Sara Fischer in this life, but in the Second World War she knew with flat certainty that she had been someone else—an English spy called Sara Weiss. Beyond that basic recall, and the blurred memories of dreams, she didn't have many concrete details. By the age of eight, annoyed by the disruptive effect of Dr. Dolinsky's tactics, her father had taught her what he had termed "applied amnesia." In effect, how to dismiss and forget the dreams. For several weeks every time she woke from a dream, her father had instantly distracted her by reading her chapters of a novel until she fell asleep. By the time they had worked their way through the full set of a popular series of children's mysteries, she had learned the knack of not thinking about the dreams. With-

out the strong link created by repeatedly recall-
ing the dreams, or talking about them, they had
literally dissolved so that, if she thought of them
at all, all she remembered was that she had
dreamed, not the content.

Her father didn't know it, and he wouldn't be
happy if she told him, but she had made some en-
quiries about Sara Weiss, and found that she had
existed, the daughter of a German businessman
and a Frenchwoman, who had been resident in
England. She had died in 1943, although she
hadn't ever been able to find any details about her
death.

Finding out that Sara Weiss had existed had
been a jolt. Up until that point, the idea that she
was remembering actual events had been a purely
cerebral reality, with no grounding in fact.

She had conducted a search on the Internet.
Seeing the name listed in black and white, the
details of a life that uncannily mirrored her own
in terms of interests and education, then discovering that Sara Weiss had died while in her early
thirties, had shaken her.

Somewhere there would be a grave. Proof of
a life lived and lost. A life that still lingered on
in her mind.

Accepting that reality was difficult enough. Being confronted with a physical link to that past in the form of Bayard was a complication she didn't need.

Three

Washington, D.C.,
Present Day

Two dead, and counting.

Marc Bayard, Assistant Director of Special Projects at National Intelligence, studied the loading zone outside the entrance to the D.C. Morgue as he stepped out of an unmarked departmental car. Agent Matt Bridges flanked him as they walked inside, automatically drifting to Marc's left and staying a half step behind, covering the firing arcs and Marc's back while staying out of the way of his right hand.

Bridges wasn't assigned bodyguard duty, and Marc didn't normally need the protection. He worked out regularly and he carried weapons. The Glock 19 was nothing exotic, just down-home firepower that was proven and reliable. These days he wasn't often in the front line. If anyone wanted to take him out, the maneuver was generally an interdepartmental or a political one, but risk was inherent in the job, so he kept his hand in. His choice of backup weapon was a six-inch blade strapped to his ankle. Not many people knew he had the knife or that he was proficient with it, which suited Marc. Living in D.C. amongst the suits and the political-speak, people saw what he projected, not the lean, fit Louisiana boy who knew his way around the woods. To coin a pun, the knife was his edge.

The dry chill of air-conditioning matched the blank neutrality of the decor as they stopped at the reception desk. A short conversation later and an orderly appeared with a clipboard. Marc checked his watch as they were directed down a corridor and into a room. He'd cut one meeting, and put a second on hold. If it *was* Jim Corcoran who had been brought in, he would clear his schedule for the afternoon.

Corcoran had been with Marc in the FBI. Marc had headhunted him when he'd made the move to National Intelligence to head the task force that had been assigned to take down two key criminal organizations: the Chavez cartel, headed by Alex Lopez, and a secretive political cabal formed decades ago by ex-SS officers.

Apart from the fact that Corcoran was a damned good agent and a friend, he was a crucial link in Marc's team. He had been personally responsible for tracking down and indicting over two hundred members of Lopez's network and shutting the cartel down along most of the Eastern Seaboard. Among the arrests had been officials in a raft of government departments, but he had bagged a couple of bigger fish—notably, two federal agents.

The door to the morgue swung closed behind him. The cold pungent smell, laced with chemical, made his jaw clench. He had known Corcoran for more than ten years. He had been invited to dinner at Jim's house and had attended his wedding and his daughter's christening. Losing Jim wouldn't just be a blow to his team; it would hurt.

The room was congested with morgue personnel and D.C.'s finest: two uniforms and a detective, who introduced himself as Dan Herschel.

Marc moved smoothly through the formalities. The two uniforms had gotten to the scene first, then Herschel had taken the case. But Marc's attention was on the two bodies residing on narrow metal tables, both encased in body bags.

The medical examiner, a slim fiftysomething woman with taut features and tired eyes, unzipped the PVC far enough that Marc could view the first face.

Shit. Fuck.

Corcoran.

The second body was that of a woman who had gotten caught in the crossfire. PVC peeled open over pale skin, dark hair and delicate cheekbones.

Sara.

Time seemed to slow, stop. Blood pounded through his veins in quick, hard strokes.

The panic was irrational. It wasn't Sara Fischer. She was safely locked into her life in Shreveport, Louisiana. He had seen her just weeks ago at her father's funeral. This woman was younger, in her early twenties, and her hair was black, not dark brown, but for long seconds those facts failed to make any difference.

A phone beeped, the sound harsh and discordant. The M.E. backed off a few steps to take the call, and Marc focused on Detective Herschel reciting facts with flat precision as he read from notes.

Corcoran had walked to a café to get lunch. The woman had been entering as Corcoran was leaving and had simply gotten in the way. The gunman had shot her first, then hit Corcoran, one to the chest, a second shot to the head. The hit had been very fast, very precise. Hampered by a paper bag and a foam cup, Corcoran hadn't had time to reach for his gun.

Marc dragged his gaze from the dead woman's face. With every second that passed she looked less and less like Sara. "Witnesses?"

"The café owner saw what happened, but only from inside the building. We're working on tracing some of the regular customers who were eating at the tables outside."

"Any description of the shooter?"

"Male, medium height, dark hair that's graying at the temples. No facial details because he was wearing a mask."

Lopez. Was it possible? "Security tape footage?"

Herschel had backed off a step. "Yes, sir, from two angles. A bank across the road and a traffic camera."

"I'll need to see both, now. And talk to the café owner."

The quick tap of heels was followed by the muted swish of the doors swinging open. Jennifer Corcoran, accompanied by a uniformed police-woman, stepped into the morgue. Her face was white, her eyes stark and already red rimmed and swollen from crying.

When she saw Marc, her mouth trembled. He reached her in two strides and held her tight, while Bridges cleared the room. The M.E. stepped back but didn't leave, her face apologetic. Marc didn't labor the point. As private as this moment was, there were formalities to be completed; she had to stay.

Two hours later, Marc stepped into his office, dropped his briefcase on his desk and jerked at the knot of his tie.

Both tapes and the café owner's recollection had been inconclusive. The tapes had been blurred by distance and obscured by traffic and passers-by. The mask the shooter had been wearing had successfully blanked out his features. Aside from the fact that he was approximately five-ten, dark-haired and no longer young, they had nothing.

Bridges's jaw was grim as he strolled over to the coffee machine in the corner of his office. "So, what now?"

Marc shrugged out of his jacket and peeled off the shoulder rig. A raft of paperwork, a press release, sat on his desk: damage control. "I'm pulling my people off the team."

Two agents dead within a fortnight wasn't enough to establish that Lopez was systematically killing men *Marc* had handpicked. A third killing would cement the pattern, but damned if he would risk losing anyone else.

The first, Powdrell, had been an experienced field agent. Corcoran had been a step up into the executive ranks. The disparity in rank aside, both of the men had been ex-FBI, headhunted by Marc. He had known them personally, and they had both chosen to move from the Bureau to National Intelligence on the strength of that personal loyalty. Maybe it was just a coincidence that "his" people were being targeted, but Marc didn't think so.

Lopez was cold and methodical. Aside from the seemingly random killing of his own bodyguard at age twelve in Colombia, to Bayard's knowledge, Lopez hadn't made one move without good reason. In light of his consistent methodology, he was certain that first killing hadn't been carried out in a psychotic fit of rage, either. At age twelve, Lopez—then known as Alejandro Chavez—had been experimenting with execution.

The unprovoked killing had set off a chain of events that still reverberated. In order to extract Alex from prison, his father, Marco Chavez, had literally held the country to ransom, machine-gunning three villages then manipulating a pardon for Alex with the donation of a hospital. Following the wave of hatred for the Chavez cartel, and the death threats that had followed Alex's release, Marco had been forced to remove his son from the country. Courtesy of the power and influence of the Nazi cabal, which had strong links with Marco, Alex had started a new life in the States under the name Lopez.

Once in the States, protected and bankrolled by the cabal, Alex had thrived, heading up the American branch of the Chavez cartel and expanding into the international terrorism market. Until that point the relationship between the cartel and the Nazi cabal had been stable and mutually beneficial. In 1984, however, with the

theft of billions of dollars from Lopez's main operating account, the balance of power had shifted.

In order to avert his own possible execution for
the massive loss of cartel funds, Lopez had
traveled to Colombia, murdered the only person
who could order his death—his father—and
taken control of the cartel. He had saved his own
skin, but, heavily in debt, and with rival cartels
circling, Lopez had been forced to go, cap in
hand, to the cabal in order to survive.

The cost of survival had been servitude, something Lopez had never had a talent for. As lethal
as an asp, approximately eighteen months previously, he had manipulated his cabal "keepers,"
threatening exposure of their secretive and politically powerful organization if they didn't allow
him entrance into their upper echelon. The cabal
had acted swiftly, executing their own people in
order to neutralize the threat and setting a trap to
take down Lopez. But with federal agencies—including Interpol, MI6 and Mossad—now locked
onto both Lopez and the cabal, the damage
control was too late.

A missile blast in Colombia had vaporized the
Chavez fortress, located in Macaro, hundreds of
miles east from Bogotá. Unfortunately, the cabal

had missed killing Lopez and his right-hand man, former FBI agent Edward Dennison, by seconds. A further attempt to take Lopez out at a meeting in El Paso had also failed, and resulted in a state of war between the two organizations. Lopez had escaped, taking a wounded Dennison and his leverage with him—a book that exposed the cabal members. He had also left behind an interesting array of corpses—one of them Senator Radcliff, a bona fide, paid up member of the cabal's upper echelon.

Lopez had gone underground, only to surface months later as the lead suspect in a series of clever murders, which had systematically decimated the upper echelon of the cabal, leaving one lone member—the powerful but elusive Helene Reichmann, daughter of Heinrich Reichmann, the original architect of the cabal.

The series of murders had been chilling and effective, demonstrating Lopez's power and destroying a number of leads in Bayard's investigation. Ultimately, the murders had proved to be a godsend, throwing the workings of the cabal wide and providing a huge investigative platform that meant Marc had been able to systematically take down both the cabal and Lopez's networks.

The rich scent of coffee filled the office, over-laying the faint, lingering scents of the morgue that still clung to his clothes and skin. He hadn't eaten—neither of them had—so while he waited for the coffee he called in some takeout.

Despite the caffeine, Bridges was a health nut. He rarely ate red meat and almost keeled over at the sight of fat, so Marc limited the selection to salads and sandwiches. In any case, after seeing Jim and the hollow emptiness in Jennifer's eyes, he didn't particularly care what he ate.

Bridges handed him a cup. "Willard's in Flor-ida. Rossi's home sick."

Otherwise Rossi would have been with Cor-coran, and the hit might not have taken place. Supposition, maybe, but Marc doubted Lopez would have risked taking on two federal agents.

The fact that Lopez had known Corcoran was on his own could have been the result of inside information, but that didn't necessarily follow. If his surveillance was good enough, and it probably was, he would simply have recognized the oppor-tunity and acted on it. "Willard's on his way back. They're both on leave until further notice."

Bayard studied the view from his office window while he drank his coffee. Ever since he had seen Corcoran, the back of his neck had been crawling. He had run through possible motivations, but the only one that linked both Powdrell and Corcoran was the investigation into Lopez. It was also a fact that the murders uncannily mirrored Lopez's assault on the cabal.

Two kills, both running with clocklike precision and no concrete leads. It took time, planning and good information to carry out a hit.

Aside from the fact that his men were being hunted, he was also certain that someone within his own organization was leaking information.

Lissa, his personal assistant, tapped on the door, breezed in, set a box on his desk and dangled an invoice. Marc peeled some bills out of his wallet and added a generous tip. The gourmet restaurant that regularly supplied the building made a point of extending deliveries into the early evening specifically for them, and the service was always prompt.

Lissa flicked open the box on her way out and checked on the contents. "Looks like chick food to me."

Bridges looked faintly outraged. "What's wrong with healthy food?"

Lissa lifted her brows and sauntered out to pay the delivery boy.

Smothering the first gleam of amusement he'd felt in a week, Marc examined the sandwiches, took the beef and mustard and left Bridges with the chicken. "She likes you."

Bridges started on his food. Lissa had been a reluctant focus for Bridges ever since he had moved into the office next to Marc's. The combination of personalities was decidedly offbeat; Bridges the warrior monk, his principles as sharp-edged as a blade, and Lissa, divorced, sweetly cynical and with a city girl's love of all things shopping. If anything ever happened it would be explosive. "You know you're driving her crazy."

Bridges checked out his suit sleeve. "No markdown ticket from Saks. It's not ever going to happen."

Just after five, Rear Admiral Saunders, Director of Special Projects and Marc's boss, stepped into Marc's office. "Any progress?"

Marc sat back in his chair. "Nothing concrete yet. I've pulled Willard and Rossi off the task force. We're tightening security."

He had closed down surveillance options around the building, but blocking every known camera wasn't a cure-all. It was easy enough to install a hidden camera, and satellite coverage was a wild card he couldn't control. If Lopez, or whoever it was who was targeting his team, wanted to watch them, there wasn't much he could do to prevent that.

He'd also put a team on running traffic cameras and collecting security tapes from every business within a four-block radius of the café where Corcoran had been shot. It was painstaking work and the results might not be conclusive, but his gut instinct said that Lopez had been the shooter and that he'd had to park a vehicle somewhere. If they could score a license plate, they would be closer than they had ever been to finally capturing him. "I've moved Jennifer and her daughter into a hotel until the funeral's over."

He had also posted security around the house and issued a gag order for the press. If the fact that Corcoran had been an agent investigating Lopez were released, they had an even bigger problem. It was a remote possibility that Jennifer and her daughter could become targets themselves, and a given that if the media spilled the full story, every weirdo and head case in the country would crawl out of the woodwork to confuse an investigation that was already in trouble.

Saunders's expression was impassive as he listened to the details. "I talked to the director half an hour ago. He's asked me to keep him briefed."

The remainder of the conversation was to-the-point and predictable. Saunders had a reputation for cleaning up messes and cutting through red tape with a facile skill that, over a career that had spanned decades, had won him more friends than enemies. That political savvy had shot him through the naval ranks and into the upper echelons of the intelligence sector. He was sharp and efficient, and it was no secret that he was standing in line for the job of Director of National Intelligence and a seat on the National Security Council. He needed a media circus now about as badly as he needed a heart attack.

The inference was clear. Any shit, and he would pin it to Marc's ass.

Saunders exited with a crisp, "Keep me informed."

Lissa stepped into Marc's office bare seconds after Saunders was out of earshot. She was on the point of leaving, the strap of her purse slung over one shoulder. "Do you think it matters to him that Jim died?"

Bayard pulled up a file on his laptop. "Trust me, don't go there."

Saunders had feelings—just not very many of them.

The first time Marc had met Saunders had been over twenty years ago at the memorial service of Todd Fischer, Sara's uncle and his friend Steve's father. At that time, Saunders had been almost single-handedly responsible for the cover-up of the *Nordika* dive tragedy in which Todd Fischer had died, and the leaked file that claimed the "missing" naval dive team had deserted. His actions, aimed at protecting the Navy's reputation, had reaped him professional advancement, but with the recent recovery of the bodies of the naval dive team in a mass grave in Juarez, Colombia, Saunders was hurting.

When Lissa turned to leave, Marc stopped her. "Did you drive in today, or take the Metro?"

Her expression was dry. "I don't have a dedicated parking space so I'm afraid it's the Metro. Why?"

"I'll ring down and get security to escort you

to the station. Until further notice, you can drive in. I'll authorize a parking space."

Her expression didn't change, but Lissa was nobody's fool. She had a double degree in foreign affairs and business administration. She ran his office like a well-oiled machine, and when it came to understanding the nuances of the intelligence world, she was as sharp as a seasoned agent. "You think it's Lopez."

He kept his expression impassive. "I'm just taking precautions."

After calling security, then arranging that one of the visitor spaces be redesignated, he studied the file on Lopez. The moment in the morgue when Herschel had described the shooter replayed in his mind. The fact that Lopez had shot Corcoran himself was significant. Lopez's network was in tatters, most of his key people behind bars. Financially, he had to be hurting.

The fact that Lopez was killing to an agenda made him predictable and vulnerable. In strategic terms, Marc had the upper hand. He could play the decoy game and use offensive surveillance tactics. With the resources at his disposal, he could guarantee Lopez's capture. He just had to get Lopez before he killed again.

* * *

Just after six, Marc drove into the garage of his apartment building, collected his mail and newspaper and took the elevator to his third-floor apartment. Leaving his briefcase in the hall, he tossed the mail and the newspaper on the dining table and walked through to the bathroom. If it had been a normal evening, he would have worked off the tension by going for an extended run, but Corcoran's death had ruled out that option. Until they found the shooter, he and his staff couldn't afford to expose themselves any more than necessary.

Feeling restless, his muscles tight—a side effect of the fierce anger that had gripped him when he had seen Corcoran's body in the morgue—he showered and changed into sweats. He could think of another way to relieve his tension, but that option wasn't viable. He wasn't into instant sex, and lately he didn't have time for relationships. Snagging the remote on the way to the kitchen, he flicked on the television and caught the end of the evening news as he sipped a cold beer and reheated day-old pizza.

Still feeling edgy, then outright pissed when he caught the sports news and saw that the Falcons had lost to the Giants, he ate, rinsed his dishes and stacked them in the dishwasher—not a complicated process when he'd drunk the beer direct from the bottle and the pizza had arrived encased in cardboard. When the kitchen was returned to its usual sterile state, he checked his mail and scanned the newspaper.

A story on the second page caught his attention. The column was small, the details sketchy. Sourced from a piece published in a local Shreveport paper after the death of Ben Fischer, the article rehashed the scandal surrounding the *Nordika*—a ship that had been hijacked out of the port of Lubek on the Baltic Sea near the end of the Second World War. The wreck sunk off the coast of Costa Rica, had become central in the investigation into both the Chavez cartel and the cabal, and had been the scene of the mass murder of the team of Navy divers that Todd Fischer, Sara's uncle and Ben Fischer's brother, had commanded.

The article mentioned the fact that Ben had brought back possessions belonging to Todd Fischer. Marc had been aware that Ben had gone to Costa Rica to assist in the search for his brother and the seven other missing divers, but to his knowledge, he hadn't brought anything back. If he had, Todd's son, Steve, a CIA agent, who had been active in the recent investigation, would have received the items and Marc would have known about it.

If Ben had brought items back and concealed them, there could only be one reason: they would somehow have added fuel to the scandal and disgrace surrounding the disappearances. If that was the case, then the items were undoubtedly connected to the investigation, and he needed to see them.

But that wasn't all that worried him.

If Ben had brought back material that could provide a lead in the ongoing investigation, then he wasn't the only one who would be interested in that fact. Lopez and Helene Reichmann—the head of the cabal—would have a stake in recovering what could be incriminating evidence.

There was also another angle. No documentation pertaining to the cache of looted gold, artwork and artifacts the *Nordika* was purported to have carried had ever been found but, thanks to the media, the legend was now public knowledge. Despite the fact that the Navy had dived on the wreck a number of times and grid searched the area, and that the *Nordika* was now cleared for recreational diving, the treasure hunters were still lining up.

He studied the newspaper article again. It had been picked up by one of the national dailies, so it was too late to put a lid on it. Chances were there was nothing in it, that whatever Ben Fischer had brought back from Costa Rica had been nothing more remarkable than his brother's personal effects. But Bayard didn't like leaving anything to chance.

Picking up the phone, he dialed Sara's number.

The phone rang several times then clicked through to her answering service. He left a message.

Just before he hung up he thought he heard a small click.

He didn't normally conduct business from his land line. When he was at home he liked to keep his life as ordinary and real as he could. If he had to make work calls, he had his cell and a satellite phone in his briefcase, but he hadn't considered a cautionary call to Sara as work.

Picking up the receiver, he listened, but aside from a faintly hollow background sound, all he could hear was the dial tone. The building was old, a grand Victorian lady with high, ornate ceilings and a creaking lift—as far removed from his high-tech day environment as he could get. Sometimes when it rained, the electrics got a little freaky, which could explain the noise. Lately, with the heat and humidity, they'd had rain most days. That probably explained the sound he'd heard.

Frowning, he set the receiver back down.

Four

Sara Fischer stepped up onto the airy veranda that wrapped around three sides of the Fischer family homestead. The house, which had been built in the 1920s by her grandfather, stood nestled in an enclave of bronze-leaved magnolias, towering oaks and a tangle of rhododendrons and dogwoods. The lawns were neatly trimmed, courtesy of a mowing service, but the fields, now empty of cattle, and the For Sale signs that had already sprouted along the roadside, gave the property a derelict air.

Suppressing the raw ache that crept up on her every time she drove to the house and had to face the reality that her father was gone, she unlocked the door and stepped inside.

The proportions of the house were nice: a wide hall, large, spacious rooms, two bedrooms on the ground floor, four above and an attic. In a wild moment, just after the funeral six weeks ago, she had considered keeping it, but the house was just too far out of Shreveport. As pretty as the drive was into town, the daily commute to the library would add an extra hour onto her working day.

Besides that, much as she loved the history and connection of the house, it had been a family home. Her father had rattled around in it by himself, and so would she. It was designed for a large rambunctious family, and that was something she couldn't see herself ever having. At thirty-four, with a short list of unsatisfactory and, quite frankly, disappointing relationships behind her—and no man in sight for the grand total of *three* years—clinging to the house was nothing short of pathetic.

The sun slanted through the sitting room, capturing the motes of dust she stirred up as she crossed the large, empty space. The furniture had gone already; there was just the piano left, which she was keeping. It wouldn't fit comfortably in her apartment, so it would have to go into storage until she moved somewhere bigger, but that didn't matter. She loved the piano and the memories that went with it: lazy summer days spent listening to her mother play classical pieces and jazz, hours spent in this room after school working her way through music books until she'd gone to college.

Reaching out, she lifted the keyboard cover and ran her fingers over the keys. The notes resonated through the empty house, clear and rich but definitely out of tune. Closing the cover, she continued up the stairs, opening windows in the empty bedrooms to let the heat out and stopping to check all the cupboards and wardrobes to make sure no personal items had been left behind.

She had already emptied the main rooms of the house, selling the furniture, taking trunkloads of her father's clothes and kitchen equipment to the charity shops, and storing anything of a personal nature until she was ready to sort through the last fragments of Ben Fischer's life, and face the unpalatable fact that, without his cheerful, no-nonsense presence, she was now utterly alone in the world. The only room left was the attic, and the urgency to clear that out had been spurred by a story that had been printed in the local newspaper.

The reporter had somehow gotten hold of photos of both Ben and his brother Todd when they had first joined the Navy. The article described the old scandal of Todd's disappearance and the fact that, unwilling to believe that Todd was missing without a trace, Ben Fischer had gone down to Costa Rica to personally search for his brother. The story, apparently supplied by a source in Shreveport—which she read to mean one of her father's old naval cronies—had gone on to rehash the subsequent dishonorable discharge of Todd's naval team and the recent discovery of the mass grave in Juarez, Colombia.

The fact that Todd had finally been vindicated had stopped Sara from becoming too upset over the story. The investigation, which had resulted in the discovery of the mass grave, was now a matter of public record. What concerned her was that the story claimed her father had brought personal items back from Costa Rica.

She remembered him making the trip, but at no point had he mentioned to her that he had retrieved any of Todd's personal effects. If he had, logically, they should have been passed on to

Aunt Eleanor or Steve, but if that was the case, she was certain she would have heard about it. The Fischer family had been close, and the tragedy had pulled them even closer. A more likely scenario was that, with the media scandal still raging, her father had kept quiet and stored the items rather than upset Eleanor any further. Now, with both Eleanor and her father gone and Steve in the Witness Security Program, there was no one at hand to ask.

If the items were in the attic, she needed to find them. The last thing any of them needed was for some antique dealer or the purchaser of the house to stumble across possessions that were not only private to the Fischer family, but that were potentially newsworthy.

The staircase to the attic was dim and claustrophobic, and the attic itself was like an oven. By the time she threaded her way through old tea chests and boxes of books to one of the matching gable windows situated at either end of the room, perspiration beaded her upper lip and every pore had opened up. Working at the stiffened latch, she shoved the window open, leaned out and gulped in cool air.

Minutes later, she had the second window

open, and a breeze was circulating as she began the task of sorting through the jumble of boxes.

Two hours later, sick of slapping at mosquitoes, she gave up on the idea of fresh air and closed both windows. With darkness blanking out the view and a single bulb her only illumination, she surveyed the junk.

She had gone through two-thirds of what was, mostly, burnable rubbish: old books that had warped and moldered, clothes that should have been thrown away twenty years ago and an assortment of mostly broken kitchen appliances and furniture. She hadn't stumbled across anything that was connected to Todd, but the more she searched, the more certain she became that if Todd's personal effects were anywhere, they had to be up here.

She sorted through another chest. Right at the bottom was a cardboard box labeled Fireworks.

Vivid memories of bonfires and Fourth of July barbecues punctuated with the high-pitched whine of skyrockets took her away from the dim, dusty attic.

One summer she and Steve had saved fireworks in order to make bombs. They had made a number of prototypes but had made the mistake of blowing up a small tree. Both sets of Fischer parents had gone crazy. She and Steve had been forced to divulge their hiding place, then watch as the remaining fireworks were dunked in water, rendering them useless. The hiding place was here, in the wall of the attic.

Pushing to her feet, she examined the area where the loose board had been, looking for prying marks that had been made by two kids more than twenty years ago. She found the marks. Holding her breath, she worked the board loose, breaking a nail in the process. Lowering the board along with its neighbor to the floor, she examined the shallow vertical cavity. Adrenaline pumped. She hadn't expected to find anything, but there was something there.

Reaching in, she grabbed a package and the canvas strap of a knapsack. A cold tingle went down her spine when the weight and the bulk of the knapsack registered.

She carried both items into the center of the room, where the light from the single bulb was strongest. Unlatching the flap, she studied the bag's contents. There was no doubt in her mind that these were the items her father had retrieved from Costa Rica; mementos too painful and too controversial at the time to keep in plain view or to hand on to either Eleanor or Steve.

Maybe it was because she still felt raw and emotional after her father's death and funeral, but Sara could remember Todd's disappearance as clearly as if those events had happened last week.

The fact that her uncle—a healthy, fit man in his prime—had *died* had been shocking to the nine-year-old girl she had been, and so had the circumstances surrounding his death. The entire family had been proud of the medals and honors Todd had won. Her father had steadfastly maintained that foul play must have been involved, that it hadn't been a case of desertion, but when the scandal had leaked into the papers, the gossip had spread like wildfire. Sara could remember the whispered comments at school, the pointing fingers in the street, and her father refusing to let anyone answer the phone but him because of the crank calls.

With hands that weren't quite steady, she unwrapped the package, which was only loosely bound, as if her father had inspected the item then wrapped it again before stowing it in the cavity. It was a camera. Any lingering doubt that the things stowed in the wall had belonged to Todd dissolved. Underwater photography had been his hobby; she could remember Steve endlessly vying to use this same camera on dive trips. The camera itself was empty of film, but the side pocket of the soft camera case held a film carton with three letters scribbled on the side: ACE. She opened the carton, although she already knew it was empty. The film had been removed from the camera for processing.

She began extracting objects from the pack. The first was a flashlight still containing batteries that were corroded with age. The heavy shape of the second item was instantly familiar. Guns of all shapes and sizes had been a matter-of-fact part of the Fischer family, and her life, for as long as she could remember. Her father had taught her to shoot at the same time Steve had been taught. As academically inclined as she had always been, she was nevertheless a natural marksman and had given Steve a run for his money during target practice.

The glow of the bulb illuminated the maker of the handgun, Pietro Beretta. She placed the gun on top of the tea chest. The knapsack also contained a magazine and a box of ammunition.

When she pulled the box out she could feel loose rounds rolling around, which meant the box wasn't full. The magazine was empty, which indicated that the missing rounds had been used. That fact more than any other hammered home the intimacy of the items she was handling. They weren't just objects, they had been the personal possessions of Todd Fischer.

The final item was a battered hardbound book. Her heart automatically beat faster as she picked it up. The camera had been an emotional journey, the gun a window into the past, but to Sara, books always carried an extra zing. Whether they contained reference information or a fictional story, she loved the mystery inherent in page layered upon page, all closed between two covers.

But she was reluctant to open this book.

It didn't have a title or anything on the spine to indicate the publisher or the contents: it looked like a diary. If it was Todd's journal, then it was private and most definitely needed to go to Steve.

She opened to the first page. It was written in German.

Frowning, she turned a page and skimmed the text. It took a few moments for her mind to click into the structure and format of the language, because her German, which she had studied along with French at college, was definitely rusty.

Flipping back a page, she found a date— 1942—and directly below that the phrase *Schutz-staffel Chiffrier-abteilung.*

Cold congealed in her stomach. *Schutzstaffel* was the full name of the Nazi SS. *Chiffrier-abteilung* meant cipher department.

Not long after her father had come back from Costa Rica, she had overheard her parents talking. She hadn't meant to eavesdrop. She had been in her room reading and they had been sitting out on the porch. In the stillness of the evening, the words had floated in her window. At first she had thought the discussion had been a general one about World War II and she hadn't paid it much attention, but when her father had mentioned her uncle's name, her ears had pricked up.

She knew the basic facts of Todd Fischer's disappearance and death. She had been secure in the belief that he had died in the Gulf of Mexico in the line of duty, no matter what anyone else maintained. But according to her father, Todd *had* been on a wild-goose chase, hunting Nazis. The Navy had covered it up, *but he had the evidence to prove it.*

Standing, surrounded by dust and old memories that had teeth, the gritty reality of the mass grave at Juarez was sharp and immediate.

Her uncle had been working undercover south of the border, but the job he had been sent to do defied belief and common sense. Neither of her parents could credit that Todd and seven other SEALs had gone missing on a mission that belonged decades back in time: a mission that in the 1980s could only be described as crackpot.

Todd had been hunting Nazis, and he had found them, along with a connection to a Colombian cartel. The combination had been brutal. Juarez had resembled the horrific aftermath of a death camp.

She skimmed the first page of the book. Halfway down the reason she still hadn't adjusted to the syntax became clear. It was a codebook.

A cold tingle went through her, a brief flash of unwanted memory. When she'd been a child, one of the nightmares that had regularly played had been about opening a book and memorizing a word. Later on, it had been an easy leap to conclude that she had been stealing a code.

The content of the book explained why the cover and the spine were blank. Despite the fact that it had been produced by a printing press—a necessity because every communications post of ground, air and sea forces had needed a copy of their own respective codebooks—it would have been a secret document, requiring a security clearance. Putting a title on the book would have been tantamount to waving a red flag.

The instant she recognized the content, translating became easier. She turned pages and studied the codes, suppressing a queasy desire to drop the book and wash her hands. As fascinating as it was, the codebook had been formulated with the express purpose of aiding Nazi secret communications. The result had been the loss of life of Allied soldiers. She knew that the armed forces had used codes and ciphers, and still did, but all the same, she couldn't control her natural recoil.

Even worse, for the book to have been in Todd's possession meant it had been a part of his investigation and had likely belonged to one of the Nazis he had been chasing. The thought that she could be handling the personal possession of a war criminal and a murderer made her skin crawl.

She had always been fascinated by puzzles and codes. Her mind, with its memory for detail and bent for lateral thinking, was suited to puzzle solving. She had studied mathematics for a while, along with language and history. One of her papers had included sections on the use of secret writing and one of her thesis subjects had been cryptography.

Silence closed around her and seemed to thicken as she continued to study the code. She had no idea where or when, but she was certain she had seen this particular arrangement of letters before. That fact in itself wasn't surprising. The Germans had been excellent cryptographers, the best in the world. The majority of books on codes and ciphers had been written by Germans. It was possible that she had studied a similar code.

Her gaze caught on a penned note in the margin, and for a split second the room faded.

Code leak traced to Vassigny Stop Find Traitor Stop

An owl hooted. She started, almost dropping the book, and the curious moment of déjà vu passed, although the puzzling phrase lingered. She couldn't remember the last time she had seen a telegram except those slipped into her parents' old wedding album. They had become obsolete decades ago.

Taking a deep breath to steady nerves that had

no earthly reason to be shot, she checked her watch. It was almost nine. With the half hour drive into town, it was long past the time she should have left, and besides, she had what she had come for.

Shoving all of the items back into the knapsack, she hitched one strap over her shoulder, picked up her handbag and descended out of the attic. After closing windows and switching off lights, she stepped onto the front porch and pulled the door closed behind her. The night was pitch-black, the temperature a few degrees cooler than earlier. Heavy clouds had blotted out the faint light of the moon and stars.

Feeling in the dark for the railing, she made her way down the steps. On impulse, she dug in the knapsack and pulled out the flashlight. When she flicked it on, there was no response, not that she had expected one. At a guess, those particular batteries had been dead for almost twenty-five years.

As she negotiated the overgrown path, she could just make out her pale silver car on the drive. She retrieved her keys from her handbag and depressed the locking mechanism. The car beeped and small sidelights flashed, relieving the smothering darkness. As she set the knapsack and her handbag on the backseat and slid behind the wheel, Sara was abruptly glad she'd decided against living in the house.

The last thing she needed was to sit alone at night in an isolated country house, turning slowly into a comfortably well-off, overorganized, *lonely* spinster.

Five

An hour later, after eating takeout, then showering and changing into soft track pants and a camisole, Sara sat down and began to sift through the week's papers. She had two national tabloids and the local paper delivered, enough editorial to see her through the week and fill her evenings.

Her gaze caught on an advertisement in the world news section of one of the tabloids and she frowned. This was where she'd seen that particular arrangement of letters in the code book, not in the puzzle section, but in an advertisement, and not once, but several times.

The ad was for a photographic restoration service. The letters ACE leaped out at her.

She stared at the advertisement, then transferred her gaze to the knapsack, which she'd placed on the coffee table. The camera inside hadn't contained any film. If there had been a film, someone had taken it out, but she didn't think that it had been her father. Ben Fischer had been meticulous. If he had gotten the film developed, she would have found the prints and the negatives when she had sorted through the family photos. If there had been something sensitive or unpleasant about the photos, he would have stored both the photos and the negatives with the other items that had been hidden in the attic. Anyway, from the way the camera and the knapsack had been stuffed in the hidey-hole in the attic, she had the distinct impression that Ben Fischer hadn't taken the time to do anything but hide the items.

Maybe there *was* no missing film—but the idea that there could be was tantalizing, and the letters Todd had scrawled on the side of the film box added to the likelihood.

It was possible Todd had sent the film off to the ACE photographic service. It looked as though they specialized in restoring photographs, but it was possible they also did—or had once done— processing. After almost twenty-five years it was a stretch to expect that any processing firm would have retained prints of work that had never been paid for and collected. The negatives, if they had reached ACE at all, would most likely have been destroyed by now.

Putting the newspaper down, she walked out to the kitchen and made coffee. Carrying her mug back into the sitting room, she switched the television on and flicked through the channels until she found a popular current-affairs program. A few minutes later, unable to concentrate on the disintegrating politics of the Middle East, she set the mug down and picked up the phone, which was sitting on a side table. She stared at the ad. It had been published in both of the tabloids, which meant the firm must be on a sound financial footing to afford the advertising bills. It was a Washington, D.C., number.

She hesitated for long minutes. Steve had told her to keep her nose out of the whole affair. She knew how dangerous the situation was, or had been. Alex Lopez was still on the loose, but the thought that he could be a threat to her in Shreveport was remote. And what harm could there be in ringing to enquire about a lost roll of film? At this time of night, she didn't expect to reach a person, just an answering service. She would leave a message and wait to see if they called back.

She dialed and, when she got a disconnect signal, replaced the receiver. She checked the number and dialed again, just in case she had hit a wrong number. When the disconnect tone beeped in her ear again, she gave up. It was possible the number had been misprinted. Whatever. For the moment that avenue was gone.

Rummaging in her purse, she took out her cell phone, found Steve's number, then hesitated, staring at a cheerful grouping of photographs on an armoire. There were old-fashioned shots of her parents, and Uncle Todd and Aunt Eleanor before they'd had children. Baby shots of both her and Steve. Steve at age eight, proudly hoisting the first fish he had ever caught; herself playing the piano, her head turning as she grinned, caught in a beam of sunlight shafting through French doors. The shot created an impression of time caught and held, as if that moment still lived.

But if she had learned one thing it was that she couldn't turn back the clock. She wasn't a child anymore, and neither was Steve. Both his parents and hers had died and now, with the exception of some distant cousins in Albuquerque, they were all that was left of the Fischer family.

She dialed Steve's number. She wasn't supposed to know it. He had broken the rules giving it to her, but she had agreed to use it in emergencies only, and on the proviso that she didn't keep any records of the call on her phone.

Steve picked up almost immediately. The first thing he wanted to know was if anything had gone wrong. Swallowing a rush of emotion at just hearing his voice, she told him about the knapsack and its contents.

"You recognized the underwater camera?"

"Yes." She had only used it once, but she wasn't likely to forget. That day in the pool had been one of the last times she had seen Todd alive.

"In that case, Bayard should definitely see it. We wondered what had happened to the camera. Monteith got the film. I found the negatives and the prints he'd had developed. I assumed Monteith had tossed the camera."

Monteith had been Admiral Monteith, the naval officer who had ordered the controversial mission. In order to protect himself, Monteith had hidden conclusive evidence that the divers and the charter boat operator, who had located the wreck of the *Nordika,* had been murdered.

"Damn…" Steve's voice had faded to a mumble, as if he was holding the phone away from his face.

She could hear his wife, Taylor, in the background, his murmured, "It's okay, honey."

He came back on the line. "I want Dad's things, but Bayard's going to need to see them first. He's not with the FBI anymore. He's working with Saunders at the ODNI, but I know he still has the case."

"I've got his home number. He gave it to me at Dad's funeral."

He gave her Bayard's office and cell phone numbers, just in case she couldn't reach him at home. She wrote the numbers down, then repeated them back. The ODNI was the Office of the Director of National Intelligence, which oversaw the entire intelligence community. Bayard had previously been a highflier in the FBI. She had no doubt that his move had been upward.

"Any problems?"

Sara's fingers tightened on the receiver, the invisible threads that held them together as a family suddenly pulling almost painfully tight.

The urge to tell him about the unsettling moment of déjà vu was briefly powerful enough that she almost gave in to it. Two solid reasons stopped her. As a close family member, Steve knew about her past problems. He had always been protective and sympathetic, but she doubted he would buy into either her past-life memories or the paranoia. Secondly, she was reluctant to upset him with any further links to a past that had already consumed enough of his life. After years of living a solitary existence hunting his father's killers, he finally had a chance at a normal life, and he was *happy*. "No, no problems. How's the baby project?"

She could almost feel his grin. "You'd better talk to Taylor."

Taylor came on the line. Sara hadn't had much time to get to know Steve's wife, but in the short time they had spent together she and Taylor had hit it off. The ordeal Taylor had endured when she had been targeted by Lopez and the cabal, followed by the discovery of the mass grave at Juarez, then the memorial service for Todd Fischer, had cut through the normal friendship preliminaries.

"Three months to go. Did Steve tell you it's a girl? He's over the moon."

Taylor's happiness was palpable, and for a moment Sara was swept into the warm heart of the small family that was forming. A familiar ache started at the back of her throat. She had felt it when her mother had died, then when her dad had gently slipped away. Then again, ridiculously, at Steve and Taylor's wedding.

She had always loved her family, loved being a part of the belonging and the warmth. She hadn't experienced any kind of maternal urge yet—she had never gotten close enough to any of her boyfriends to even start thinking about commitment, let alone having a child. The crush on Bayard, like a lot of the wilder, more intense teenage feelings she'd seen her friends go through, seemed to have passed her by. But that didn't mean she didn't eventually want children of her own, and a husband. She had just never met anyone she had wanted enough to marry.

Steve came back on. They had just moved into a house in Michigan. Instead of the sea, they had lake views, but he wasn't complaining. He finally had what he wanted, and both he and Taylor were blissfully happy.

When she finally hung up, the sense of separation was acute.

Fingers shaking, she set the phone down on the table. She was having trouble breathing and she was ridiculously close to tears. The emotions had come out of nowhere, hitting her like a fist in the chest.

She rang Bayard's home number. It rang once, then clicked through to an answering service. She waited for the prerecorded message but there was just a muted beep, then a hollow sound as if a tape was running.

Frowning, she waited several seconds, just in case there had been a mistake and the recorded message cut in late. When it was evident there was no recorded message, she left a brief message, stating that she had found possessions belonging to Todd Fischer that he needed to see, including a book and a camera, then quietly set the receiver down.

She had goose bumps all down her arms and the back of her neck was tingling, which was ridiculous. She was certain she had rung the correct number. She hadn't heard Bayard's voice as she had expected to, but that in itself wasn't alarming. She had been talking to a machine but she couldn't shake the weird sense that someone was present, listening.

Suddenly, she wished she hadn't made the call.

Six

Bayard had been almost asleep when the phone rang once, then stopped. Lifting the receiver on his bedside table, he listened. When he heard the dial tone, he flicked on the bedside lamp and checked his answering service. No message had been left.

Reaching for his cell phone, he dialed Bridges, who was a telecommunications expert.

Bridges picked up immediately. Marc could hear the television in the background. "Don't you have a life?"

Bridges grunted. "I've got the same one you've got. What's happening?"

"My phone's been compromised."

"I'll be there in twenty."

* * *

Juan Chavez peeled off his headset, picked up the cell phone on the desk beside him and hit speed dial.

A small sound had him swinging around in his seat. He terminated the call, a shudder going through him at the swiftness and silence of Lopez's arrival. He hadn't heard a vehicle pulling into the garage, which meant Alex had either parked out on the road, or he had been here already. Given that they had hit Corcoran that afternoon, he was going with the second option. Normally, Alex gave the order and stepped away from the process, letting him take care of the details.

But these killings were different, not related to drugs or any other aspect of business. To Juan, killing federal agents made no sense. They couldn't kill the entire justice system, and they couldn't stop it. All Alex would do was make life more difficult for them and, perhaps, finally accomplish his own death.

The thought of Alex's death was something Juan refused to let himself consider for more than a fleeting second. If he did, he was afraid it would show on his face and, despite the fact that Alex was his cousin, he wasn't stupid enough to rely on family ties to save his skin. Alex was distinctly different from the entire Chavez clan. If he didn't see Alex's father, Marco Chavez, in his cousin's features, he would doubt his paternity. But Chavez he was. And despite the fact that Juan and his brother, Benito, were family, Alex would kill either of them as quickly and coldly as he had shot and killed his own father.

He turned back to the laptop. "He made one call to Sara Fischer, and she tried to call him just a few minutes ago."

His fingers moved over the keyboard as he pulled up a window and hit the play button on the conversations that had been intercepted and recorded. Bayard wouldn't know that Sara Fischer hadn't received his call, and vice versa.

Alex listened without expression, his gaze showing no trace of the excitement that had infected Juan when he had realized exactly who it was Bayard had called.

Juan had done all the research. Sara Fischer was thirty-four, a librarian based in Shreveport. She was also Steve Fischer's cousin. Fischer had been a major thorn in Lopez's side and, along with Bayard, had made a huge dent in his organization.

Lopez's expression didn't alter. "Put a tap on Sara Fischer's phone."

"You want me to put a tail on her?"

"I'll see to it. Replay the call."

The sense of chill deepened as Juan hit the replay button and listened to Bayard's deep, even voice. Alex's expression remained impassive, but Juan could detect the predatory glitter in his eyes, the sharp attention to every nuance—an almost animalistic seeking for some sign of weakness in his enemy.

He experienced a familiar sinking sensation. He had shot Powdrell. The hit on Corcoran had been high risk and opportunistic, and Lopez himself had carried it out. "You want me to set Bayard up?"

Lopez's gaze bored into his and for a brief moment Juan's breath seized in his throat at the possibility that he actually did want to take this as far as killing Bayard.

"Not yet," he said softly.

A split second later, Lopez was gone, melting into the shadows of the hallway like a wraith. The smooth, gliding way he moved, the air of cold purpose, sent a trickle of unease through Juan.

Bayard was powerful, focused and prewarned.

If Lopez really did want to kill him, he should have done it first and gone after his soldiers later.

To Juan, none of this made sense. Marco had been a ruthless and brutal leader. Alex was no less, but his desires bordered on the psychotic. To kill Helene Reichmann, the head of the cabal and a dangerous opponent who sought to kill Lopez himself, was understandable; it was a survival issue. Picking off federal agents and going after Bayard was not. Governments changed, and so did their personnel, but the agencies themselves didn't disappear. Creating a media storm that would live long in the memory of the agency itself was tantamount to suicide. They would be hunted relentlessly.

In his opinion Bayard would move on, eventually. All they had to do was stay quiet, operate in a low-key way that wouldn't attract any undue attention. They could survive Bayard. If they went after him directly, they were all dead.

Lopez stepped out onto the street, extracted a key from his pocket and unlocked his car. The locks made a discreet thunking sound, but no lights flashed. Sliding into the driver's seat, he watched as a four-wheel-drive truck pulled into a space outside Bayard's apartment building. If he hadn't already recognized the license plate, the flash of blond hair would have identified the visitor: Bridges.

Picking up his phone, he called Juan. "Get out, now. Bayard's found the wire."

Juan's reply was brief. They had always known tapping Bayard's phone was a risk, and a one-time deal. They wouldn't get another opportunity. Pulling out from the curb, Lopez headed for his hotel. Thirty minutes later, he was packed, checked out and on his way to Dulles. While he waited for his flight, he studied the story on the second page of the newspaper.

Bayard's message to Sara Fischer had been brief, just a request to call him and his number, Sara's call had been far more interesting. She had found items belonging to Todd Fischer, including a book. Bayard hadn't got the message, this time. When he finally did, it would be too late.

Lopez intended to get to Shreveport before him.

Seven

After trying to watch a sitcom for the better part of an hour, Sara checked the locks on the apartment and went to bed.

An hour of tossing and turning later, she turned on the bedside light and reached for a novel. Her head felt heavy, her eyes grainy. She had sleeping pills, but she was reluctant to take one. The battle to relax into sleep was in her mind and therefore controllable. Annoyed as she was at still being wide-awake when she needed to be asleep, she hated the thought of being dependent on any drug.

She stared at the lines of print, forcing herself to concentrate on the story line. Gradually, the novel worked its magic and she became hooked on the story and began to relax.

Outside the wind had picked up. Rain rattled against the windowpanes, the monotony of the sound, soothing her even more. The words began to merge, blur. Her eyes drooped, shutting out the bright, intrusive gleam of the bedside lamp.

The book slipped from her fingers as she dropped into sleep.

France, 1943

Cold seeped through the stone walls of the Château Vassigny as Sara Weiss stepped into the cavernous reaches of the library.

She bypassed Oberst Reichmann's desk and retrieved the set of keys hidden behind a leather-bound tome on the bookshelf.

Moving quickly, she unlocked the door to what had once been an anteroom but which, since the Germans had moved in, had been converted into a makeshift strong room. Stepping inside, she closed the door. She selected a second key and opened the small, squat safe positioned against one wall.

Ignoring the neat piles of francs and the boxes of jewelry that Reichmann and his Waffen SS had "confiscated" during their occupation of Vassigny, she removed a correspondence file, the SS codebook and a second book, this one bound in brown leather, which she hadn't ever seen before.

The codebook itself was nondescript. Bound with board, it was about the size of a school exercise book or a journal. Some codebooks were enormous volumes, but this one fell into the medium range: comprehensive but pared down for portability and ease of use by soldiers in the field. The SS, like the other branches of the German military, also used encryption machines. But as highly efficient and notoriously hard to break as the codes transmitted by their Enigma machines were, the "clear"—that is, the uncoded message—was often encoded before it was encrypted for added security, making the messages even more difficult to decipher.

Ears straining against Reichmann's return, she opened the codebook and turned pages. A bright red thread floated onto the carpet. Reichmann's additional security. The thread was always positioned between pages fifteen and sixteen.

She found the reference she wanted and committed it to memory.

One entry, no more.

She had been steadily stealing the code, one word at a time, for the past few months, ever since Reichmann, the head of the local Waffen SS had employed her as his personal secretary. Sometimes she didn't have access to the safe for weeks. At other times, she managed to get several words or phrases in a day. To date, she had stolen more than seventy percent of the code.

Placing the codebook on top of the correspondence file, she pushed the spectacles she wore for close work higher on the bridge of her nose and opened the second unidentified book. For long seconds what she was reading didn't make sense. Then her stomach clenched in automatic recoil and bile rose in the back of her throat. The book was a ledger, a list of the Jews Reichmann and his SS had sent to the death camps.

Her mind slid back three years, to darkness and horror and grief. Her parents, Dietrich and Janine Weiss, had been living in Paris under assumed names, running an underground paper for the French Resistance. It was safe, they had assured her. At the first hint of trouble they would leave and join her in England. Just days later they had been arrested. Shortly after, they had been transported to Ravensbruck and executed.

She flipped through pages, frowning. The documentation was highly unusual. It provided proof of genocide, something the Germans were determined to conceal. The book shouldn't exist, and it shouldn't be *here*.

Vassigny was a small, quiet village, a producer of vegetables, milk, cheeses and wine, and a provider of accommodation for the SS. Reichmann billeted his men and ran his operation from the Château, but the prison at Clairvaux held larger concentrations of German forces, better security and an administration center. Any sensitive documentation should have been kept there.

Stomach tight, she flipped pages. Account numbers and figures leaped at her, and the reason for the book's existence became clear. It wasn't an official record. Reichmann was a former Swiss banker, and this was his own personal ledger. A secret accounting of murder and the transfers of the money he had stolen from the people he had condemned.

She stared at the neat lists of dates, names and bank accounts spanning more than two years, the dizzying amounts of money Reichmann had stolen.

Her task in Vassigny was to coordinate airdrops of supplies from Special Operations Executive in England for the local French Resistance, the

Maquis, and run the escape pipeline. The fact that the job with Reichmann had fallen into her lap, giving her access to the codebook, had been a bonus. The code breakers at Bletchley Park in England needed the information she supplied, but Reichmann's ledger represented another priority.

Her jaw tightened at the sheer numbers Reichmann had sent to the camps. The ledger was proof of genocide, and of Reichmann's unconscionable greed.

Reichmann wasn't just stealing from the Jews, he was stealing from the Reich. With access to the accounts of Jews sent to the death camps, before those accounts were declared to the Reich, he could transfer money into nominated accounts. The theft would be concealed behind a serpentine raft of paperwork, and was, no doubt, supported by the connivance of a bank. Reichmann might not be entirely suited for his SS command, but when it came to moving money, he was at the top of his game.

Her parents' names wouldn't be recorded here, because at that time Reichmann had been based in Lyon. But whether or not they were listed, it didn't matter. Her parents had given their lives to stop this kind of evil. She needed the book for them—and for every individual and family listed in it.

A name registered. Simon de Vernay.

Shock reverberated through her. She checked the ledger entry. The amount of money transferred made her mouth go dry. She didn't know any one person could have such an amount.

The de Vernays were very well-known, an old Jewish family that had settled in Angers, their principal business, the diamond trade. No diamonds, as such, were listed, but that made sense. The de Vernay's were traders, not jewelers. Their stocks of diamonds would have been concentrated in Antwerp, the main diamond-trading center and, since war had broken out, no doubt in other, safer centers offshore.

Setting the book down, she opened Reichmann's private correspondence file, which contained personal and classified materials that never crossed her desk. A telegram, received that morning, was sitting on top.

"Code leak traced to Vassigny Stop Find traitor Stop"

Her heart kicked hard, once. With fingers that shook slightly, she replaced the telegraph in the file and returned it to its correct place on the shelf, placing the ledger and the codebook on top. She locked the safe, then closed and locked the door to the strong room and returned the key to its hiding place.

The echo of footsteps in the front hall signaled that Reichmann had returned from his meeting. She slipped out of his office, walked through to her own room and sat down behind her desk. She checked her wristwatch. Almost fifteen minutes had passed while she had been in the strong room. The risk she had taken was huge. Normally, three minutes was her maximum turnaround time, but the information she had gathered had been crucial, not only for her own survival, but for the Maquis.

Code leak traced to Vassigny Stop Find Traitor Stop.

There were two possibilities, perhaps a third. Her radio transmissions to SOE HQ in England could have been intercepted. The success of their sabotage program could have aroused suspicion. Or they had a traitor.

The leak, if there was one, couldn't be local. Her cover was simple. She was married to Armand de Thierry, the former occupant of the Château and the marriage, on paper at least, was real. Armand, a wealthy landowner, was seen as a valued Nazi collaborator, owing to the fact that he owned a great deal of productive land and was able to supply the German soldiers with wine, fresh meat, vegetables and cheeses. He was also the head of the local Maquis, a small, but effective group of French Resistance fighters.

Armand was in his fifties, but the fact that he was wealthy meant his second marriage, after the death of his first wife, to a much younger woman was not considered strange.

For Sara, the cover was natural and impeccable. The fact that her mother was a Parisienne, and her father German, that she had spent her childhood in Berlin, her formative years in Paris and most of her adult life in Oxford, England, suited her uniquely for this mission.

During her time in Vassigny, she had been cared for and protected. Armand and the Resistance had gone to great lengths to integrate her into the village and their lives. The fact that she had devised the present cipher system that the Allied ground forces used to communicate with each other was the one glaring weakness in her suitability as an agent, although that risk was offset by the fact that her link with the cipher had been kept secret.

Armand and the SOE had protected her, but

her time in Vassigny was over. There were a limited number of codebooks, and only a handful of people with access to the Château. It was only a matter of time before Reichmann, or more likely, Stein, the local Gestapo officer, unmasked her. When she transmitted the code information at her next scheduled radio contact, she would make arrangements to leave.

Reichmann bypassed her office and walked directly into his. Breathing a sigh of relief, Sara walked through to his office and bade him good-night.

Returning to her desk, she stripped off her spectacles, carefully stored them in her glasses case and slipped the case into her purse. Shrugging into her thick lined coat, she wound a woolen scarf around her neck, tucking it in against the cold. Collecting her purse, she straightened and caught a glimpse of her face in the ornate gilded mirror opposite her desk. Her skin was as pale as the empty marble fireplace, but that wasn't what held her attention.

The scarf was bright red. The significance of the color drained the blood from her face.

She had forgotten about the thread in the codebook.

* * *

Sharp pain shooting up her shins jerked Sara awake. She stared blankly at the dimly lit room and the rectangular shape of a coffee table, for long seconds unable to grasp where she was.

A shudder swept through her when she identified the cozy familiarity of her sitting room. Dim light flowed from the hallway—her bedroom—which meant that when she'd fallen asleep, she must have left her bedside lamp on.

Gripping the nearby arm of the couch for support, she sat down, her hands shaking as she rubbed away the pain in her shins.

The sharp clarity of the dream, the jolt of raw terror, had already faded, sliding into automatic, practiced blankness.

Pushing to her feet, she flicked on the lights and poured herself a glass of ice water from the fridge. Sitting on a stool at the kitchen counter, she slowly sipped the water and waited for her pulse to even out.

There was an easy explanation for the dream. Something had happened when she had picked up the codebook. She had experienced a flash of déjà vu, which had, in turn, triggered the dream.

The purity of the logic didn't help her with the

fact that she had the dreams in the first place or that she had started sleepwalking again.

Or the certainty that her past was inextricably entwined with the now.

Eight

Edward Dennison, ex-FBI agent, ex-drug cartel member, and now a dead man walking, wiped down the counter of the bar he owned. The Shack was a seedy joint on the waterfront renowned for cheap beer, mean chili and a distinct lack of any discernible comfort.

In terms of excitement, tending a bar scored low on Dennison's barometer but, after escaping Alex Lopez's last attempt on his life by a matter of seconds, Dennison was all over boring and routine.

He loved the seedy dim bar and the predictable clientele. In the months he had owned it, his customers generally fell into two categories: tanned tourists wearing gaudy clothing and smelling of sunblock, and the regulars. The tourists, annoyed by the stink of drying fishing nets and sour beer, didn't stay long. The regulars—fishermen and plantation workers, mostly—hung out at the bar and propped up the pool table, providing a quality that had been sadly lacking in Dennison's life for more years than he cared to count—continuity.

Rain or shine, the same faces appeared, the same beer was ordered and the same music on the jukebox was played. Conversations were predictable and laconic. Dennison hung on every word and loved with passion the static world he had landed in.

Just months ago, in custody in D.C., with the CIA squeezing him for information about Alex Lopez and the wealthy cabal that backed him, the future had been clear: a prison sentence, followed by a cartel hit. No matter where the CIA locked him up, or how secret they tried to keep his location, Lopez would have found him.

In a bizarre run of luck, Dennison had managed to escape custody and the hit. Weeks later, after scanning the Internet for news of his escape and the ensuing investigation, he had found, instead, his death notice.

He had sat staring at the briefly worded statement, a piece of prose that utterly eliminated all
the highs and lows of his life and distilled his
existence down to two dates and a deceased wife,
and wondered who had killed him off, and why.

The answer had been simple. Marc Bayard,
the intelligence executive running the Lopez and
cabal investigations.

Bayard was sending him a message. The
door was open, and he wanted him to come in
out of the cold.

The terms were tempting. Dennison was officially dead, which meant the heat was off. The
FBI wasn't actively hunting him. Neither were
the CIA, the NSA, Interpol and whatever other
agency had been hunting his ass for the past
twenty-four years. It was even possible that Lopez had bought into the death scenario.

There would be incentives to sweeten the
pot—no doubt amnesty for his crimes and the
opportunity to live on American soil under a new
identity on the Witness Security Program—so
long as he testified.

Another search had turned up the apparently
unconnected fact that Agent Harris, one of the
CIA agents who had been minding him, had been

shot and killed in the line of duty on the same day Dennison had "died." The only conclusion he could draw, incredibly, was that the CIA agent he had left handcuffed and unconscious on the floor of the motel had been executed by Lopez's people in his stead. And Bayard, the methodical bastard, had used the situation to extend him an amnesty.

The implications had been huge. Harris had looked a little like Dennison, close enough to create uncertainty. If Lopez's hit man had been working from a photograph, or he had simply been in a hurry, it was entirely possible that he thought he had killed the right mark. If no one in Lopez's organization had found Harris's death notice and tied it to the time of the hit, it was logical to assume that Lopez really did think he was dead.

So…dead and free, for the moment. He didn't fool himself that it would last. Bayard could revoke his "death" whenever it suited his purposes. In one smooth stroke he had offered Dennison a deal, a grace period and a threat.

Life was good…but the clock was ticking.

He tossed the cloth under the bar, grabbed a broom and began sweeping sand through the cracks in the scarred hardwood floor. A cockroach the size of a small bird scuttled from beneath a table and made a run for the nearest piece of warped skirting board.

Dennison didn't bother to make a swipe at the insect. Live and let live, that was his motto, and it was a fact that cockroaches were a part of island life. No matter how many you killed, they kept on coming.

A bit like Lopez and his limitless supply of hired guns.

When the bar was swept and the trash emptied, he walked out back where Louis Jamais, his only permanent employee, was preparing bar snacks—a big pot of seafood gumbo, slabs of island baked bread and a rich, spicy chili that was Louis's own recipe. Picking up the latest copy of an American tabloid he subscribed to for the express purpose of keeping up with the Lopez/cabal investigations, Dennison walked outside to enjoy a few minutes respite before they opened for the lunchtime crowd. Sitting on the back step, he flipped through pages.

His gaze skimmed the lead stories without much interest, then snagged on a small special interest piece. His attention sharpened as he read. The focus of the story was an epitaph of Ben

Fischer, the brother of Todd Fischer, and a rehash of the *Nordika* tragedy, with one exception. Ben Fischer had made a trip to Costa Rica to search for his brother. He hadn't found Todd Fischer, but when he had returned to Shreveport, Louisiana, he hadn't gone home empty-handed. He had taken Todd Fischer's personal possessions with him.

Instincts honed by years of working for Alex Lopez and too many close scrapes with death sprang to life. He stepped back into the kitchen, ignoring Louis's query as he ratted around in the box where they kept old newspapers, which were useful for wrapping up food waste. He found several editions of the same tabloid, but, frustratingly, no more front pages.

"This what you're looking for?"

Louis tossed him a paper he'd been about to use to wrap up fish bones and vegetable peelings. Dennison unfolded it. The front-page coverage of the graves at Juarez jumped out at him and his pulse rate rocketed. He checked the date at the top of the page. It was several weeks before the edition he had been reading. "Thanks."

Ignoring Louis's curiosity, he walked back outside, reread the article and studied the blurred photograph of mourners. He didn't recognize any of them and he hadn't expected to. The CIA had vetted all coverage in order to guarantee the security of its own personnel.

The photo, or the fact that the grave had been found, didn't interest him so much as the story behind the killings—one he had researched on and off during his years in Colombia.

Heinrich Reichmann and his fellow SS Officers, along with Reichmann's daughter, Helene, had escaped Germany in January 1944 after hijacking a ship called the *Nordika*—along with a number of genius children who were the supposed genetic seed pool of the Third Reich. The ship had sailed from Lubek, a port on the Baltic Sea, reportedly loaded with gold bullion and art treasures.

Reichmann had been an aristocrat, a banker and an SS Officer, but his primary talent had been theft.

One of the rumors—perhaps more than a rumor—was that the crates of treasure had been hidden in a series of caves on the coast of Juarez.

Dennison had spent weeks searching Juarez, cruising the coast in a launch, walking the seashore and slogging through jungle, but he hadn't found anything that remotely resembled a system of caves large enough to hide a substantial cache.

The previous year, however, the story had been given unexpected credence by the discovery of a mass grave containing both the bodies of the original crew of the *Nordika* and a naval dive team that had investigated the wreck in the eighties. For a brief time, the legend of the treasure had been resurrected, and Juarez had crawled with treasure hunters.

Dennison hadn't bothered. The gold bullion had undoubtedly been stored in Juarez, but he was willing to bet that it had been for a very short time. Reichmann had used it to buy protection from Marco Chavez, and when he had moved into the States, he had likely taken what was left of the gold with him.

While Dennison had lived at the Chavez compound, he'd had years to go through Marco's papers. He hadn't found much, just a few leads. One of them had been about the late George Hartley, one of the original SS officers who had sailed on the *Nordika*. Hartley had betrayed Marco and the cabal, providing the Navy with enough information to instigate the original investigation that had ended in the dive tragedy. If

Hartley had known where the *Nordika* was scuttled, then to Dennison it had followed that he could have known the location of the treasure.

Checking into Hartley's past had largely been a dead end, but he had pulled up one significant fact after holding a gun at Hartley's lawyer's head and forcing him to hand over a journal.

The journal had been in German. It had taken Dennison weeks to decipher it, and the process hadn't been without its frustrations. Hartley had been laying the groundwork for his memoirs. Unfortunately, aside from the relatively short interval Hartley had worn the SS uniform and then turned to organized crime, his life had been uneventful. But Dennison had turned up one interesting snippet of information.

It was known that Reichmann had stolen money, gold, art and artifacts. According to Hartley, he had also stolen diamonds.

Specifically, a large cache of polished and cut stones from the diamond-trading de Vernay family.

Dennison found the newspaper that had carried the story about Ben Fischer and reread it. It was a long shot, but Todd, Ben Fischer's brother, had been researching the Nazi cabal just before he was killed. It was a matter of public record that one of the people he had interviewed had been George Hartley. If Ben Fischer had retrieved his brother's personal possessions from Costa Rica, it was possible that he had information that Dennison could use.

He studied the details of the epitaph, then walked into the tiny cramped office that opened off the kitchen, booted up his laptop and dialed up a search engine. Seconds later he studied the telephone pages for Shreveport. Rummaging in a drawer, he found a pen and some notepaper and wrote down the details. He had his street address.

Shutting down the laptop, he packed it into his briefcase. He folded the piece of notepaper and the newspapers he wanted on top of the computer, fastened the case, then walked back out to the kitchen and placed the keys to the bar on the kitchen counter. "I have to go away for a few days. You're in charge."

Louis's expression was outraged. "I can't look after this place on my—"

"Employ someone," Dennison snapped, his mind already locked on the task ahead. "I've got unfinished business to attend to."

Nine

Sara locked up the library and stepped into the parking lot. She had spent her lunch hour researching the codebook she had found. The amount of material on World War II codes was staggering, and most of it had to do with the race to break the Enigma codes. The mechanized enciphering machines had been supremely efficient and the codes difficult to break. The addition of double coding—that was, encoding the clear before it was enciphered—had made the task doubly difficult.

She caught a blur of movement out of one eye. A split second later she was jerked back against a hard, male body and a gun was jammed against her throat. The sour smell of sweat and the unmistakable scent of marijuana filled her nostrils.

"If you want my bag, take it."

A hand clamped over her mouth. He began to drag her away from her car and the light, toward the deep pooling shadows of a service lane. His continued silence sent adrenaline pounding through her veins. She was abruptly certain this was no ordinary attack. If he had wanted her bag, he would have snatched it and left, although if he was high, his ability to reason might be nonexistent.

The other alternative was that he was a rapist, which would fit his need for darkness. Her car was parked in the brightest part of the lot, and was easily visible from the road and the park.

She sagged, letting him take all her weight, and at the same time pulled her feet up so that she dropped to the ground.

He grunted with surprise as she sprawled on the asphalt and rolled free. Hard fingers wound in her hair as she surged to her feet. Ignoring the stinging pain, she chopped at his wrist, the movement instinctive. The gun discharged and spun away. A blur of movement off to the left registered, the slam of a car door. One of a group of lanky teenagers dressed in team uniforms tackled the assailant.

The two men grappled on the ground. Seconds

later, her attacker scrambled to his feet, scooped up the gun and ran.

The kid sprang to his feet. "Jay, he's got a gun!"

Jay, who was pounding down the street, stopped at the corner. In the distance, Sara heard the roar of a powerful engine. The fact that her attacker had a car surprised her. She had assumed he was some kind of vagrant.

A young woman helped her to her feet. "Are you okay?"

She pushed strands of hair out of her face and stared at the wink of taillights as the vehicle rounded a corner and accelerated away. Her pulse was still pounding, and she was shaking. Her hand hurt where she'd chopped at his wrist, although she didn't think she had broken a bone. "I'm fine. Thanks for stopping and helping me."

She worked out and, a couple of years ago, she had done a self-defense course. She had seen the physical activity as a necessary balance in a life that at times was too quiet and too studious, but now she was glad she had taken the course.

She had seen his face and she had an idea of his height and build. He had clearly been Latino, and his face had been pockmarked with scars.

Maybe it wasn't the most distinctive description but, with any luck, in a town like Shreveport, it would be enough.

A young man in sweats handed her her purse. "Do you need help getting to the police station? We can take you if you'd like."

She looked at the young fresh faces around her. They were all maybe seventeen or eighteen—technically young enough to be her children. Great. Not only was she shaking like a leaf, now she felt like an old lady.

When she finally got home, it was just short of midnight. Parking her car in the lot behind her apartment building, she turned off the engine and the lights and studied the lit area outside the apartment entrance. Tension that just hours ago hadn't existed gripped her, although the idea that the man who had attacked her would know where she lived or stake out her apartment in order to finish what he had started was patently ridiculous.

Grabbing her bag, she exited the car, and pressed the remote-control key, locking the vehicle as she covered the few yards to the door. She inserted her key card and punched in her PIN number. When the lock disengaged, she stepped inside, closed the door and stared out into the parking lot—for a moment back at the library, the smells of sweat and marijuana turning her stomach.

She strode down the hall and fitted the card into her door. When she had searched for an apartment, she had specified a ground floor property. She had wanted the additional luxury of being able to step outside onto grass, of having her own small piece of garden. Now she would gladly trade it for one of the cheaper upper-story apartments.

She had laid a formal complaint with the Shreveport PD and given her statement. An APB was out on the guy she had described, although the officer she had dealt with hadn't been optimistic about their chances of finding him. The cities of Shreveport, and its close neighbor, Bossier, just across the Red River, had their share of crime, including a busy homicide list. The fact that her attacker was armed was cause for concern, but the scenario of an armed man attacking a lone woman in a parking lot wasn't unusual. She should count herself lucky that she had gotten away unscathed, and that nothing had been stolen.

Stifling a yawn, she checked her answering

machine, her stomach tensing slightly as she remembered the call to Bayard the previous evening. The light wasn't blinking, which meant there were no messages.

After showering and changing into a pair of cotton drawstring pants and a tank top, she made herself a hot drink and a snack, brushed her teeth, then propped herself in bed and turned on the small television set she kept in her bedroom.

She flicked through game shows and documentaries and settled on a sports channel. The NFL game was as simple and straightforward as apple pie—utterly divorced from the attack in the parking lot—but even so, every time she relaxed and began to drift off, a flashback to the attack would snap her back to alertness.

At one in the morning, her head finally drooped on the pillow. Awareness of the flickering picture, the monotonous drone of the sports commentator, faded as darkness rushed to meet her.

The frozen chill of a Vassigny winter seeped into Sara's bones as she stared at the bright red scarf wound around her neck.

Maybe the thread she had left on the floor by

Reichmann's safe wouldn't matter. He already knew someone was stealing information.

Although, she reminded herself, *not from his safe*.

The leak could have originated from Stein, who also held a codebook in his possession.

Reichmann was arrogant and cruel, an aristocratic Teuton with a touch of vanity that made him easy to handle. Alexander Stein, on the other hand, showed no tendencies toward any form of self-indulgence. He was cold, methodical and very efficient. He seldom showed any emotion at all.

A small shudder went down her spine. His previous posting had been in Lyon at the Ecole de Sante Militaire—the location of one of the Gestapo torture chambers.

Lately, Stein had also been resident in the Château, but his rooms were more accessible than Reichmann's. He also had an office at the prison at Clairvaux, where he carried out much of his interrogation work, a third potential source for a leak.

But the telegram had specifically named Vassigny, not Clairvaux.

At one point Sara had considered obtaining information from Stein's book and discarded the idea immediately. Unlike Reichmann, he didn't take risks with the book. It was kept under lock and he carried the only key with him at all times on a chain around his neck.

Her heart clenched. Fear was a sour taste in her mouth.

Survival. Preservation. The concepts had been drummed into her during the two-month training course at Inverie Bay in Scotland. The SOE instructors had been ex-military and ex-agents. Everything they had taught they had learned through personal experience, some in the First World War, and on the beaches at Dunkirk.

She needed to get back into Reichmann's office.

Stripping off the coat and scarf, she dropped them across the back of her chair, opened her correspondence file, took out a letter she had taken down in shorthand that afternoon and began typing.

Ten minutes passed, then twenty. It was past five. Outside the sky had darkened; she could smell the savory scents of food being prepared in the Château's kitchens.

Finally, Reichmann left his office. She listened

intently, nerves stretched taut as she registered the distinctive sound of his boots on the wooden stairs. He was going to his rooms.

Picking up the letter she had typed, she placed it on a clipboard and carried it through to Reichmann's office. Halfway across the room, she stopped. She had forgotten her spectacles. Heart pounding, she walked back to her desk, found her bag, extracted the spectacles from their case and slipped them on the bridge of her nose. They were a detail, but an important one. She needed the layer of protection her guise as a shortsighted secretary provided. She usually kept her head down, her voice soft, the image of a mouse uppermost in her mind. If Reichmann or Stein ever looked past her dowdy clothes and hair and the delicate glasses, she wouldn't last five minutes.

She knocked on Reichmann's office door. When, as expected, there was no answer, she strode into the room, collected the key and unlocked the strong room. Leaving the door open so she could hear if Reichmann was on his way back, she unlocked the safe, picked up the thread and inserted it between the correct pages of the codebook.

With jerky movements, she locked the safe

and exited the room. Footsteps rang on the stone flags as she locked the strong room door and replaced the key in its hiding place.

Walking swiftly, she stepped out of his office and closed the door behind her just as Reichmann stepped into her office.

She smiled smoothly. "Herr Oberst, I didn't realize you had gone out. I have the letter you required for the morning." She handed him the clipboard and watched as he removed a gold pen from his pocket. "If you don't require anything else, I'll go home."

Reichmann's expression was oddly distracted as he signed the letter and handed it back to her. "By all means. You have already worked past your normal hours."

"Then I'll leave. Armand has guests tonight."

"Another soiree, madame?"

"Unfortunately, no." The only "soirees" they had were the small parties thrown by Armand for the leaders of the occupational force—a political necessity to maintain his privileged position. With nothing but sprouting potatoes, shriveled apples and spoiled wine to serve, because the Germans had all but emptied their storerooms, there was no chance for anything but grim survival. "Business, I'm afraid. Armand is trying to convince some of the farmers to modernize their farming methods."

His gaze was clear and cold, his contempt for what he considered the peasantry, clear. "Commendable."

Placing the clipboard on her desk, she reached for her coat and scarf.

"Just one more thing, Madame de Thierry. We have had a little…emergency. I'll need you to come in tomorrow."

Heart pounding, she slid her arms into the coat and wound the scarf around her neck. "The usual time?"

"That's correct."

"I'll be here."

She could feel his gaze boring into her back as she picked up her purse and left. She kept her pace sedate as she walked through the vaulted hall and down the front steps, quelling the panicked urge to run.

Four hours later, warm air plumed from Sara's lungs, forming a fine mist in the icy air as she waited with Armand.

Shadows flickered at the edge of the forest.

Jacques de Vallois and his men, with their "package," an American SOE agent by the name of Marc Cavanaugh.

As soon as Cavanaugh flowed out of the forest, a Sten gun held in one hand, as at ease with the cold, alien landscape as any of de Vallois's men, her stomach did a familiar little flip. Cavanaugh had been an instructor at Inverie in Scotland, training recruits in close quarters combat and survival skills. During those two months, he had barely spoken a word to her that wasn't part of the course, and she had been utterly focused on passing each unit and getting to France, but as stubbornly as she had repressed it, the awareness had grown.

Cavanaugh's mother was originally from Lyon, which explained his fluency with the language. For the past year he had been working on and off clandestinely in France, helping to train Resistance groups, and coordinate their activities. They had been instructed to shelter and assist him.

De Vallois lingered to collect food supplies and ammunition, and to exchange information about the movements of the SS and the Milice— French Collaborators—a group in which he had a spy. With the mounting activity in Lyon and swelling numbers of troops indicating an imminent assault, he and his band of Maquis were moving camp and traveling deeper into the forest. The fighting philosophy of the Maquis was to inflict damage with minimal losses to their fighting force. They had no wish to become involved in a pitched battle with an SS panzer division.

When de Vallois and his men melted back into the forest, Sara turned and issued orders in rapid French.

"You have a vehicle nearby?"

She swung around to find Cavanaugh looming over her, his shoulders broad in a dark jacket, his eyes calm and remote. "Yes, but only for the forest roads. After that we walk. This close to the SS garrison, it's risky to use a vehicle at all after dark. Anyone caught on the roads after seven risks being shot."

When they reached the cover of the trees, she found her knapsack, rummaged in it and handed him a dark woolen coat. "Wear that. The wool makes you disappear, and when you brush against trees and shrubs it doesn't make any sound."

Armand grinned. "You'll have to excuse Sara. She likes to give orders."

Cavanaugh shrugged into the coat. "In this case, she's going to have to take some."

Armand's expression cooled. "Who are you?"

Sara placed a hand on his arm. "It's all right, Armand. I know him. Don't forget, he's not an airman, he's an agent."

Cavanaugh's gaze fastened on her. "I know your work on encryption systems. I've been instructed to get you out." He unzipped a pocket in his jacket and handed her an envelope. "I have your orders."

She ripped the envelope open and skimmed the letter it contained. It had been signed by Colonel McCleod, her commanding officer. Her stomach tightened. In retrospect, she shouldn't have been surprised by Cavanaugh's arrival. The second she had seen the telegraph in Reichmann's safe she had known it was time to leave. If she stayed and got caught, and Reichmann or Stein found out who she really was, she risked jeopardizing much more than Armand's network. She met Cavanaugh's gaze. "You already know about the leak."

"We intercepted a message two days ago."

Her jaw tightened. Two days. That meant he had left immediately. "I can't go. Not yet. If I disappear, the entire network will be in jeopardy."

Armand was suddenly there, a solid rock between her and the American. His dark gaze bored into hers. "What leak? What have you found out?"

"I haven't had time to tell you. I saw a telegram in Reichmann's safe. They've narrowed the code leak to Vassigny."

Cavanaugh's gaze sharpened. "Then we leave. Now."

Sara kept her own gaze level, her voice flat. "We can't. Reichmann has asked me to work tomorrow. If I don't turn up at the Château in the morning he'll know something's wrong. He'll tear the village apart. I need time to construct a cover story—a sick relative in another town, perhaps—something that will make sense. Besides, the next scheduled border crossing is in forty-eight hours. Leaving tomorrow night will give us a twelve-hour start. We'll be in Switzerland by the time Reichmann finds out I'm gone."

It would also give her time to break into Reichmann's safe and get the ledger.

An hour later, Sara stopped at the concealed entrance to a warren of underground tunnels.

Armand lit an oil lamp. Light flared, golden and warm, making her aware of how cold she had become despite the long walk. She glanced at Cavanaugh, seeing him clearly for the first time that night. He was as dark as Armand, but younger and much taller. In terms of looks, he could easily pass for French, or even Italian. Shrouded in the dark wool coat, he could have been one of Armand's men, except for the eyes. They, she decided, were what made him different: cold, remote and used to command.

The ease with which he held the Sten put him firmly in context. He'd had military training and active service before he'd moved into intelligence work. "You won't need a gun." *Yet.*

Sara woke with a start, bright lamplight hurting her eyes.

Vassigny. Stein.

Cavanaugh.

She stared, disoriented, at the color and noise blaring from the television screen, still tangled in that dark cold world and the unpalatable fact that Bayard seemed to be as inextricably part of that last life as he was of this one.

Fumbling through the rumpled covers, she

found the remote and killed the TV. She'd spent years avoiding Bayard, but in the past few months she had bumped into him several times. At the memorial service for Uncle Todd a few months ago, then Steve and Taylor's wedding. He had also turned up at her father's funeral.

The dreams and memories had stopped when she was twelve, and had resumed briefly when she had come into contact with Bayard when she was eighteen. Since then she had been utterly normal—until now.

Pushing the covers aside, she shrugged into a robe and walked out to the kitchen, made herself a cup of hot milk, then walked through to the bathroom and found the small bottle of sleeping pills her doctor had prescribed shortly before her father had died.

She hadn't used them then. She'd had weeks to prepare for her father's death, and shuttling to and from the hospital, her father's house, her apartment and work had left her perpetually exhausted. Whenever she had the opportunity, she had literally fallen into bed.

She shook a pill into her palm. It was after three in the morning, the wrong time to take a sleeping pill, but she was desperate.

She swallowed the pill, chasing it down with the warm milk and walked through to her bedroom. As a precaution, she set her alarm just in case she overslept.

Vassigny.

She frowned. She was certain it was a place name. On impulse, she walked out to the sitting room, found her atlas and ran her finger down the index.

The name leaped out at her. Not Louisiana, or anywhere in the States.

France.

She noted the grid reference and turned to the map of France and all the fine hairs at her nape lifted. Vassigny was a small village at the base of the Langres Plateau, not far from the Swiss border.

A crumbling Château, dark pines, vast silences…

She snapped the atlas closed.

The sleeping pill was working. Her head felt heavy, and—probably because she was already exhausted—she felt clumsy and uncoordinated. But that didn't change the clear, sharp knowledge in her mind.

It was happening again.

The dreams, the horror.

And this time, it *was* intruding into her real life.

Ten

Sara checked with the Shreveport PD before leaving for lunch at twelve. Rousseau, the detective who had taken her statement the previous evening, wasn't in yet. He worked second shift and didn't start until two. Her call was transferred through to the field office and picked up by a crisp-voiced officer who identified herself as Detective Canon.

A few minutes later, Canon found the file. Rousseau had done some checking, and the man she had described didn't have any kind of profile in either Shreveport or Bossier. It was possible he was new in town, or just passing through. His description had been circulated and they would keep looking, but unless he attacked someone else and they managed to get a license plate or Sara could add to the information she had given them, the likelihood that they could locate him was slim.

Bright sunshine made her wince as she stepped out of the dry, cool, air-conditioned environment of the library just after one. Moist heat enveloped her, making her break out in an instant sweat, and a surge of dizziness hit, an unpleasant side effect of the sleeping pill she had been battling all morning. She gripped the railing until the dizziness passed. A few seconds later, she continued on down the stairs and headed in the direction of the nearest café.

Ten minutes later, a deli sandwich tucked in her purse and a take-out coffee in one hand, she strolled back in the direction of the library. Smothering a yawn, she paused for a pedestrian crossing. When the walk sign flashed, she started across the road.

The throaty roar of a car sounded. Car horns blared and someone screamed. Pedestrians scattered. For a split second time seemed to slow, freeze, as her sluggish mind processed the fact that the car was torpedoing straight toward her.

Coffee splattered across the road as she flung herself to one side. Hot exhaust filled her nostrils as she hit the asphalt and rolled, pain exploding in her hip, her shoulder, her head.

The roar of the car receded. Shakily, she pushed to her feet. An elderly man picked up her purse, which she must have dropped, and helped her to the sidewalk.

She leaned into him, limping and ridiculously weak. She was bruised and sore, she had wrenched her ankle and her palms were bleeding, but she was alive.

He helped her to an empty table at a nearby café. A waitress hurried over with water and a supply of paper napkins. "Do you need an ambulance?"

Sara blotted her palms, which were leaking blood and watery fluid. She realized her white blouse was spattered, and so were her beige pants. The lurid stains made her injuries look a lot more serious than they were.

"I'm fine." She peeled the napkins off the heels of her palms. The bleeding had almost stopped, making them look raw and sore. "If I could use your bathroom to clean up, that's all the help I'll need."

"No problem." The waitress indicated the restroom doors just visible at the far end of the café.

As Sara pushed to her feet, the elderly man handed her her purse. "Are you sure you're okay? Shock is a funny thing. It can sneak up on you."

She put more weight on her sore ankle. When it held, she straightened and let out a breath. She didn't feel good; aside from the dizziness and the fact that she was shaking with reaction, her head was throbbing. She didn't think she had a concussion, but the bang on top of the sleepless nights and the sleeping pill hadn't helped. "A couple of painkillers and a good night's sleep and I'll be fine."

He stared in the direction the car had sped off. "Damned maniac. People like that shouldn't be allowed on the road." He handed her a piece of notepaper. "I wrote down the license plate. If you don't want to call it in, I will, but there's more chance the cops will haul that guy off the road if you put in the complaint."

Sara took the number. "Don't worry, I'll do it. I'm on my way to the precinct as soon as I clean up."

Ten minutes later, after she had soaked most

of the stains out of her blouse and slacks and rinsed and dried her hands, she used her cell phone to call in sick at work, explaining that she'd had a small accident. Feeling closer to normal, but still undeniably shaky, she limped out of the restaurant and caught a cab.

The precinct was only three blocks over. She could have limped there, but given that she was almost certain the driver of the car that had nearly hit her had been the same guy who had attacked her last night, she didn't want to risk it.

The detective who took her statement was concerned about the near accident, but ultimately dismissive about her theory that the driver of the vehicle had been deliberately trying to run her down.

Shreveport was a university town and there were a lot of kids with hot cars. Add the casinos on the waterfront and the drug trade, both of which generated a significant "underworld" factor, and they had their share of the weird and the wacky.

In the few minutes she had been seated in the interview room with Detective Thorpe, he had made it plain that he thought it was more likely the driver had been either a kid pulling a prank, or an addict, high on whatever drug he had pumped into his veins, than a killer.

He studied the file on her attack the previous night. "How could you tell it was the same guy who attacked you in the library parking lot?"

"I recognized his face."

He glanced at the statement she had just filled out. "You say here that the driver was wearing dark glasses."

"That's right." *And last night the assault had taken place in the dark, but she had been clear enough about what he looked like then.*

He tapped his pen on the desk. "Aside from the fact that he had dark hair and tanned skin and was wearing the glasses, was there anything else about him that you recognized?"

Sun had been slanting across the windscreen, glittering off the chrome grill....

She shook her head, unable to pinpoint exactly what it was that had made her so sure it had been the same guy.

"Nothing. I'm sorry."

He made a note on his report and checked his watch.

She checked her own wristwatch. She had been here for approximately an hour. Her lunch hour was long gone. At a guess she had caught Detective Thorpe just as he was going off for lunch.

Thorpe sat back in his chair. "We have the license plate, so that's a start. With any luck, we should be able to ID the driver, providing the vehicle wasn't stolen."

A second detective stopped by his desk. "We've checked the plate. It's a rental, hired out of Dallas-Fort Worth Airport by one J. F. Delgado. Plus, I just pulled this off NCIS. Looks like your boy's got a record."

Sara stared at the black and white. The photo was of a much younger version of the man who had attacked her. "That's him."

Thorpe frowned. "Damn, that's strange."

The other detective grinned. "I was wondering when you were going to pick up on that little detail."

Thorpe flipped the sheet around on the desktop so she could read the note at the bottom of the page and her blood ran cold. According to the file, Joe Delgado had died more than ten years ago.

At two thirty-five in the morning, she woke to find herself in the front hall of her apartment, her fingers curled around the door handle.

She had taken the chain off the door. Just a few more seconds and she would have been in the corridor. She could have made it outside and maybe even walked onto the road, if the soreness of her palms hadn't jerked her awake.

Shaken, she put the chain back on and flicked on lights. According to the clock on the sitting room wall she had slept for just over five hours. She had needed a good night's sleep. Instead, she had walked again.

She limped to the window and twitched the drapes aside. The city shimmered quietly, sprawled out and familiar. In the distance, she could just glimpse the hot pulse of a casino sign. The moon was up—

Shining with the same cold light that had flowed over the dark hills and forests around Vassigny.

Recoiling from the flash of memory, she turned on her heel and walked through to the bathroom, flicked on the light and rinsed her face, gritting her teeth against the sting of grazes on her palms. She dried off with a towel and stared at her reflection. It was the same face that had stared back at her all of her adult life. She had been born in Shreveport and brought up here. She had attended LSU in

Shreveport. Apart from a postgraduate course at Oxford, she hadn't traveled. In a family of foot-loose soldiers, she was plain, ordinary, stay-at-home Sara.

She had studied both German and French, but she had never been to either country. There was no way she should know about a place called *Vassigny,* let alone remember that she had actually been there.

Walking back into her bedroom, she shrugged into her robe. She would make herself a hot drink and read until she was relaxed enough to sleep again. Courtesy of her late shift the previous night, she didn't have to be at work until one, so she could sleep in if she wanted.

Minutes later, chamomile tea steaming gently on a side table, she examined the piles of maga-zines and books on the coffee table. The knap-sack caught her eye, reminding her that she still hadn't heard back from Bayard, which was un-usual. If she didn't hear from him tomorrow, she would call again.

Unfastening the knapsack, she took out the codebook. Other than the cursory look at the first few pages when she had been in her father's attic, she hadn't touched it.

She flipped to pages fifteen and sixteen, automatically expelling a breath when there was no red thread lodged between the pages.

A wisp of memory intruded—a code reference.

Feeling certain that, like the red thread, the code wouldn't be there, she turned pages. On page thirty-five, she stared at a table code and the combination: 8, 1, bridge.

It was the code in her dream.

Eleven

Half an hour later, Sara had printed out a number of files from the Internet about German code-books.

The subject was huge and most of the online material was collated and presented by private citizens, which meant a great deal of the information was slanted toward a particular topic, or shallowly researched and repetitive.

From her own study of cryptology, she had a basic knowledge and understanding of codes and ciphers, although most of her research had been based on secret writing before World War II. Regardless of when the code or cipher was invented, the techniques for deciphering were based on mathematical systems. In a cipher, every letter of the original message was replaced. Once the key to unraveling a cipher was found, the entire system was broken, and any message written using the cipher could be easily read.

With a code however, this was not the case. Codes were not based on replacing every letter—in effect, creating a new alphabet—but on a code dictionary, or codebook. One word or phrase might be decoded, but the rest of the code dictionary would remain secure. The major weakness of a code over a cipher was that the codebook could be stolen, thus exposing the entire code.

On impulse, she picked up the codebook and the newspapers with the ACE advertisements and sat down at her desk. Pulling a piece of paper toward her, she began checking the line of code against the entries in the codebook.

Minutes later she stared at the result, which was utter gibberish.

Unwilling to give up she began working to "decipher" the text using the St. Cyr Slide—a system using two alphabets, one sliding beneath the other. A key letter is chosen—for example, the letter *P*—and positioned beneath the *A*. From that reference, the clear message was coded into the corresponding letter on the slide.

Applying the method she had used was like reaching into a haystack and expecting to pull out the needle first time. The impulse to try the St. Cyr system had simply popped into her mind. It shouldn't have worked—but the result was grammatically perfect.

Five Down One To Go

She studied the phrase. Her mind instantly made the connection to the well-publicized fact that five members of the cabal had been murdered, most of them by Alex Lopez and, in theory, just one was left. It was more than likely that the message was a game or a joke and had nothing whatsoever to do with the cabal. But that wasn't what worried her. She shouldn't have been able to break the cipher so easily.

She shut down her laptop and closed the codebook, bracing herself against the automatic recoil that just touching it caused. It was just a book, an unpleasant chunk of history.

Too late to wish she had never found it.

The library was cordoned off when she arrived for work at one. The back entrance was blocked by a police officer.

She produced her ID, but he politely refused

to let her in. There had been a homicide. Every-one inside the building was being detained and questioned and no one was being admitted until they were finished. He didn't know how long the process would take, but he guessed another hour at least.

For a split second the world spun and she felt the blood drain from her face. Although the idea that Delgado had come back to finish the job he'd started was definitely wild. "Who was killed?"

"One of the library staff. Her name hasn't been released yet."

Sara walked around to the front of the build-ing and threaded her way through a gathering crowd. Police cruisers and an ambulance were pulled up outside the library doors. A news crew was already covering the scene. The coroner was crouched over a sprawled body, which was mostly covered by a tarpaulin.

Nicola Gilbert, one of the librarians who was on late shift, and a longtime friend, was standing nearby, gripping her arms, her face white.

When she saw Sara, her eyes widened as if she had seen a ghost. *"You're safe."* She shuddered as she indicated the mounded tarpaulin. "I thought that was you."

"It's my half day."

"I forgot," she said softly. "Well, I guess that narrows it down. I got a glimpse of her before they put the tarpaulin over. I didn't see much, just long dark hair in a knot." Tears leaked from the corners of her eyes. "It has to be Janine."

"Did anyone get a description of the killer?"

Nicola searched in her purse and came up with a damp tissue. "An elderly couple saw the whole thing. Apparently she walked out of the front door on her way to lunch, and a guy walked up the steps, pulled a gun and shot her."

A brief flash of Delgado's mug shot tightened Sara's tension another notch. It couldn't be related. Why should it be? "Where are they?"

"Over there." Nicola indicated a police cruiser, the two back doors open. She recognized Detective Rousseau sitting in the driver's seat, taking a statement.

The coroner drew back a corner of the tarpaulin. For a few seconds, Janine Sawyer's face was starkly visible.

Grief and sadness pooled. Janine had a daughter at LSU and elderly parents who depended on her. Her death would devastate her family.

Sara watched as the evidence team moved in.

Medics with a stretcher and body bag stood off to one side. "Did he take her purse?"

"According to the couple, he didn't stop to take anything. He just shot her and ran."

The reality of the shooting sank in along with a frightening twist. Nicola had thought it was Sara. On any other day it could have been, because she shared the same lunch hour with Janine.

Another salient fact registered. Janine had looked a lot like her, with pale skin and long dark hair. Today her hair was pulled into a neat French twist, a style that Sara often wore, and she was wearing a white blouse and camel pants, a similar outfit to the one Sara had worn to work the previous day.

The idea that the killer had been the same man who had attacked her—twice—and that he had mistaken Janine for her was a leap, but she couldn't ignore the possibility.

Ducking under the crime scene tape she strode toward one of the uniforms guarding the scene. The officer, who was holding a news team at bay, looked harassed.

"I need to talk to one of the detectives involved with Janine Sawyer's shooting. I have information that could help with the investigation."

Seconds later, Rousseau directed her to a police cruiser. He took the driver's seat and she sat in the front passenger seat. He flipped his notepad open, not bothering to list her personal details, because he had taken her statement the night she had gotten mugged in the parking lot.

Sara stared at the barrier being erected around Janine's body. "I think I know who shot Janine. Check with the report on the complaint I laid yesterday."

Rousseau's gaze was sharp. "What are you saying? That it was the same guy?"

"It's possible."

Rousseau looked skeptical. She couldn't blame him. She had trouble believing it herself. "I could be wrong. I *hope* I'm wrong, but in the past two days I've been attacked in the library parking lot, almost run down crossing the road and now a coworker who happens to look a lot like me has been shot on the library steps. Maybe those events are coincidental. All I'm asking you to do is check."

"If he's trying to kill you, what's the motivation? Is he related to you in some way?"

Rousseau's expression was utterly neutral, his voice flat, but Sara got the distinct impression that he couldn't imagine why someone might want to either mug or kill a thirtysomething librarian.

She could see where he was going with the question. She was comfortably well-off, but she wasn't drop-dead gorgeous and she didn't drive a flashy car or wear much in the way of jewelry. "His name is Delgado, but I don't know who he is or what he wants."

She had a theory, but it was so wild there was no way she could air it here. Somehow she had done exactly what Steve had warned her against, and had gotten sucked into the Lopez/cabal investigation. The only reason she could come up with was that somehow, someone knew she had recovered Todd Fischer's personal effects.

"Let me get this straight. You're saying the killer may have shot Janine by mistake."

"He left her bag. If he didn't want money, why did he shoot her?"

The expression on Rousseau's face didn't change. "Meth? Crack? Who knows? Maybe he was just having a bad day."

"No." If it had been Delgado, he had been having exactly the day he had planned.

"Okay, but you're still not telling me what I

need to hear. Why would someone be gunning for you?"

"Ever heard of Alex Lopez and the Chavez cartel?"

It was midafternoon by the time Thorpe, who had been given the job of interviewing her, finally showed her to an empty office and she was able to explain about her family's connection to the Chavez cartel.

Thorpe's gaze sharpened. "You're Steve Fischer's cousin?"

She was used to the reaction. Steve had been an officer in the Navy, a SEAL and a CIA agent. He was a local hero and he had gotten a lot of press lately with the discovery at Juarez. Sara had stayed out of the limelight as much as possible, her focus on her father's illness then death. Only the people closest to her knew that she was related to *that* Fischer family.

Thorpe made a notation, then excused himself. Through the glass door she could see him talking to Rousseau. At that moment Rousseau looked toward the interview room and raised a hand.

Thorpe returned and took his seat.

A few minutes later, Rousseau joined them. He

placed a file on the desk. "We've got an ID on the shooter, which *does* match the description of the guy who attacked you the other night." He opened the file. "According to this, the same guy—Joe Delgado, *deceased*—nearly ran you down yesterday. We have a few facts, a lot of supposition. What we need is motivation."

And solid evidence, which she couldn't supply.

"You're not going to like what I've got to say." And there was no way she could tell them all of it. She was aware that any credibility she had hinged on the fact that Janine Sawyer had died.

Taking a deep breath, she outlined her discovery of the items in the knapsack and the connection with the ongoing investigation into the Chavez cartel and the cabal.

Half an hour later, they broke for coffee and Sara took the opportunity to use the bathroom. Her face was white and there were dark crescents beneath her eyes, courtesy of lack of sleep and the fact that her mascara had smudged. She splashed cold water on her face, dried off with paper towels then took the time to apply fresh makeup, using the exercise to steady herself, although working with taped palms was difficult.

Thorpe was waiting in the interview room

when she returned. "I rang ACE Photography. It's a disconnected number. I did an Internet search to double-check. A number of hits came up with the keyword *Ace* but nothing for ACE Photography."

"ACE exists. They've been advertising in the newspapers."

Rousseau sat on the edge of the desk, his arms folded across his chest. "The situation with the Chavez cartel and ACE Photography aside, is there any other reason you know of for someone to want to kill you?"

"No."

Thorpe and Rousseau exchanged glances.

Rousseau leaned back in his chair, his expression guarded, his voice flat as he spoke. The Shreveport PD was hamstrung; they had to go on the facts and the major one was that Janine Sawyer had died, not Sara. The homicide investigation had to focus on Janine's life. Sara's angle was interesting, but at this point the possibility that Janine had been the target all along, and not Sara, was far more likely than a case of mistaken identity.

Thorpe shrugged. "We'll do what we can. Check with the papers' advertising departments, run a credit check on ACE. If there is an organized crime connection, we can run the data through the IRS."

He checked his watch. "I'll get a cruiser to drop you back at the library so you can pick up your car. Are you going to be alone tonight?"

Sara suppressed a grim smile as she pushed to her feet and picked up her purse. Both detectives had given her every courtesy but they had made it clear in the politest possible way that they thought she was paranoid, even bordering on hysterical. She couldn't blame them. She was entertaining the same possibility. "I live on my own."

"Then maybe you should think about spending the night with a friend or a relative."

And chill out. Lose the paranoia.

"Thanks, I'll think about it."

A police cruiser dropped her on the sidewalk just along from the library. As she stepped outside into the heat of late afternoon, the fluttering crime scene tape blocking off the library entrance was a chilling reminder of what had happened.

She lifted a hand as the officer accelerated away. The late-afternoon traffic was a steady hum behind her as she strode toward her car, the only vehicle left in the lot. She checked the shadowed loading bay and the back entrance, and skimmed the shrubs clustered around the parking lot. In contrast to the noise and activity out on the street, the library and the parking lot, usually busy at this time of day, seemed encapsulated in silence.

Sliding gingerly behind the wheel, because she was still stiff and sore from the previous day, she locked the car and fastened her seat belt. Seconds later, she was in traffic. According to Thorpe, the evidence techs were finished with the crime scene and the library would be open for business as usual in the morning. Tomorrow was Thursday, one of their busiest days. She would be expected at work at nine. She had approximately sixteen hours to decide whether or not she was going to show.

Twenty minutes of rush hour hell later, Sara turned into her street. Thorpe had suggested she stay the night with a friend or relative. He had been concerned for her state of mind, but it occurred to Sara that there was another very good reason for staying away from her apartment. Wild theory or not, if whoever had shot Janine had intended to kill her, then she had a serious problem.

It made sense to act as if there was a threat. If the killer was after her, logic dictated that the reason had to do with items she had retrieved from her father's attic. It also followed that if the items were that important, then he would want to retrieve them, which meant he would search her apartment.

Instead of turning into the parking lot, Sara cruised slowly past, scanning the parking lot and the windows of her unit. She stopped at an intersection and checked her rearview mirror. She had taken note of the cars following her. One in particular, a beige Lexus, was still on her tail, although that didn't necessarily mean anything. It was a busy road. A lot of traffic was flowing both ways and there was a major shopping complex up ahead. The lights changed. She accelerated through the intersection and turned into a quiet residential area. The Lexus cruised straight ahead through the lights, toward the mall.

When she was satisfied no one was following her, she doubled back and parked down the street from the apartment block so that her car was hidden from sight by a bank of thick, shady magnolias. She was beginning to feel faintly ridiculous. This was Shreveport, Louisiana, not Colombia. On the flip side, the Chavez Cartel had killed a lot of people in a great many locations. If she was right, Janine Sawyer was the latest in a long line of hits.

Grabbing the key to her apartment and tucking her purse beneath the driver's seat so it would be one less thing for her to carry, she locked the car, walked through the shady trees fronting the parking lot and skirted the open space. Maybe it was overkill, but she didn't want to expose herself by crossing the parking lot.

The air-conditioned cool of her apartment was a relief after the heat and humidity outside. Walking through to her bedroom, she kicked off her pumps and changed into a pair of cotton pants, a tank and a pair of running shoes. Dumping her crumpled blouse and suit into a laundry basket, she walked through to the sitting room, found the knapsack and stuffed the codebook, the newspapers and the notes she had made into it.

Minutes later, she had retrieved her passport and the personal papers she needed, plus the family photos and the few personal items she couldn't leave behind, and had packed them in a cotton tote bag. On impulse, she found a plastic bag in the pantry and packed it with items from the fridge that would spoil—fresh milk, cheese, tomatoes and salad greens.

The parking lot was visible from her kitchen window. Most of the parking spaces were empty, which was predictable at this time of day.

There was a car in her parking space.

She studied the late model Japanese import positioned just yards away from her window, but it was partially screened from view by shrubs. It was a completely different make and model from the one that had almost run her down, but she could tell from the license plate that it *was* a rental.

A faint noise in the corridor made her heart pound. Leaving the items on the counter, she gathered up the knapsack, the tote and her briefcase, which contained her laptop, and walked quickly through to her bedroom. She couldn't risk using the back door because it was directly opposite her front door and if someone was breaking into her apartment, the likelihood that he would see her was high.

Closing the door, she opened a window and lowered the items onto the garden.

An audible click, followed by silence alerted her. He was in.

Ears straining, she climbed out of the window and dropped silently to the ground. Pushing the window closed, she shouldered the knapsack, slung the strap of the tote over one shoulder and grasped the briefcase. Staying low, she backed through the thick layer of shrubs, far enough that she was concealed, but could still see in her windows.

A face appeared at the kitchen window.

Delgado.

He spun away and she realized he had discovered the items from the fridge that she had left on the counter. All he would need to do was touch them to realize from their coldness that she had taken them out of the fridge just minutes before.

Edging deeper into the garden, she turned on her heel and ran.

Twelve

Sara pulled into a parking lot in a mall. Just over twenty minutes had passed while she had driven aimlessly around the suburbs. She had used her cell phone to ring the number Rousseau had given her. She had been shunted through to his answering machine and had left a message about the break-in and the fact that Delgado was driving a different rental. Unfortunately she hadn't been able to supply him with the license plate. By the time she had thought about that, she had already been in her car and driving.

She had also rung the Shreveport PD after-hours number and talked to the duty officer. They had dispatched a car to check on her apartment, but they would be too late; Delgado would already be gone. The biggest gain in making that call had been to get the break-in on record, so that when she next spoke to Rousseau or Thorpe she would have solid evidence to back her story.

Her easiest option now was to get out of town, but before she did that she needed to get hold of Bayard. If she was right, and Delgado was one of Lopez's people, he needed to know.

Grabbing her purse, she locked the car and strode into the mall. She hadn't had time to pack her toothbrush or any spare clothes or fresh underwear. Aside from that, she needed to shop for clothes. Delgado knew how she dressed, how she wore her hair. Maybe in a town the size of Shreveport-Bossier it was overkill to expect that he could find her, but she wasn't about to take any more risks. Until she got some protection, or Delgado was caught, she needed to change her appearance.

Her first stop was a clothing franchise she normally never used. The designs were cheap, bright and about twenty years younger than the tailored suits and silk blouses or low-key casual wear she usually wore. She grabbed tops, skirts and pants and walked through to a dressing room.

Minutes later, after choosing an eclectic mix of limes, pinks and interesting shades of turquoise and chartreuse, she bought underwear and a couple of pairs of light, strappy heels. Walking into a ladies' room, she changed into turquoise pants and a fitted pink sweater and slipped on a pair of high heels. Unpinning her hair, she brushed it out and pulled it back into a ponytail at her nape.

She wasn't quite in disguise, but she looked different enough that Delgado wouldn't recognize her right off. Next up she bought a cheap suitcase. Zipping her purchases into the suitcase, she loaded it in the trunk of her car, then headed for the supermarket.

Fifteen minutes later, she had the toiletries and convenience food she needed. It was after seven, but before she checked into a motel, she needed to change her car. Once Delgado realized that he had killed Janine instead of her, he would start checking motels and hotels, using her license plate to find her. The car would be the equivalent of an arrow pointing straight at her.

She drove to a used car lot. Half an hour later, she had traded in her pristine sedan for a cream soft-top convertible. The convertible was a major change of style, which, like the clothes she'd bought, was completely not her. It was possible Delgado would trace the sale and purchase, but that would take time, and she was willing to bet that right now he was concentrating on finding her, not checking car dealerships.

Sara chose one of the seedier hotels down by the waterfront and signed for a suite with a small kitchenette, using a false name. After slipping the receptionist a fifty-dollar bill when she asked for ID, she lugged her things into an elevator that looked like a certifiable antique.

Her room matched the elevator, with seventies decor, peeling paint and a musty smell. Grimy windows overlooked rooftops and a back alley filled with Dumpsters.

Leaving the suitcase and knapsack in her bedroom, she carried the grocery sack of food through to the small kitchenette then used her cell phone to dial her apartment and access her answering machine.

She had four messages. Bayard's voice was deep and faintly raspy, a northern curtness overlaying the southern drawl. He was home; call him. He had left his cell phone number.

The second call was from Nicola. She was concerned and was just ringing to check that Sara was okay.

The third and fourth calls were from Bayard, the last one curt and edged with frustration.

She called Bayard's cell. He picked up immediately.

Swallowing to clear the sudden tightness in her throat, she filled him in on the items she had found and the events of the last three days. Bayard's questions were clipped and concise.

She gave him the name of the hotel and her room number.

There was a rustling sound, a faint click as if he had unlatched a briefcase, then Bayard's voice filled her ear. "I've got a funeral to attend in the morning, but I can be in Shreveport by tomorrow afternoon—three o'clock at the latest. In the meantime I'm sending an agent over. He won't be obtrusive. He's just there to make sure you're okay, but if he thinks you're in trouble, he will act to protect you. I'll ring back in a few minutes with his name."

With fingers that shook slightly, she placed her cell phone on the counter in the kitchenette. Calling Bayard had been an admission that she needed help, hammering home the fact that she was a fish out of water with this stuff.

While she waited for him to call back, she unpacked the few grocery items she'd brought to save either having to go out and buy food, or wait on ordering from dicey room service. Making a cheese sandwich, she ate it at the counter, washing down each bite with a sip of water. The food steadied her and helped her think, but the mundane chore of eating did nothing to dissipate her tension.

Within fifteen minutes Bayard rang back. "His name's Alan Hicks, he's an FBI agent and he'll be there in about twenty minutes. Call me as soon as he makes contact."

Hicks, a lean, fit man in his early forties, with salt-and-pepper hair and glacial blue eyes, took just over the twenty. When she rang Bayard he almost bit her head off.

Her fingers tightened on the receiver. "Calm down, he's here. Do you want to talk to him?"

There was a pregnant pause. She had the definite impression that Bayard was furious, which, she decided, was so not her problem.

"Not necessary. I'll see you at your hotel tomorrow afternoon."

He disconnected before she could say anything further, and she swallowed her own spurt of reaction and anger.

"Was that Marc Bayard you were talking to?"

"Yes."

Hicks's brows shot up. "If it's okay with you, I'll take the couch."

When the kitchen was cleaned and the dishes she had used were put away, she carried the knapsack through to the bedroom. After dropping a pillow and a spare blanket on the couch, she showered and changed into jeans and a tank top, unwilling to wear anything too flimsy to bed in case she sleepwalked again.

She said good-night to Hicks, who had the television playing softly and seemed to be immersed in some technical magazine, and closed the door. It wasn't late, it had only just gotten dark, but she was out on her feet. Aside from a symphony of aches from the near hit-and-run, she badly needed to sleep.

Although not just yet.

Unfastening the knapsack, she extracted Todd's gun and the magazine, loaded the empty clip and, using the blanket to muffle the sound, slid it home.

She listened intently to see if Hicks would

respond to the metallic click, half expecting the door to burst open. When it didn't, she let out a breath she hadn't realized she was holding and examined the weapon.

The gun would need cleaning. It was possible that after all these years, it would either fail to fire or misfire, but right now the risk didn't concern her. For now, despite the fact that Hicks was here, she was just happy to have a gun that could work in her hands.

She searched the bottom of the knapsack just in case any shells were rolling around loose. Her fingers brushed against something cool and flat. A metal tag with a key attached was caught part-way beneath the stiffened piece of canvas lining the bottom of the knapsack.

She studied the key. The tag, printed with a name and address, made it clear enough what the key opened: a safe-deposit box in a Shreveport bank. The bank was the same one that both she and her father had used, but there was only one person the safe-deposit box could belong to: Todd Fischer.

The sense that she was trespassing on very private ground, that Steve should have been the one to find the items her father had hidden behind the wall in the attic and not her, was overpoweringly strong.

The mystery of Todd Fischer's disappearance and death had deeply affected the entire Fischer family. Steve had adored his father. He had focused his life on finding his father and bringing Todd Fischer's killers to justice. He had defied the odds and succeeded in unraveling the mystery and finding Todd's body. Several of the cabal members who had been implicated in the naval killings had been found dead—but none of them, to date, had ever officially been brought to justice.

But, right or wrong, she didn't want to involve Steve. In just a few weeks he would be a father. After the trauma he and Taylor had been through, the last thing they needed was to be sucked back into the investigation. Besides, Bayard would be here tomorrow.

Slipping the handgun under her pillow, she crawled into bed.

At two in the morning she woke up. She couldn't remember dreaming this time, but something had happened. She felt different, sharper. Clearer.

The dreams pried open the door to memories,

but this time something else had happened. A door had opened in her mind and it hadn't slammed shut.

Maybe it had been her decision to research the codes, which had meant that for the first time since she was a child she was actively trying to remember instead of forget. Maybe it had simply been the contact with Bayard. Whatever, this time she hadn't remembered actual events. She had remembered *what* she had been.

Knowledge flowed through her like a cold electrical current. In that moment her senses were almost painfully heightened. She was acutely aware of the scents and sounds of the night, the cool draft of air from the conditioning unit against her skin.

She had been Sara Weiss, a scholar. Some things, it seemed, never changed. Like iron filings to a magnet, she had clung to the academic life.

But she had also been something more. Intellectually, she had known what her real profession had been. Now she knew it in a flat, matter-of-fact way that was faintly chilling. She had been a spy.

Flicking on her bedside lamp, she shoved back

the covers and crossed the room to stare into the mirror fixed to the wall above the dresser.

Outwardly, she looked the same. She was still Sara Fischer, a thirty-four-year-old librarian from Shreveport. Inwardly she was essentially the same person, but with a difference. The new knowledge had burned away the paralyzing uncertainty. Last night, despite her gut instinct, she had let Rousseau and Thorpe fob her off. Now she knew better.

At eight-thirty in the morning, Sara called work and requested time off. Her boss was sympathetic. They were short staffed, but they didn't expect to be busy. Already the front steps were overflowing with flowers. With the funeral in just two days time, they were keeping opening hours short and they would be closed the day of the funeral.

The funeral.

Sara's fingers tightened on the receiver. The thought of having to sit through another funeral service, of having to watch another casket lowered into the ground, made her feel hollow inside. "Thanks. I'll call next week, when I feel better."

As soon as she hung up, she informed Hicks

that she needed to go to the bank. He didn't like it, and insisted on calling in backup. Sara calmly told him to do whatever he had to, so long as he was ready to go at nine when the bank opened. And before Bayard got into town.

She had told Bayard about every item in the knapsack except for the key, which she had found after the phone call. She had thought about simply handing him the key along with everything else, but one fact stopped her. Todd Fischer's safe-deposit box belonged to the Fischer family before it belonged to anyone else. For all she knew it contained items of a private and very personal nature, meant for either his wife or child. If that was the case, she didn't want Bayard and who knows how many federal agents looking through what should have gone directly to Steve. On the other hand, it could contain evidence or information pertinent to Bayard's case. Either way, she wanted to check it out before Bayard got in. A final, practical consideration had sealed her decision. With the nature of deposit boxes, Bayard wouldn't be able to access it without either her or Steve there, anyway.

At ten past nine, with Hicks still grumbling and a second agent, Crombie—a younger, more muscular version of Hicks—flanking her, she walked into the bank. She was shown into an interview room. A short time later she was joined by Lydia Clement, her personal banker. Lydia had helped her through the process of closing her father's accounts and also of dealing with the loose ends involved with Steve's financial affairs when he had entered the Witness Security Program.

She studied the key, then checked a computer file. When Lydia quietly stated, "The safe-deposit box belongs to Todd Fischer," Sara got goose bumps. It wasn't exactly a hand from the grave, but close.

"Can I access the box on Steve's behalf?"

Lydia closed the file and pressed a key to activate the screen saver. "You have a power of attorney for Steve and the bank holds a letter from him appointing you as his agent while he's on WITSEC. Under the circumstances, that's acceptable."

Fifteen minutes later, she studied the contents of the box—a large manila envelope, which contained a sheaf of photocopied sheets, and a smaller envelope of black-and-white snapshots. From the dated clothing of the snaps, they appeared to have been taken decades ago—perhaps in the 1940s or 1950s.

She studied a group of young people sitting on a riverbank and a name popped into her head.

Helene.

A small tingling started at her nape as she studied the blond child. The quality of the print wasn't good. She could barely make out facial features, but something about her had sparked recognition. This time the recall had been easier, smoother—simply *there*—like an ordinary memory.

She returned her attention to the sheets, which were written in German. The originals were faded and old before the photocopies had been made. The date made her pulse quicken. November 22, 1943, just weeks before the *Nordika* had sailed.

The contents of what appeared to be a manifest were varied. In some cases the original print had been so faded that the words had disappeared when the reproductions had been made, but she instantly recognized what she was looking at. The manifest of a warehouse in Berlin which, just before the fall of the Third Reich, had held a fortune in art, artifacts and gold bullion.

Now the attacks on her, and Delgado searching her apartment, made even more sense.

She studied the list of goods. On the last page a name was scrawled in blue pen, probably by Todd. The name—George Hartley—meant nothing to her.

Minutes later, the papers and the photographs stored in a manila envelope, she left the vault.

Helene.

The name teased at the corners of her mind.

Another name swam up out of the murk. *Reichmann.* Helene Reichmann.

Shock momentarily held her rigid. For a bleak moment she considered the very real possibility that her mind was playing games with her, that her subconscious had thrown up a name she knew was part of the investigation into the cabal.

No. Quiet certainty filled her. The name was familiar because it had been a part of her dreams long before she had known anything about either Alex Lopez or the cabal. Until that moment she hadn't remembered that it *had* been a part of her dream. Like most of the finer details, it had slipped beyond her reach when she awoke. Now the connection was shocking and unavoidable. She had read the newspaper reports, and listened

to Steve's clipped explanations. Heinrich Reichmann had hijacked the *Nordika,* murdered members of the crew and perpetrated numerous other
atrocities. He'd had a daughter called Helene,
who was the current head of the cabal, and who
was wanted on charges of murder and conspiracy.

Hicks and Crombie joined her as she stepped
out into the main reception area of the bank.
Minutes later, she was ensconced in the passenger seat of Hicks's car, which he had insisted on
bringing. Crombie was driving a second vehicle,
watching their tail.

The air-conditioning hummed to life as Hicks
pulled out into traffic, sending a flow of cool air
over her. Her hands tightened around the envelope,
and for a moment she needed the anchor. Most of
the time the memories were faded, distant, and
confined to dreams as if they did belong to
someone else, but now wasn't one of those times.

She checked the rearview mirror as Hicks
drove. Crombie had slotted into traffic about four
cars behind.

Heat shimmered off asphalt, sunlight glittered
off passing cars.

*Not an icy wind, Alps towering in a clear blue
sky, Reichmann's eyes, pale and empty...*

Her jaw tightened. The past was over. Finished. Reichmann was dead.

But his daughter wasn't.

Thirteen

Edward Dennison pocketed the newspaper clipping of Ben Fischer's funeral that he'd had printed off the online records maintained by the library where Sara Fischer worked. The photo of Sara was distant and blurred, but that, and the fact that she was Steve Fischer's cousin, made her easy enough to identify.

He had only seen Fischer twice, both times in circumstances he preferred to forget, but the family resemblance—dark hair, dark eyes, distinctive cheekbones—was clear.

The fact that she had a couple of feds with her made her even easier to identify and underlined that his instincts were right. Something *was* happening.

Climbing behind the wheel of the Lexus he had rented shortly after he had exited his flight into Shreveport, he turned in the opposite direction, heading toward the Fischer farmhouse and away from the feds.

She had been carrying an envelope tucked under one arm.

She hadn't had the envelope when she had walked into the bank. It was possible it contained investment material but, with two agents watching her every move, he didn't think so.

He had searched her apartment, and found nothing of interest. Judging from the mess, someone had beat him to the punch.

If he didn't miss his guess, she had found something important—information or items that either Sara's father or Todd Fischer had secured in a safe-deposit box.

If the box had belonged to Todd Fischer and hadn't been accessed since his death in 1984, then Dennison was willing to bet that it had contained material that had been part of his undercover work.

From the information that had been leaked to the press over the years, Dennison was certain Fischer hadn't taken the Costa Rican job that had cost him his life seriously, but if he had taken the precautionary measure of securing information before he had gone south, that meant he had found *something.*

It was possible he had gotten hold of sensitive information pertaining to Admiral Monteith, Fischer's commanding officer.

Monteith had been in hip deep with George Hartley on some deal. The pair had instigated the dive on the *Nordika,* and he didn't think it had been for reasons of national security, as stated. Monteith had been as corrupt and greedy as they come. In his opinion, they had done it solely to panic Helene, which they had, only not to their advantage. By the time the crisis Monteith and Hartley had instigated was over, Helene had used the excuse of Hartley's security leak to restructure the cabal. Think major blood-bath.

When the killing spree had stopped, all links to the upper echelon had been severed. Helene had ruthlessly dropped almost all organized crime activities and, from what he had gathered from newspaper articles, had liquidated assets and poured what was left of the cabal's resources into the vast, amorphous sea of global commercial business interests. Within the space of a few days the cabal had morphed into a group of extremely wealthy and powerful shareholders hiding behind a complicated maze of shell companies. Monteith had resigned and Hartley was dead.

Helene's continuing contact with Lopez and the Chavez cartel and some high-risk dabbling in terrorism had been the only aberration. The risk had been huge and in the end it had bitten her on the ass. It was a glaring lack of foresight that had always puzzled him.

Back to the envelope. It didn't in any way fulfill his idea of the "personal effects" Sara's father was supposed to have brought back from Costa Rica, and it had been relatively flat—no diamonds.

He could be too late, and the lead on the cache of gold and diamonds the *Nordika* was supposed to have carried was in the envelope she had been carrying. But he was the eternal optimist. He was certain there was more to find than an envelope.

He was clutching at straws, but he was used to that. And he had a gut feeling.

Now *that* didn't come along very often. He would keep digging.

* * *

Sara checked her watch as she finished packing her suitcase, carried it out to the sitting room and set it beside the envelope and the knapsack. Aside from the visit to the bank, the morning and the early afternoon had dragged by, the boredom relieved by making sandwiches and coffee and watching TV. Bayard, who had been delayed, was due any minute. She never thought she'd be so glad to see him.

She needed to disappear. Now.

She had almost reached that conclusion anyway, but the moment she had realized that she had a photo that could help identify Helene Reichmann, the necessity had become real.

The photographs and the warehouse manifest were hard evidence against Reichmann and the cabal. The fact that she had been the one to recover them made her a witness for the prosecution. Whether she was being actively hunted now or not, the moment her name became linked with the case, she would become a target. She would need ongoing protection.

A tap at the door jerked her head up.

Hicks opened the door. Bayard strolled into the room his gaze pinning her. He was obviously dressed for work in a dark suit, a light shirt—no tie. If she didn't miss her guess, he was wearing a shoulder-holstered gun.

She became burningly aware of her rumpled jeans, pink sweater and the shadowy hint of cleavage. Normally, she was toned down and controlled, her hair neatly pinned, and with a strategy in place to avoid Bayard.

After a brief conversation, Hicks departed. Crombie had gone earlier, as soon as they had gotten back from the bank.

Bayard closed the door and put the chain back on. "Okay. What's going on?"

She moved into the cramped kitchenette, deliberately putting space between them as she briefly chronicled the events of the last few days, omitting the information she had gotten through the dreams.

Bayard's questions about the progress of the police investigation were clipped. She watched as he began examining the contents of the knapsack. Rousseau and Thorpe hadn't believed her. Bayard was reserving judgment, but he had the advantage of an intimate view of the Chavez Cartel, the cabal and the details behind Todd's death. What sounded crazy and wild to most people was real to him.

The fact that he hadn't dismissed the idea that she had been targeted made her feel oddly shaky. She hadn't realized how much she had needed someone to believe in her.

While Bayard handled the objects in the knapsack, she ran water, filled the coffeemaker and added ground coffee.

A few minutes later, he joined her in the kitchen, leaning on the counter while she poured coffee. She placed a cup beside him on the counter. "No milk or sugar. Sorry."

"I don't take either."

That figured. Sharp and strong and absolutely no frills. She reached for her own cup.

Instead of drinking, he took her cup and set it down beside his. "Are you all right?"

"Fine."

He pulled her close. "Liar."

Her breasts brushed his chest. His clean, masculine scent filled her nostrils, along with the hint of some citrusy cologne. The awareness that had been hovering at the edge of her consciousness sharpened. She stiffened, her fingers sinking into the taught muscle at his waist, off balance and at a definite disadvantage. He had hugged her at Uncle Todd's memorial service, then again at her father's funeral. This shouldn't have been any different. A split second later the unmistakable bulge of his erection brushed her hip.

Bayard released her, seemingly unconcerned by the fact that he was semiaroused, or that she knew it. He drank the coffee, then asked to see the photos and the warehouse manifest she'd retrieved. While he studied the items, Sara leaned against the kitchen counter and sipped her coffee, glad for the respite. He made several calls on his cell phone, his voice laid-back but incisive. When he was finished, he slipped the phone back in his pocket. "That's it. We're out of here."

She eyed him warily. There was something different about Bayard. She just couldn't put her finger on it. "Where are we going?"

"For tonight, my mother's house."

House was an understatement. Mariel Bayard lived in a Grecian Revival mansion just minutes from the Fischer homestead. The house was more like a museum than a home, which was one of the reasons Bayard had spent so much time in Fischer territory.

He unlocked the front door, dropped the cartons of Chinese takeout he'd bought before they'd left town on a side table, and showed her into the sitting room. "Mom's in Florida, but Amalie's here during the day. It's after six, so I'll have to make up a bed."

He disappeared down a hallway, reappeared with an armful of linen and jerked his head at the stairs. Reluctantly, she followed him. Whenever she visited the Bayard mansion, she always felt as though she was on the movie set of *Gone With The Wind*. The room Bayard showed her to ran true to form. It was massive and airy, with a bank of tall windows draped in muslin, dark polished floors and a king-size bed dwarfed by the proportions of the room.

When the bed was made, Bayard disappeared, then returned with towels, a length of what looked like pink silk and a shirt. He deposited the pile on the end of the bed. "The nightgown belongs to Mom, the shirt's mine. You can use either to sleep in until we get your clothes from your apartment. I'm just next door if you need anything."

"Thanks, but I won't." Ever since she'd been seven, she was aware that Bayard was dangerous. It had been a well-documented fact that he had gone through girlfriends like a hot knife through butter. It hadn't been a hard choice to decide she was never going to join that particular queue.

But, like it or hate it, he still attracted her.

When he was gone, Sara examined the nightgown. When she'd shopped for clothing, she hadn't thought to buy nightwear, a fact she had admitted to Bayard when he had questioned her on the drive out of town.

She folded the nightgown and placed it on top of a dresser. There was no way she was wearing one of Julia's outrageous confections. The soft white shirt was more her style, although the fact that it was Bayard's made her hesitate. In the end she decided that, cliché or not, she was too tired to give a damn. She had slept in her clothes last night and she could do it again, but the thought wasn't appealing, and the soft shirt was large enough that she wouldn't need to wear jeans to preserve her modesty.

After eating reheated Chinese in the large, airy kitchen while Bayard conducted a number of curt conversations on his cell, she made her excuses and escaped upstairs. Walking through to the ensuite bathroom, she showered, changed into the shirt and brushed her teeth. Next door, she could hear Bayard's shower running. Half an hour later, after reading a novel she found in one of the top drawers of the bedside table, she tied her wrist to the bedpost using a thin cotton belt that had come with the turquoise pants she had bought and switched off the light. Immobilizing her arm wouldn't make for a comfortable night's sleep, but if she did sleepwalk, this time she wouldn't get very far.

Vassigny's predawn darkness was close to impenetrable, the temperature, as Sara lit a candle, icy. After stoking the wood range in the kitchen to warm the house and boil water for coffee, she dressed carefully for work, wearing a crisp blouse, a shapeless but warm jacket and an unfashionably long woolen skirt that reached almost to her ankles. With her hair clipped back in a neat French braid and her spectacles in place, the effect was low-key but businesslike. She wished to emphasize the fact that she was efficient and utterly devoid of personality, a tactic that, so far, had worked. Reichmann knew she held a doctorate in mathematics from Oxford and that she had lectured at the Sorbonne, and yet her credentials had barely registered.

Her German citizenship had been her passport

to this job. Reichmann acknowledged her background and her education, but he had made it clear that he considered her inferior on two counts: she was female, and she had married a Frenchman.

The cold of the Château bit deep as she sat down behind her desk just before eight. Reichmann called her into his office and introduced her to Gerhardt, a slender, bespectacled man in a neat, dark suit. Stein was also present.

The reason she was required to work on a Sunday, Reichmann explained, was that Gerhardt, a Gestapo officer from Lyon, was conducting an audit of their systems, and she was to show them a full set of accounts and their filing system.

Gerhardt wasn't in uniform, but that wasn't surprising. The Gestapo weren't required to wear a uniform, and, like Stein, usually wore the uniform of whatever unit they were stationed with. When Stein deferred to Gerhardt, indicating that he outranked him, she stiffened.

Stein had been in residence at the Château for approximately a month. The Gestapo, now a part of the SS, was the Reich's secret police. The death's head units ran the concentration camps. They had carte blanche to investigate anyone they considered to be a threat to the regime, including

German civilians and the military. Their powers were wide-ranging, with a license for murder.

For a small posting like Vassigny, a resident Gestapo officer was overkill. The arrival of a second officer signaled that they were more than ordinarily interested in Vassigny. Sara was almost certain they were here to investigate the code leak.

By lunchtime Gerhardt had finished going through the accounts with a fine-tooth comb and, assisted by Stein, was immersed in correspondence files.

Gerhardt stopped by her desk. For most of the morning he had ignored her, but his sharp, colorless gaze was a reminder that she couldn't allow herself to relax.

"You know shorthand, madame."

Alarm feathered through her. Shorthand had originally been secret writing. It was commonly used nowadays, but nonetheless was one of the many branches of cryptography. The only conceivable reason Gerhardt could have for mentioning it was to test her in some way.

She met Gerhardt's gaze briefly.

Always make brief eye contact. Not for long, just long enough that they're convinced you're not avoiding their gazes. Not too long in case you betray yourself.

"I learned the Pitman's system at Oxford. It has been useful. It certainly made note taking easier."

She opened a drawer and extracted a flimsy sheet of carbon.

"Oberst Reichmann tells me you have a doctorate in mathematics."

And she had spent eighteen months using her natural flair for puzzles and patterns to design codes and ciphers, before her parents had been executed and she had decided that designing encryption systems was no longer enough.

"That's correct, yes."

"And yet you don't teach."

"I'm married to a Frenchman, Herr Gerhardt. Armand requires my presence in his home."

"You could teach in the village."

"Perhaps. I tutor some of the students in my spare time, although not often. There isn't much call for calculus in Vassigny."

Movement flickered at the window.

Shock held her immobile for a split second. Cavanaugh was in the grounds, just meters away, with a scythe in his hand. He was dressed in thick, dark clothing which he must have borrowed from Armand, a hat pulled low on his head. A woolen scarf was wound around his neck, concealing the lower part of his face, but to her he was instantly recognizable.

A second movement, this one farther out. Armand and two of his men were in the adjacent field.

Cavanaugh briefly met her gaze, his message clear. Emotion swelled in her chest. They wouldn't leave until she did. If anything happened, they would act. Armand would have stored weapons nearby. The risk was unconscionable. With SS troops barracked at the rear of the Château, engaging in a firefight was tantamount to suicide.

"Is everything all right, madame?"

Keep calm. Breathe. Sara transferred her gaze to Stein, who had entered the room and was watching her closely. Her cheeks felt as cold as marble. "Yes, thank you. I was just surprised to see Armand and his work crew at the Château today."

"You didn't expect your husband to be working here?"

She kept her smile brief and austere. Stein was aware that she didn't like him; he would be suspicious if her manner was warm and relaxed. "Armand doesn't always have time to share his schedule with me, and last night we had guests."

Stein stared out the window. "The Oberst mentioned that you had a dinner party."

Sara placed a backing sheet on her desk, carefully layered copy and carbon paper, and finished off with a sheet of good quality bond on top. "We have little, but we share what we have."

Stein didn't answer. His gaze was fixed on Cavanaugh as he scythed the frost-burned border of grass and weeds.

She rolled the paper onto the platen of the typewriter and loosened the tension to align the sheet of carbon, which had slipped slightly.

Gerhardt's gaze lingered on her hands. "That is a very pretty diamond you're wearing, Madame de Thierry. Your husband is to be congratulated on finding such a flawless stone."

Sara froze for a split second.

Not just the code leak, then. *De Vernay and the diamonds.*

Maybe it was too much of a leap. The ledger had recorded money, not diamonds. But if Reichmann had taken one, why not the other?

Now she understood why Stein was based at

the Château. Not because the accommodation was better than at Clairvaux, he was here to investigate Reichmann. Somehow he had become suspicious about Reichmann's activities. The reason was undoubtedly de Vernay. Reichmann had bitten off more than he could chew when he had added de Vernay to his list of victims. The loose end of de Vernay's extreme wealth had been left dangling. If Reichmann was found out, Gerhardt and Stein could have him tortured and executed without trial.

The code leak was a separate issue, but that, combined with Reichmann's crimes, meant that Stein, and now Gerhardt, had Vassigny under a microscope.

She held out her hand so the diamond would catch the light. "You sound like you have an expert eye, Herr Gerhardt."

He smiled without warmth. "Before the war I was a jeweler. Did you choose the ring yourself?"

She was abruptly certain that he *was* looking for the de Vernay diamonds. "My husband bought it in Paris," she said steadily. She mentioned a well-known jeweler.

Gerhardt's gaze narrowed. "I recognize the fine workmanship."

With a curt nod, he returned to Reichmann's office. Stein remained in the doorway for long seconds before swinging on his heel, striding out of the office and down the hall in the direction of the front door.

Alarm jerked through her. She kept a discreet watch out the window, but Stein didn't walk around to where Cavanaugh and Armand were working. Seconds later, she heard the sound of a car engine.

Shortly afterward, Reichmann saw Gerhardt off the premises.

Sara glanced out the window, her stomach doing a nervous somersault when she saw Cavanaugh and Armand still in place. What they were doing was crazy.

She jerked her thumb in the direction of their house, indicating to Armand that they should leave. He lifted a hand in reply. To her relief, they finally went.

Reichmann left almost immediately after Gerhardt, driving in the direction of Clairvaux.

Adrenaline humming through her veins, Sara pulled the letter she had just typed out of the typewriter, attached it to a clipboard and walked through to Reichmann's office. Seconds later she was in the strong room and searching through the safe. The codebook was there, but Reichmann's ledger was gone.

Of course. She should have thought of that. With Gerhardt going through his office with a fine-tooth comb, he wouldn't have risked leaving the book in the safe. In any case, yesterday was the first time she had ever seen it, which meant he normally kept it in a place where Stein wouldn't stumble over it. He had probably slipped it in the safe as a stopgap measure.

The only other place Reichmann would store the book was in the privacy of his rooms. She was going to have to risk searching his suite.

She locked the safe and the strong room, remembered to grab the clipboard, which she'd left on Reichmann's desk, and walked sedately back to her office. Shoving the clipboard in a drawer, she shrugged into her coat, slipped her spectacles in their case and grabbed her scarf and purse.

The need to leave immediately and forget about the book was so strong she almost broke into a run. Taking a steadying breath, she slipped her spectacle case into her purse, wound the scarf around her neck and walked to the door to listen. The corridor was empty. Distantly, she could hear the clash of pans in the kitchen. With more than forty mouths to feed at the Château alone, the kitchen was a hive of activity from two in the afternoon onward.

The corridor was empty. She wasn't certain if Stein was still away or not. He could have returned while she was in the strong room and she wouldn't have heard his vehicle. She checked her watch. It was after four. Most mornings and evenings he drove to Clairvaux to check with his prison staff, but not always. Stein didn't keep to a regular schedule. He enjoyed surprising people, keeping them off balance—particularly Reichmann.

She waited a moment longer, then slipped her shoes off her feet. Holding them in one hand, her purse in the other, she glided across the foyer and up the stairs.

Reichmann occupied the master suite, a massive grouping of rooms stuffed with heavy, ornate furniture. A fire was laid in the hearth but hadn't yet been lit. She would have to be careful. Dengler, one of Reichmann's junior officers, usually acted as driver and valet. He was presently out on patrol, dismissed while Reichmann was dealing with Stein and Gerhardt, but the instant he returned he would walk upstairs to light the fire.

Pulse pounding, she searched drawers and cupboards, praying that he had hidden the book here and not taken it with him.

She checked the small sitting room, the balcony, and made a quick tour of the neighboring rooms, both belonging to officers.

No. Reichmann would keep the book close. It was his ticket to a new life, and unimaginable wealth.

She checked the time. She had less than five minutes.

She studied the floor and walls. Feverishly, she began checking behind paintings, and hit gold.

Not a wall safe but an alcove, probably designed to hold a religious artifact or icon, and the perfect size for storing the book.

Grabbing the ledger, she stuffed it into her purse. The feel of the damp brown leather was repellent. It stuck out, but she couldn't help that. Outside, the roar of vehicles filled the silence.

Adrenaline almost stopped her heart. She checked out the window. Dengler was returning with the patrol. She couldn't see either Stein or Reichmann.

She had to leave, quickly, and not by the front door.

Walking swiftly, she took the narrow servants' stairs. They were dark and dusty and in a state of disrepair, too dangerous for everyday use. The stairs came out at a small door that opened into one of the kitchen pantries. The small, dark room was hung with hams and sausages.

She slipped her shoes back on. The tang of rich, smoked sausage made her mouth water uncontrollably, reminding her that she had barely eaten all day. It had been more than a week since she'd had meat, but right now food was not a priority. She paused in a darkened alcove just short of the main kitchen and glimpsed a familiar lined face framed by wisps of gray hair tucked beneath a scarf. Nanna Guignard, the cook. Raisin-dark eyes met hers. A hand signaled that she should stay out of sight.

The old woman turned and snapped out an order. She needed herbs, various kinds, and she needed them now. And more potatoes. The two women from the village helping prepare the meal scurried out to the vegetable garden, snatching baskets as they went. A German soldier, a tall, gangling boy of no more than fifteen or sixteen who supervised the cooking, gestured at the half sack of potatoes propped against one wall.

The woman was unmoved. The Oberst had a special guest tonight. A special effort was required. Those old potatoes were for the men in the barracks.

Shrugging, he ducked his head to avoid the low lintel and disappeared in the direction of one of the garden sheds.

The woman jerked her head. *"Allez,"* she whispered. *Go.*

"Attend! La couleur. Rouge."

Mouth now bone-dry at the mistake she had almost made, Sara unwound the red scarf and handed it to the old woman. Seconds later, she stepped outside and walked swiftly to the cover of the thick tangle of overgrown shrubs that marked the beginning of what had once been exquisitely groomed gardens.

Keeping low and taking care to always keep shrubs and trees between herself and the Château, she scrambled over a low stone wall and started across a bare expanse of field.

Her stockings were ripped, her shoes wet and her feet were already numb with cold.

The jagged croak of a raven jerked her head around. The birds launched, black wings beating the air. The sense that someone was watching her was suddenly overpowering.

The ravens wheeled, swung east then settled in the distant, skeletal branches of a tree.

She stumbled on, calculating the distance. Two more fields, an icy stream to cross, a short walk down a lane and she would be at the back of Armand's house.

She checked behind her constantly. Her spine felt tight, her skin crawling with tension.

The cold water from the stream froze her feet and ankles. She slipped as she climbed the bank. Her flimsy shoes were worse than useless; they were an impediment. Leaving them behind a tree, she walked to the edge of the lane and checked the road.

The roof of Armand's house, smoke curling from the chimney, came into view. She broke into a run, clasping her purse and the book to her chest, relief making her clumsy. Home. Freedom.

Until that moment, she hadn't realized how badly she needed out of Reichmann's and Stein's twisted world.

Fourteen

Armand wasn't in the house.

Stripping off her office clothes, Sara dressed swiftly in thick woolen trousers and a woolen shirt and sweater, with a double layer of socks for her feet, which were still frozen. She didn't have time to warm them, which was dangerous, but not as dangerous as staying one second longer than she needed in Vassigny.

She took her knapsack out of the closet and stuffed it with Reichmann's ledger, spare socks in case her feet got wet again, her gun, a well-oiled Luger and a supply of ammunition.

Shrugging into a thick, dark coat, she ran downstairs and packed the food and drink she had prepared before she had left for work that morning. She wasn't taking much. They would be on the move for a day, maybe two if they encountered problems, then Switzerland, and home.

Although where home was now was a moot point. She loved France, and she had transplanted easily. If she had to label herself, she was more French than either English or German, but staying wasn't possible right now. She would go to England. Perhaps even America.

Excitement of a different kind made her heart speed up, and her face burned as she laced on leather boots, shrugged into the knapsack and checked her watch. Cavanaugh would be waiting.

Her pulse jumped another notch. What she was feeling was crazy. It shouldn't matter who was waiting.

Armand stepped in the door, removing his hat and scarf, and walked through to the kitchen. "You're ready to leave."

"And you're not."

Armand was also packing, although he wasn't coming with her. He was joining de Vallois and the Maquis. It had been decided that the entire unit of the Resistance had to pull out of Vassigny. It was regrettable, but there was no other way.

She gripped his arms and kissed him on both cheeks. His hug was brief and hard.

"Don't wait, Armand. Leave now." He should have left this morning. Instead, he had deliberately waited until she was safe.

He grinned. "Don't worry. I'll be right behind you."

Her eyes were burning. "I'll miss you."

"Don't worry, you'll see me again. I'm a survivor."

She blinked back tears and reluctantly let him go. They were married on paper, but Armand was the brother she had never had. For the past two years they had shared a waking nightmare and she had a vested interest in his well-being. "You need to leave, now. Stein's up to something."

His expression was unmoved. "Soon. Yvette and Pascal are due to arrive shortly. I can't leave until they get here."

Yvette Dutetre was his daughter, Pascal, his seven-year-old grandson. They lived on a farm, closer to St. Laurent than Vassigny, and south of the escape route. Armand had to get them out. If Armand were hauled in for questioning, Stein, without doubt, would use Yvette and Pascal as collateral. But with the compressed time frame and the difficulty of movement on the roads, re-trieving his family was fraught with risk.

"Don't delay. I've got a bad feeling about Stein." It had chased her across the fields and was still sawing at her nerves. If possible, she was even more on edge than she had been at the Château.

She hugged him again, tears burning behind her eyes. "*Bonne chance* and Godspeed. I'll never forget you."

Armand pushed her toward the back door. "*Et tu m'amie*. Now go. *Vite, vite!*"

Cavanaugh was waiting in the tunnel. The first touch of his gaze intensified her fierce need to survive and correspondingly filled her with fear. Always before she had risked herself for others, never herself. She hadn't wanted or needed anything but the work she was doing, and she had been prepared to pay with her life.

Now, she wanted to live, so powerfully that raw panic filled her. She couldn't help thinking that something she needed so badly could so easily be taken from her.

Sara lifted a lamp off a hook on the wall and used matches from her knapsack to light it. Their shadows flickered wildly over the rough walls of the tunnel. "Keep your head low, and don't talk until we stop walking. Sound travels along the tunnels. Sometimes conversations can be heard in unexpected places."

"Does anyone else besides you use these tunnels?"

"No, only the Maquis. The villagers know about it, but no one would jeopardize us."

She gripped his arm, halting him. "If I'm caught and I can't shoot myself, you'll have to do it."

His dark gaze was steady. "We won't get caught."

She didn't relinquish her grip. She had seen Stein at work, heard reports of the atrocities at Lyon and Clairvaux. He was brutal, efficient. If he had a shred of humanity in him, she had never been privileged to witness it. If he discovered that she had not only stolen their codes, but written an Allied cipher, he would be merciless. "Don't hesitate. *S'il vous plaît.*"

Cavanaugh shrugged into his coat. His gaze met hers, and she had a brief moment to wonder what his story was, why he was here risking his life. As powerfully as he attracted her, she only knew him on an instinctual, visceral level. She trusted him with her life. Perhaps it was the best way to know someone, but that didn't change the reality that she knew nothing of a personal nature about him.

"Don't worry, *madame.* I'll take care of you."

"Not *madame,* not anymore. Just plain Sara Weiss." This part of the war was over for her. She wouldn't miss the deprivation, the fear and brutality, but she would miss the comradeship. Armand and his band of Maquis, de Vallois and the SOE operatives she liaised with, had become more than friends—they were her family.

Minutes later, they exited the tunnel and stepped out into the damp chill of evening. Two of Armand's best men were waiting, dark, lethal shadows who went by the names Rene and Guillaume.

As they entered the edge of the massive forest that fringed the eastern slopes of Vassigny, the sense of foreboding that had dogged her even before she had left the Château coalesced into knowledge. In the distance the sound of vehicles jerked her head around. From their vantage point she could clearly see Armand's house, and two vehicles parked outside it. One of them Stein's.

Panic gripped her. Stein knew what Reichmann was up to and he had been spying on him. She hadn't seen him this evening, which was unusual. She should have paid attention to her gut instinct. When she was crossing the open fields the sensation that she was being watched had been almost suffocatingly strong. *Because Stein had been watching her.*

Fear hammered in her chest. She had an urge to retrace her steps. To *run.*

Armand should have left by now. He should be behind them, although he wasn't leaving France. He and his daughter and grandson were joining de Vallois and his men in the forest. They would remain with them until it was safe for Yvette and Pascal to be moved south to stay with relatives.

A second later Armand stumbled out of the house, one of Stein's troopers following behind. A small figure was hauled out of one of the cars and Sara's heart contracted with shock.

"I need to go back. I'm the one they want. They've got *Pascal.* He's seven years—"

"No."

Cavanaugh gripped her arms, his gaze locked with hers. "If you go back, you'll make things worse. You'll put the proof they're looking for in their hands. Armand knows the game. Let him play it."

Her jaw clenched. If Armand were captured he wouldn't talk, no matter what they did to him—or his family. That was how they survived, the code of silence combined with absolute trust and absolute loyalty. But his death would be on her head. He had harbored her, protected her. *She* would be the reason he died.

Cavanaugh shook her. "De Vallois will get him. *Ne souci pas.*"

Don't worry. Tears were streaming down her face. She couldn't hear what was being said, the wind was too strong up here, snatching away all but the loudest sounds. Pascal, despite being pushed around, was upright and stoic. He was seven going on thirty. He had seen things that no child should ever see, and he knew what a monster Stein was.

She could see Armand gesturing. She knew what he would be telling them, that she had gone to Bourg-En-Bresse to tend her sick aunt, and that she would be back in a few days.

A fist caught him on the cheekbone. She flinched, sound erupted from her throat as he crumpled, blood streaming down the side of his face.

Cavanaugh's grip tightened as one of the vehicle doors was flung open and Yvette was pushed out. Pascal darted across the road to his mother and they clung together as Armand pushed to his feet. Surrounded by Stein and his armed squad, all three looked pitifully frail.

A flicker of movement caught her eyes.

An old man was drifting along the road, ostensibly returning home from the fields. Abelard, one of de Vallois's lieutenants.

Fierce relief filled her.

Cavanaugh was right. De Vallois was there and he had control of the situation. It was possible they would fight. There were no guarantees, but with Armand and his family involved, they couldn't afford to lose.

Abruptly, Cavanaugh hauled her close. The heat of his body engulfed her, she could feel the steady beat of his heart. His hold loosened. His gaze caught hers, held, and the secret she had pushed aside and tried to stamp out, because it was an impossible luxury, was suddenly as clear and sharp as the icy winter sky.

Emotion pierced her, raw, urgent. Something

altered in his gaze, and in that moment the secret was shared. His hands framed her face and his mouth came down on hers, touched, clung. The numbing cold dissolved and for a few dizzying moments she burned.

When he lifted his mouth, his gaze was once again implacable. "Now we go, *n'est-ce pas?*"

Not a question. A command.

They walked in silence as full dark fell, following goat trails, each step careful. A twisted ankle or a broken bone now would spell disaster.

Two more of Armand's men met them at the intersection of two streams that ran through the forest. Here the trees were thinner and the moonlight illuminated the open areas. Rene and Guillaume squatted down to top up their water bottles. Sara indicated she needed privacy.

Cavanaugh's gaze was sharp, his voice toneless. "Don't go far."

She retraced her steps until she found a secluded area not far from the water. They would be traveling for two days, minimum. In that time there wouldn't be any luxuries, and few opportunities for her to relieve herself out of sight of the men. She pushed her trousers down, squatted and systematically emptied her bladder. When she was finished, she used one of several cotton squares she had brought to dry herself. When her trousers were refastened, she buried the scrap of cotton under a thick layer of pine needles.

A breeze rustled through the trees, the cold penetrating her layers of wool clothing as she washed her hands in the stream, then, on impulse, splashed water on her face. When she straightened an arm clamped around her throat, choking off her breath.

Cold steel jabbed into her side. "Don't make a sound."

Stein.

She drove back with an elbow and wrenched at his arm. He jerked her back, the movement short and vicious. Long seconds passed, her chest burned, her vision began to blur. Stein was pressing on her carotid.

Then they were moving, her feet stumbling, dragging. The viselike hold on her throat eased, oxygen flooded her lungs. She gasped. Stein's hold tightened, once more cutting off her air supply. Distantly she could hear shouts, gunfire.

Moonlight dazzled her eyes. They were out on a road. Stein pushed her into the back of a truck.

Two soldiers she didn't recognize gagged her and tied her hands behind her back. Two more clambered over the tailgate, their weapons clattering on the rough wooden deck. Then the truck was moving.

A sharp pain in her wrist and shoulder catapulted Sara out of sleep. Moonlight glowed off white muslin drapes, white embossed wallpaper and lavish white bed linen.

She was standing beside the bed in her room in Bayard's house, her arm rigidly extended, held in place by the belt.

Heart pounding, her mind still locked in a paralyzing no-man's-land between dream and reality, she loosened the belt and slipped her wrist free. A small shudder ran through her at the thought of what could have happened if she hadn't tied herself to the bed. The Bayard house was enormous, the towering landing and the sweeping staircase potential death traps.

The digital clock on the beside table read just after two. If there was any form of rationality to the dreams it was that they always seemed to occur at the same time within her sleep cycle.

Fragments of the dream resurfaced as she

massaged her wrist, sharp edged and vivid
enough to make her heart pound. Too awake to
attempt going back to sleep right away, she
padded downstairs into the sitting room. Moonlight washed through the windows, almost as
bright as day. Flicking on a lamp, she found the
knapsack and the envelope, which Bayard had
stored in an armoire. She slipped the photographs
out of the envelope.

*A color photo in a silver frame on a carved oak
desk.*

Blond ringlets, blue eyes, milk-white skin.

Reichmann's daughter.

Helene Reichmann would be in her seventies
now, but that didn't change the fact that she had
been involved in the execution of Todd Fischer
and seven other naval divers. The impact of that
one single crime on Sara's family alone had been
immense. Now, suddenly, the dreams that had
haunted her since she was small weren't just a
weird mental aberration; they were *connected*.
She didn't know how or why that had happened,
just that it had.

She had never met Helene Reichmann in the
flesh, but she had met her father, Heinrich.

Maybe it had been a mistake to look at the

photos, with the night chill biting into her skin, the old memories and old fears biting even deeper, but now that she'd started she couldn't stop.

She flipped through the photos. All the hairs at the back of her neck lifted as she stared at a snapshot of a lean, tanned older man, his hair bleached white by the sun. His bearing was erect despite the fact that he was out of uniform, the hawklike cheekbones unmistakable. Reichmann, the author of Reichmann's Ledger, the book that had almost cost Steve and Taylor their lives.

A soft footfall brought her head up.

Bayard glided into the room, large and catlike in the shadows. A sharp jolt of recognition went through her and suddenly the dream was back, clear and cold, as real as the solid walls around her—part of her.

"Couldn't sleep?"

Not since I was seven.

She glanced away from his muscled chest, the unconscious seduction of dark trousers clinging to narrow hips, the heightened awareness forced on her by the dream. "I sleep better in my own bed."

With a carefully constructed routine built up from childhood, filled with nightly rituals that impressed upon her mind that her life was normal and there was nothing to fear from sleep.

Bayard took the snapshot from her fingers and tossed it on the coffee table with the others. "Never look at photos of criminals at night. Trust me, you'll never sleep."

"What if I can't sleep anyway?"

He picked up a remote and flicked a switch. An obscenely large wide-screen TV flared to life.

Question answered: watch football.

He flicked through a couple of channels, found the one he wanted, grabbed her hand and pulled her down on the couch with him. He propped his bare feet on a leather ottoman, offered her space if she wanted it, and groaned when the Cardinals' quarterback was sacked and the Steelers' defensive back came up with the ball.

After ten minutes of watching the ebb and flow of the game, two touchdowns and a major ruckus about an offside call, she forgot about her bare legs and finally relaxed, amazed at how happy she felt watching twenty-two men go to war over a piece of pigskin that would fit inside a bread box. Fifteen minutes in, Bayard offered her a warm beer, and a half share in a box of saltines— all he could find in the pantry.

The halftime whistle blew and the intermission replays started, along with blow-by-blow dissections of the major plays. Sara curled her legs up on the couch and settled in. Bayard slid her a sideways look. "By the way, you look good in my shirt."

Fifteen

Sunlight flooded through the tall bank of windows in her bedroom, dazzling her. The small clinking sound that had woken her came again. Bayard was sitting on the window seat, dressed in black pants and a soft, black T-shirt that molded his broad shoulders and chest—with the addition of a jacket, ready for work, she realized. A tray of aromatic coffee was on the seat beside him, the knapsack and the manila envelope were on the floor.

She pushed upright, taking a fistful of snowy linen with her. The shirt covered her like a shroud, but the soft fabric clung where it touched and she wasn't about to trust its opaqueness in the sunlight. A button had come adrift in the night.

She decided to ignore it. He would be lucky to see more than a faint shadow of cleavage. "You shouldn't be in here."

"How did you sleep?"

"Like a log. Thank you." After watching football for an hour and a half and sipping her way through the beer, she had barely been able to keep her eyes open. When her head had started to nod, she had left Bayard to it and gone to bed. She had slept so deeply, she couldn't remember dreaming. She had even forgotten to tie her wrist, for which she was now profoundly grateful.

Bayard added sugar to one of the mugs, stirred and handed her the hot drink.

Like the white mansion, the bedspread and filmy curtains, the mug was stylishly white. She sipped, her mind for a brief moment blank to everything but the sheer pleasure of rich, mellow coffee freshly brewed. When she opened her eyes, Bayard was watching her.

She took another sip, steeling herself against the urge to blush like a schoolgirl. "What does it feel like living in a movie set?"

Amusement gleamed in his dark eyes. "You'll have to ask my mother. I don't live here."

"So what's your place like? Black leather, glass, chrome?"

This time his mouth twitched. "*Chérie,* you won't ever catch a man like that."

The lazy use of the French endearment, the faintly edged exchange sent a shaft of heat through her. "Maybe I don't want one."

"So I hear. Although you never struck me as a coward."

She overcame the urge to enquire who exactly had slipped him that piece of gossip. It had probably been his mother. Mariel Bayard had moved out of Shreveport several years ago, but she visited often. On average, Sara had lunch with her two or three times a year. The last time had been less than a month ago. "I'm not a coward. Just…unmotivated."

The silence stretched while she sipped her coffee, which she noted was hot, which meant Bayard hadn't been in the room long. The thought that he had been watching her sleep made her feel decidedly uncomfortable.

He opened one of the deep sash windows and propped one shoulder against a broad white sill. A warm breeze wafted through the opening, bringing a hint of the scorching heat to come and laced with the scent of freshly mown hay.

He replaced his empty mug on the tray, irresistibly drawing her eye. Like a punch in the stomach, the old attraction hit her full force. Bayard might have a high-flying career in the intelligence community, but with the sunlight glancing off tanned biceps and the breeze molding the T-shirt to his torso he looked male, earthy and borderline dangerous. He obviously kept himself fit, despite the fact that he no longer played football.

Bayard crossed his arms over his chest. "I've made some calls. You were right. Delgado is Lopez's man. He uses a number of aliases. He flew out of San Diego under one identity, then used another to rent the car. I've informed Rousseau. They've already put an APB out on him."

She sipped her coffee and let the rich bite of it take her mind off the fact that if she hadn't gotten out of the apartment when she did, Delgado would have shot her.

"We're checking on ACE and the newspaper ads and we've got a cryptanalyst working on the codes."

"You have a cryptology department?"

His mouth twitched. "We are the secret service."

She refused to let him charm her. "I need to talk to the cryptanalyst."

"Derrin's a professional. He'll have the code-book. There's no need for you to get any more involved than you have been."

"The messages are double coded for security." She hesitated. "There's a cipher involved. It's not noted down in the codebook."

She set the coffee down and slid out of bed. She really needed to use the bathroom, and she badly needed to be dressed. The shirt came to midthigh and the length of leg revealed wasn't anything that couldn't be seen on a city street, but climbing out of bed with Bayard in the bedroom, her legs *felt* naked.

His gaze sharpened. "Where did you get the cipher?"

"I'll tell you in a minute." She grabbed a pair of jeans. First she had to figure out what to say.

I remembered it.

I don't know how I know it, I just do.

The bathroom was as airy and spacious as the bedroom, with marbles tiles, a sunken bath and a walk-in shower. She took her time, washing her hands and face and drying off on one of the fluffy towels. She rewound her hair into a tighter knot and stared at her taut features for long seconds. There was no way she could lie to

Bayard. He was an intelligence expert; he would slice her story to pieces in seconds. Taking a deep breath, she pulled on the jeans, fastened them then walked back out to the bedroom.

Bayard hadn't moved. "If the cipher isn't part of the codebook, then how did you know to use it?" he asked softly. "I know you studied cryptology, but I didn't think you were an expert."

"I'm not." The fact that he knew anything at all about what she had studied surprised her. On both hands she could count the times she had seen Bayard since she had gone to college. She knew he had kept in touch with Steve, but he seldom, if ever, came back to Shreveport—especially since his mother spent most of the year in Florida. "I studied mostly pre-World War stuff—the Zodiac Alphabet, the Vigenère and St. Cyr Ciphers, the Louis XIV Cipher. Whoever is publishing the codes is using a codebook and the St. Cyr cipher, which makes sense. If he had used an Enigma cipher, whoever is on the receiving end would also need an Enigma machine and the correct settings in order to feed the enciphered message through and get the clear."

His expression didn't change. "Then the clear would have to be decoded." He lifted the flap on the knapsack, pulled out the codebook and examined it. "A naval code?"

"No. One that was used by ground forces."

That got his attention. During the Second World War, most of the code breaking effort had been directed at naval codes. It had been crucial to gain accurate intelligence about the German navy's movements because their U-boats had effectively ruled the English Channel, hampering the Allies' ability to conduct a war in Europe by blocking off their main supply route. No food and ammunition meant no war.

"You said you don't have a written record of the cipher?"

"That's correct."

"Then how did you know to use it?"

She shrugged, avoiding his gaze. Bayard's methodical questioning made her feel as if she was being cross-examined in a court of law. Suddenly the leap between the career in law he had walked away from and what he was doing now didn't seem so huge. "I tried it, and it worked. Run it by your expert if you don't believe me."

He replaced the codebook, picked up the envelope and tipped the snapshots out on the window seat. He had studied them at her hotel.

Before they had left Shreveport, he'd had the photos scanned and emailed to his office in D.C. One was clearly of Heinrich Reichmann, but he had yet to make any comment or accept her statement that the small blond girl in the shot was Helene.

He singled out the photo of Helene. "We have one blurred photo of Reichmann dating back to the 1940s, an archival shot taken when he assumed command of his SS unit. That information is classified and has never been released to the press. We don't have any images of Helene."

She could feel his gaze on her again, calm but relentless, like water wearing away stone.

"So how," he asked softly, "do you know what Heinrich and Helene look like, if you haven't ever seen them?"

Such a good question.

Bayard was clinical, logical. He liked the quantifiable. So did she. Unfortunately, neither of them were going to get it this time. "I don't know how," she said bluntly, "but I have…memories of them."

"Are you telling me that you have memories of people you've never seen?"

He didn't believe her. Well, she had never expected that he, or anyone else, would. The only person on the planet who had understood had been her father, and he was gone.

"Has this got something to do with what happened to you as a kid?"

Tension drew her up even more tightly. "What do you mean?"

"The nightmares. The sleepwalking. Come on, Sara. It wasn't common knowledge, but we were neighbors. I knew."

She stared out at the view. Her parents had talked to professionals about her "condition." Obviously, at some point, her mother had confided her problems to Mariel Bayard.

She could feel herself tightening up, closing off. Having people know she was different, maybe even view her as mentally ill, was like being naked in public. When she was a child, doctors and teachers had stared at her as if she was an object. For some weird reason, they hadn't wanted to meet her gaze, as if in doing so they would somehow connect themselves too closely with a "sick" person.

Highly paid professionals hadn't been able to understand what she had been going through, or find a neat, scientific reason for the phenomena listed in their textbooks. Psychic experiences didn't exist, therefore she had to be mentally abnormal.

"What, exactly, did my mother say?"

She knew for certain it hadn't been her father. He had not only understood what was happening, he had kept a lid on her condition as much as he could. But her mother had neither understood nor accepted Ben Fischer's view.

He shrugged. "She was worried when you started talking German in your sleep."

She stared at the hard contours of his face. "And what did you think?"

"I was a kid. I thought speaking a foreign language was cool. Now?" He lifted his shoulders. "You were seven years old. I don't pretend to understand what was going on."

But he suspected she was weird and unstable in some way. "All I'm doing is supplying information. If it doesn't pan out, ignore it."

She shoved a loose strand of hair behind her ear and began straightening the bed, although she knew that Amalie, Mariel's housekeeper, would probably strip it down anyway.

"I don't think you're weird. I just need to understand what's going on."

"Then do some reading, Bayard, broaden your understanding—"

"I already have."

His phone buzzed, breaking the taut silence. He turned away, facing the sunlit vista of acres of uncut hay shimmering in the breeze as he took the call.

Sara let out a breath. She stared at the strong line of his back, the darkly tanned skin of his arms. Bayard had always been formidable, even as a child. Faintly arrogant and declarative, used to having what he wanted. The friendship with Steve had worked because they had been alike in many ways: strong, mentally brilliant and competitive. But she and Bayard had never been a comfortable fit.

The choice of metaphor sent a jolt of heat through her. Thinking about Bayard naked and on top was a pastime she'd banned years ago.

He slipped the phone in his pocket. "Delgado's been sighted in Shreveport. A car matching the description of the one you saw outside your apartment is parked down on the waterfront. I need to go. There's no food in the fridge, but Amalie will be in at nine. She'll cook you breakfast if you want it."

She shook her head. "I can look after myself. I'm going for a walk." She needed time to think, to find her balance in the silent beauty of the fields.

He frowned. "I'd prefer it if you stayed here."

"I'll only be gone a couple of hours and I'll have my cell phone on me. Don't worry, I won't go to Dad's place."

She picked up one of the pillows that had slid off the bed. When she straightened, he was right behind her.

"Why don't you leave your hair loose?"

She felt a faint sting as he tugged out pins. She whirled, annoyed with his games. His hands landed at her waist and her breath stopped in her throat. "Don't."

They had only kissed once, twice if she counted the dream, but she could still remember the response that had jerked through her—both times. She stepped free, automatically twisting and pinning her hair.

Bayard caught a loose strand and let it slide through his fingers. "I'm not walking away this time."

She watched as he slipped the photos into the envelope and shouldered the knapsack. Minutes later, she heard the crunch of tires on gravel as he left.

A week ago she would have run without hesitation, but something had changed. *She* had changed. Sometime over the space of the past week she had finally accepted the memories for what they were, a part of that past life. Her experiences were neither good nor bad, they simply "were."

She changed out of his shirt and slipped on a cotton tank, not bothering with a bra, because it was already hot enough that a light sheen of perspiration was coating her skin and she intended to swim in the river anyway. She packed her clothes and tidied the room, placing the paperback on the bedside table.

When she'd checked that she hadn't left anything in the bathroom, she carried the suitcase out onto the landing, folded Bayard's shirt and went in search of his room, which was easy to find, because his bed wasn't made.

She studied the room, which, unlike the rest of the house hadn't been on the receiving end of Mariel's themed decorating. The walls were blue and still covered with sporting posters, the bedspread a dark chocolate color. The drapes were patterned in blue and gold. A shelf held school sporting trophies, and there was still a study desk with a lamp positioned against one wall.

She placed the shirt beside his shaving kit, which was sitting on the bed. The room smelled subtly of Bayard, making her stomach tighten and her nerves hum. He had said he wasn't walking away this time.

For Bayard, that was tantamount to a blunt statement of intent.

Sixteen

Marc walked into the Shreveport Police Station just before ten, and was shown through to Pete Rousseau's office.

Courtesy of a fax from his office in D.C. and a raft of information on Delgado and his connections with the Chavez cartel, Rousseau had agreed to share information about both the Sawyer and Fischer cases. The detective was polite, but wary. Marc understood the reaction. With the Lopez case, local and federal jurisdictions had always been an issue, but current legislation allowing wide-ranging powers for the investigation of organized crime gave him the muscle he needed. Rousseau was also aware that Marc could pull rank if he wanted.

Rousseau took him through the notes on Sara's file. Marc frowned when he read about the attack at the library. Sara had mentioned that Delgado was stalking her; she hadn't said that he'd held a gun to her throat. Her account was confirmed by statements from a number of LSU students. Delgado was a professional hit man, but on this occasion, his method hadn't been clinical. He had chosen to get up close and personal rather than shoot from a distance, probably because he had made the mistake of underestimating Sara. He had no doubt thought that because she was a librarian, she would be a pushover, and had blown the job. But if those kids hadn't intervened, Sara *would* have been executed in the parking lot.

Rousseau slid Janine Sawyer's file across the desk. The gunman had fired twice into her chest, killing her almost instantly. Sawyer was older, but from a distance, dressed in homogenous business clothes, she could easily be mistaken for Sara.

The phone rang. Rousseau picked up the call. Seconds later he hung up and reached for his sport coat. "Looks like they just found Delgado. He's floating in the river just south of the Cities.

He's been shot—two in the chest, one in the head. Looks like your boys are going to be looking for a new hit man."

Outside the air-conditioned paradise of the Bayard mansion, the air was hot enough to shimmer in the distance. The sun beat down, burning into Sara's bare shoulders and arms, and the light was harsh enough that dark glasses were a necessity. As she walked across manicured lawns and stepped through a white picket gate into the wilderness of vast hay fields, the smell of grass spun her back to long, lazy summers spent running barefoot and wild. She and Steve and Bayard had climbed trees, built huts and swum in the water hole just below her parents' house.

She climbed a stile and stepped into a mown hay field. The grass was short and spiky and browned off where the sun had burned the delicate lower stems. In a neighboring field, restrained by a taut wire fence, a few of Vance Pettigrew's prize Black Angus breeding cows grazed, their coats impossibly sleek and glossy. The pungent smell of the animals drifted on the warm air, blending with the herbaceous top note of grass and the cooler, underlying scents of the river.

A fine film of sweat broke out on her skin as she walked, the heat and the easy rhythm of the exercise leaching away the tension that had strung her tight ever since she had seen Delgado in her apartment. When the heat became too intense, she scrambled down the riverbank and walked in the dappled shade of acacias and willows.

The peaked rooftop of the Fischer house appeared through the trees. She continued to follow the line of the river, which curved around the house. A pair of swallows dipped and darted through the air. Automatically, her eye followed the movement and fixed on the attic window of the house.

It was open.

Chills chased across her skin. She distinctly remembered closing the window when she'd left the other night, and she hadn't been back since. Someone was in the house.

She reached for her phone, and searched for Bayard's number. Before she could short dial, it buzzed. She picked up the call on the first ring.

"Where are you?"

Bayard. Her stomach tightened in automatic response to his voice. She kept her voice low.

"I'm on the riverbank, on the bend directly below Dad's place. Someone's in the house."

"Stay where you are. Get under cover and don't go near the house. I'm on my way."

When Bayard hung up she deleted the ring tone and switched the phone to vibrate. Slipping the phone back into her pocket, she retreated farther into the deep shade of the trees lining the bank. Bayard had told her to stay where she was and she understood his reasoning, but if she walked a few yards upriver she would still be under cover, and she would have a better view of the house.

She walked soundlessly between trees shrouded with rampant morning glory creeper, and scrambled around rearing slabs of basalt until she found the vantage point she wanted.

The breeze lifted, sifting through the trees and blocking out sound. A dark-haired man moved through the trees at the edge of the lawn, his step swift. He emerged into a small sun-dappled clearing, his head up and alert.

An image flashed into her mind. A Nazi SS officer, striding across an open field with that same predatory glide, his head moving as if he was scenting the air.

For a split second, the heat and the scents of the river dissolved and she was plunged into icy cold and darkness, pines towering over her.

Stein.

A small sound squeezed through the sudden constriction in her throat. A second later the clearing was empty, as if the man had vanished into thin air.

He must have heard her and reacted. Sara froze in place. She probed the shadows where he had been just seconds ago. He had to be nearby, probably concealed behind a tree.

Long seconds ticked by. The heat and the humidity increased as the cloud cover thickened, making the grove of trees even gloomier. Sweat trickled between her breasts and cooled on her skin as she strained to hear, but the breeze was gusting now, muffling sound.

A faint movement made her stiffen, and suddenly she could see him. Not behind a tree, but in front of one. He must have heard the small sound she had made, but he had probably thought it had come from a bird or a small animal.

His head turned. Light glanced off cheek-bones, the sprinkling of gray at his temples, the line of his jaw.

Relief loosened some of her tension. He was dark, definitely Latino, and not tall enough to be Delgado.

Movement from the attic sent another spurt of adrenaline through her. The window had just been closed. Whoever was in there had probably finished what they were doing and was on the point of leaving.

When she checked on the dark stranger, the place he had been standing was empty. He must have moved while she'd been distracted by the window closing, and she didn't know in which direction he had gone. The only certainty she had was that he hadn't retraced his steps, because if he had he would have crossed her line of sight.

The two men were probably together, one searching the house for the items she had already removed and who knew what else, the other prowling the grounds keeping watch. She had gotten a good look at the Latino, enough that she could describe him to the police. If she could work her way closer, she would be able to see the second guy as he came out the front door.

Moving as quietly as she could, she retreated a few more feet so that a thick clump of vegetation screened her from the place the Latino guy had been, then she worked her way back down to the rocks, which would hide her completely. When she was certain she was out of sight, she walked around the bend of the river, far enough that she could safely cross without being seen. Then she walked into the water until it lapped at her thighs. Taking off her watch, she tossed it along with her cell phone onto the far side of the bank.

She took her sunglasses off and held them in one hand. Taking a deep breath, she crouched down and pushed off, sliding silently under and through the deep, green water to cut down on noise. In contrast to the steamy heat, the water was icy. One breaststroke and scissors kick with her legs and she was across and pulling herself up the bank. Seconds later, after pulling the pins out of her soaking hair and letting it fan over her shoulders and back so it would dry and also provide her bare shoulders and arms with some makeshift camouflage, she slipped her dripping sunglasses on top of her head. The sound of a helicopter registered. Retrieving her watch and the phone, she paused at the edge of the lawn in time to see a thickset, balding older man folding himself behind the wheel of a rented Lexus. The car was beige and she was abruptly certain that it had been the same vehicle that had followed her to her apartment the previous day. Her spine tightened when she noted that he had driven away without a passenger.

A faint sound jerked her head around.

Black metal gleamed. Adrenaline pumped when she identified the shape of a handgun.

Dennison pressed his foot on the accelerator, the Lexus fishtailing as he arrowed down the drive. The feds were circling. He had seen the chopper crest the horizon from the attic window, which was why he had cut short his search.

He couldn't believe that Bayard had managed to track him from Grand Cayman. In an effort to avoid detection, he had flown to Mexico, then driven across the border in a rental, changed his identity three times and paid for everything in cash. He should have been invisible.

A flicker of movement in the trees caught his attention. A familiar, cold, dark gaze locked with his, and Dennison's heart seized in his chest. Then he was past, the rooster tail of dust behind him obscuring the view from his rearview mirror.

Moments later the rear window exploded and

blood blossomed on the back of his hands as tiny shards of glass peppered his skin. A second shot whined past his ear, vaporizing the front windshield.

Blood trickled down his dark glasses and adrenaline pounded through his veins as he stomped on the accelerator, his gaze glued to the ribbon of road ahead as the car slid around a corner. A second helicopter appeared in the distance, much larger than the first. A Blackhawk, probably with a SWAT team on board.

Now the big-budget bust made sense. The feds weren't after him; it was Lopez they wanted.

He braked for the turn onto the highway. Back in the direction of the house the smaller chopper lifted off near the spot he had glimpsed Lopez and comprehension dawned. That chopper belonged to Lopez, not Bayard.

Dennison jerked the smeared dark glasses off his face and tossed them on the passenger seat. The smaller helicopter had already disappeared from sight. Lopez had escaped by the skin of his teeth.

But that wasn't the biggest tragedy.

His retirement plans had just developed a fatal flaw.

Lopez knew he was alive.

* * *

Dark eyes locked with Sara's as the heavy beat of a second helicopter filled the air. Bayard.

She let out a breath. He lifted a finger to his lips and signaled that she stay where she was. Then he was gone, moving soundlessly past her. She noted that he was wet to his thighs, which meant he must have forded the river downstream where it was shallower. He was also wearing a shoulder holster, the webbing almost invisible against his black T-shirt.

Time passed. She remembered her watch, and refastened it to her wrist. Water from her wet hair trickled down her spine, and her clothes clung stickily to her skin, making her feel even hotter. The brightness of the day dimmed as clouds rolled in. Thunder rumbled and fat droplets of rain began to patter on the leaves. The rain thickened, then just as abruptly, stopped and the sun reappeared, turning the landscape into a steam bath.

In the distance the heavy pulse of the second, much larger helicopter deepened as it lifted off. Minutes later a whisper of sound was all the warning she had before Bayard materialized out of inky purple shadows.

He was wet, his hair dripping, his T-shirt

clinging to his shoulders and chest. He still had the gun in his hand. "Did you see him?"

"Not clearly. He got picked up by a chopper. My team missed him by seconds. The other two had a four-wheel drive parked down by the barn."

The tension that had gripped her when she had seen the man in the shadows coiled even tighter. That made *four,* including the guy who had been searching the house.

Bayard's phone vibrated. While he took the call, setting up surveillance detail for the four-wheel drive which they had *let* get away, she studied the thick shrubs that enclosed the house gardens. As the crow flies, the barn wasn't far from the house, but it was situated on a small farm road that forked off about halfway down the drive—a condition that her mother had imposed when she'd agreed to move this far out of town. She might live on a farm, but she hadn't wanted to stare at sheds and have farm vehicles and equipment clogging her driveway. Her father had good-naturedly put in the separate road and planted a line of trees to conceal the barn from the house.

Bayard hung up.

She watched as he holstered the gun. "I saw

two of them. One was in the house." Briefly she described the first man she'd seen, then the older balding guy who had left in the Lexus. "Sorry, I didn't get a number for the Lexus."

Bayard's expression was curiously resigned. "Dennison." He used his phone to call in the description, with instructions to check the rental car companies.

Sara frowned. She knew the name, but she couldn't put her finger on who he was. "Who's Dennison?"

He slipped the phone in his pocket. "He's ex-FBI. He was also Lopez's right-hand man for about twenty years, until he turned on Lopez and became an informant. We've been watching him for months now, but he gave us the slip a few days ago."

Sara remembered a newspaper article she'd read to her father while he'd been ill in hospital. Ben Fischer had been fanatical about keeping up with every aspect of the investigation, and Dennison had had a significant role. He had been responsible for retrieving the original copy of Reichmann's Ledger and had been taken into custody shortly afterward. "I thought he died."

"Only on paper." Bayard leaned back against a tree trunk, his gaze skimming the shadows.

"So he didn't die."

"Someone who looked like Dennison did. We used the opportunity."

The flat series of statements didn't shock her as much as they should have. Bayard had a job to do. It wasn't pretty and she wouldn't want to do it, but she understood the necessity. "The Latino guy. It wasn't Delgado."

"Delgado's dead. They fished his body out of the river this morning."

The sense of cold deepened. "So who was it then?" And what did he want in Shreveport, at *her* house?

"How old would you say the Latino guy was?"

"Not young. He had gray at his temples, although he moved like a young man." Her stomach tightened as she relived the few moments when she had seen him gliding through the trees. "Maybe forty-five. Fifty at the most." She nodded toward the house and the front door, which was still flapping in the breeze. "When it's clear, I need to check out the house. I won't touch anything."

Bayard's expression was remote. "Not yet. Rousseau's sending a team over."

Long seconds ticked by. Her clothes were drying against her skin, although her underwear was still uncomfortably damp—and the insects were biting. She slapped at a mosquito. She was beginning to itch and burn, signaling that she had been bitten in a whole lot of places she hadn't noticed. Bayard didn't seem to be affected.

She checked her watch. Foot to the floor, it would take Rousseau and his men a good twenty minutes to drive out here.

Less than a minute later, an unmarked car and a police cruiser crunched to a halt on the graveled drive, which meant Bayard must have called for backup before he had gotten here.

Bayard's palm landed in the small of her back, sending a small shock of awareness through her as he urged her out from beneath the concealing shadows of the trees. Sliding her dark glasses down onto the bridge of her nose, she tried to shrug off the feeling of exposure that stepping out of the shelter of the trees elicited. Whoever had been here, they were gone.

As they crossed the open grassy space, she lengthened her stride, but instead of taking the cue and letting his hand drop, Bayard easily matched his pace with hers, maintaining the contact.

Maybe it was the humidity, or the fact that

she'd just had another scare and was still high on adrenaline, but her body's response to Bayard's proximity was intense and unsettling. A sharp ache flared in her loins and her nipples contracted into hard points, painfully erect against the fabric of her damp shirt.

Rousseau lifted a hand as he climbed out of the unmarked car. He shrugged out of his suit jacket and tossed it in the backseat of the car, revealing the fact that he was armed, and walked across the lawn to meet them.

Rousseau nodded at Sara and shook hands with Bayard. When she attempted to politely step away from Bayard's touch, his arm curved around her waist, keeping her close. When she stiffened, he sent her an impatient glance, the message clear; he wanted her close.

Already hot, with his palm spread across her rib cage, within a bare inch of her breast, she felt even hotter. She could sense Rousseau's curiosity, see it in the darting glances he sent her way as he caught Bayard up on the smoothly coordinated surveillance of the two vehicles.

Thorpe arrived, grimacing as he stepped out into the heat, and instantly shucking his jacket and loosening the collar of his shirt. He acknowledged her with a quick nod, then they moved into the house, which had already been checked out by two uniformed officers. As she stepped into the cool dimness of the hallway, Sara was uncomfortably aware that Rousseau was staring at her.

When she caught a glimpse of her reflection in the glass doors that opened into the sitting room she understood why. The only times he had seen her she had been dressed for work in quiet, low-key clothing, her hair pulled back in a knot. Other than a cursory glance that acknowledged that she was female and the courteous manners he would extend to any woman, neither he, nor Thorpe, had paid her any attention. Now, with her hair tumbling in damp coiling tendrils over her shoulders and down her back, *she* barely recognized herself. Added to that, she wasn't wearing a bra and the cotton tank she was wearing was still clinging to her skin.

Bayard's gaze caught hers, narrowed and glittering. She felt her cheeks heat. If she'd thought *he* hadn't noticed, she was wrong.

An hour later, after Rousseau's team had been through the house, taking prints off door handles and window fastenings, she did her own checking.

It was clear from the mess that Dennison had spent his time in the attic, which made sense since, apart from the sitting room which contained the piano, the rest of the house was empty of possessions. When she had finished checking the window fastenings, she walked downstairs. Bayard followed her into the kitchen.

She felt shaky and more than a little emotional. Part of the reason was that she hadn't eaten. Even worse, she hadn't had anything to drink and in this weather that was fatal. She found the glass she had left in one of the cupboards for just that reason, filled it with tap water, drained it and refilled it, drank, then left the empty glass on the counter.

A cloud of dust moving down the drive signaled that the last of Rousseau's men had departed. She leaned against the kitchen counter while Bayard drank a glass of water. She watched as he rinsed the glass. "Ready to go?"

His hands landed on either side of her on the bench. "Not yet."

His hips pinned her against the kitchen counter, and suddenly, there was no air. His mouth when it touched hers was soft, giving her the opportunity to pull back if she wanted. Instead, she cupped his jaw and angled her head to deepen the kiss. The pressure of his mouth increased. His tongue in her mouth sent a shaft of heat through her.

Her arms coiled around his neck as she fitted herself more tightly against him. The hard bulge of his erection burned against her stomach. His hands cupped and molded her breasts through the fabric of her T-shirt, his forefingers and thumbs squeezing her nipples into tight, hard points, the hold possessive and flagrantly sensual. His mouth lifted then sank back down on hers.

The message was clear. He wanted her and he was going to have her. She could lie all she liked about wanting him, but they were going to have sex. It was just a matter of when and where.

When he ended the kiss and stepped back, her mouth was swollen and damp, her body as tight as a bow.

Somehow, in the space of a few hours "not ever" had changed to "not yet."

Seventeen

Bayard parked in the visitors' space at the rear entrance of the police station. Heads turned as they strolled down corridors and through a field room. His hand stayed firmly in the small of her back despite the fact that she'd changed clothes before they'd driven into town. This time, she'd included a bra, and she'd smoothed her hair into a neat knot.

Rousseau showed them directly into his office. "Help yourself to the phone. I'll get coffee."

Bayard made a series of phone calls in quick succession. The nearest FBI office was in New Orleans, but he bypassed that and requested the information he wanted from someone called Lissa in his D.C. office.

Rousseau arrived with foam cups of coffee, several sachets of sugar, creamer and plastic stirrers. Sara loaded her cup with creamer and sugar and sipped. The rich sweet taste exploded across her tongue and made her realize how hungry she was. What she needed was food, but until she could buy something to eat, the coffee would have to do.

Bayard slipped a faxed copy of a photo in front of her.

She studied the slightly blurred shot, which looked as if it had been taken with a poor quality cell phone camera and, like a switch flicking, she was once again swimming in shadows and murky heat.

Stein.

Although it couldn't be. Stein had to have died. But then, so had she.

Bayard placed another photo in front of her, this one taken from a slightly different angle.

"That's him," she said flatly.

"Are you sure?"

"Yes." The murky quality of the shot, the way his head was angled, made the resemblance to the man she had watched from across the river even stronger.

"You just positively identified Alex Lopez."

Rousseau let out a low whistle.

The sense of cold she'd experienced the moment she had recognized Stein deepened. "I thought there were no photos of Lopez."

"When Dennison turned federal witness, he supplied us with these images."

Rousseau's gaze narrowed. "Now we're going to have to talk. What's Lopez doing in Shreveport?"

Bayard gathered up the photos and slipped them back in the envelope. "He's playing on a couple of levels. We've checked back on every advertisement placed by ACE in the last year, and found a list of telephone numbers—all with one-time use, then disconnected. The code traffic goes two ways between Lopez and, we think, Helene Reichmann. They've been using the code to correspond."

Sara sipped her way through her coffee as Rousseau flipped open a file and took notes. Bayard's flat delivery of the facts made sense. The situation between the Chavez cartel and the cabal was well-documented and ongoing. Put simply, it was two criminal organizations, which had once been intimately linked, trying to take each other out. The prize was equally simple—a great deal of money was involved. If the Nazi gold and artwork Reichmann had taken out of Berlin was also up for grabs, the prize pool could conceivably double.

She set her empty cup down. "I can understand why Lopez wanted the safe-deposit box, but killing me doesn't make sense. All he had to do was let me collect the items, *then* steal them."

Bayard sat back in his chair. "That's where the second agenda comes in. Over the past couple of weeks, two of my men have been killed in D.C. The second killing was almost certainly carried out by Lopez."

Sara dropped her empty foam cup into the trash. She knew Bayard had lost two agents but, in conjunction with the attempts on her life, there was now a more sinister connotation. Last year Lopez had systematically killed off almost the entire upper echelon of the cabal. The series of murders had been designed to isolate and terrify Helene Reichmann. Presumably, Lopez's ultimate aim was to kill Helene, he just hadn't succeeded yet. "Are you saying that Lopez is now trying to kill you?"

"Looks like it."

Bayard's gaze was calm, but that didn't change the fact that she wanted to shake him. He had to have known since the death of his second agent that Lopez was targeting him and he hadn't bothered to mention the fact to her. "Okay, so he wants to kill you, but why Lopez himself? Why didn't he send someone else?"

He shrugged. "Over the past few months we've closed down an estimated eighty percent of Lopez's operation. He's lost personnel, and he's had to pull key men out of the Colombian end of the business. Recently a rival cartel stepped in and took a chunk of his coca territory in Colombia. It's an equation. Less product coming out of Colombia, and his distribution system is almost nonexistent. Lopez is on the verge of going broke." Bayard checked his watch and pushed to his feet. "Which is probably why he used a low-rent killer like Delgado in the first place. Delgado was cheap, and dead, he was free."

Bayard gathered up the faxed sheets and slipped them back in his briefcase. He shook hands with Rousseau and Thorpe.

When they stepped out into the parking lot, Sara turned on him. "Why didn't you tell me what Lopez was doing?"

"There was no need for you to know."

For a brief second, she was so angry she couldn't speak. "It would have been nice to know a little earlier that he's trying to kill you."

His gaze narrowed. "I didn't know you cared."

Bayard unlocked the car, tossed his briefcase on the backseat and held the passenger-side door for her. His phone buzzed as he turned into traffic. The conversation was brief and monosyllabic. When he hung up his expression was remote. "I sent an agent over to check out your apartment. You've had another break-in."

Her jaw locked. With Delgado, Lopez and Dennison in town, and any number of "treasure hunters," it was logical that her apartment would be searched. But that didn't make the violation of her privacy, and her life, any easier to take. "I need to go there."

"Sorry, that's not an option. Rousseau's already on his way, and I've made arrangements for it to be cleaned and everything put in storage."

She stared at the glittering streams of traffic, the heat rippling off the highway. Despite the fact that she knew she had to step away from her apartment and her life in Shreveport, that didn't make leaving her home any easier. "So, what now?"

"We pack. I've got a flight booked for this afternoon. You're coming to D.C. with me."

Sara was woken by the flight attendant just before they touched down in D.C. Smothering a yawn, she folded the light blanket, handed it to the attendant and fastened her seat belt.

Bayard, who occupied the seat next to her, and who had been in work mode ever since the meeting with Rousseau, disconnected his laptop, slipped it into his briefcase and stored the briefcase in the overhead locker. His black T-shirt separated from the waistband of his pants, revealing a slice of flat, tanned stomach as he reached up and closed the locker.

His gaze locked with hers as he sat down, and suddenly they were back in male-female territory. "Feel better?"

"A little."

From the moment she had identified Lopez, time had been compressed. With a few phone calls, Bayard had organized one of his men, who had been involved in tailing Dennison, to go to his house, pack their things and meet them at the airport. His assistant, Lissa, had made the travel arrangements, a chartered private jet to Atlanta landing in time to connect with a regular flight to Dulles. The seats had been first class, something of a revelation after the economy class seats Sara usually booked. Aside from the fact that the seating was actually comfortable, the cabin was hushed and the food had been wonderful.

The plane banked. She looked out of the window, saw the carpet of lights below, the unmistakable shape of runways that denoted they had arrived at Dulles, and checked her watch. With the time difference, it would be close to nine o'clock.

Just after landing, a member of airport security directed them to a VIP lounge, where Lissa, who turned out to be a tall blonde with the kind of fine-boned face that photographed like a dream, was waiting.

Their luggage was hand-delivered almost immediately, and Lissa led them out through a private exit to where a glossy SUV with tinted windows was parked in a security clearance area.

A lean guy with short blond hair and a Southern accent, who was introduced as Bridges, was at the wheel. When their luggage was loaded, Bayard climbed into the front passenger-side seat and Lissa and Sara climbed into the rear.

This late, traffic was light, and the SUV was

comfortable enough that she actually fell asleep. Forty minutes later, Bayard shook her awake. Instead of a hotel, he had brought her to his apartment.

Too tired to argue, and aware of the security practicalities of trying to protect her in a hotel or motel, where she could be tracked with relative ease, she climbed out and let Bridges carry her suitcase.

The apartment building was large and in the Victorian style with soaring ceilings and lavish moldings, although the security features were up-to-date, with access card locks, bright lights flooding the entranceway and foyer, and cameras bristling from a number of locations. Bayard's access card even came with an attached GPS system, so that if he lost the keys, he could locate them.

Bayard's apartment was on the third floor. He gave her a brief tour of large, elegantly proportioned rooms. After showing her to a guest room, which Lissa had arranged to have made up for her by Bayard's cleaning lady, he handed her his keys, unlocked a file drawer in his study and found a spare set, then left for his office and a late-night meeting.

Sara was just as happy to be on her own. They had eaten dinner on the flight, so she wasn't hungry, but despite changing earlier in the day, she badly needed to shower and wash her hair.

An hour later, she was wearing a set of soft sweats she'd managed to buy from a mall near the Shreveport airport. Her hair was combed out and drying. Now wide-awake, courtesy of her cat-napping on the flight and during the trip into town, she unpacked. She shook out shirts and trousers and hung them in the closet, then loaded underwear into the top drawer of a chest. When she pulled open the second drawer, she discovered it was filled with a neatly folded assortment of football T-shirts and sweaters. The logos denoted they were from a number of universities, a legacy from Bayard's college football days. The next drawer down was empty, so she unloaded the rest of her clothing into it.

After storing her suitcase in the closet, she flicked on lights and walked out onto the narrow wrought-iron balcony that opened off the French doors and tried to orient herself. Since arriving, the night had chilled down and dense clouds had moved in. A cool breeze flowed against her face as she studied the amorphous glitter of the city and the darkened area directly out from the balcony, which indicated that the building over-looked a green space—either a park or a school.

None of the buildings visible were high-rises, which indicated it was an older part of town, probably with building code restrictions and historical covenants slapped on many of the existing buildings.

A gust of wind brought a scattering of rain. Shivering, she walked back inside and closed the doors. When she had goaded Bayard about chrome and glass, she had been joking, but she hadn't realized how wide off the mark she'd been. The apartment was definitely not a modern, minimalist bachelor pad.

She checked her watch. It was after ten, but she still wasn't anywhere near sleepy. Picking up a pile of newspapers, which Bayard's housekeeper must have left on the kitchen counter along with his mail, she made herself a cup of tea and walked through to the sitting room.

The second she unfolded the first paper she saw the ACE ad. Her pulse rate lifted a notch as she studied the line of code. She walked through to her room and found her purse. She didn't have the codebook, because Bayard had taken that, along with all the other items she'd found, but she had her working notes on the previous codes she had solved and her own homemade version of the St. Cyr slide. And, with any luck, her memories of the code from her time in Vassigny.

Sitting down, she began the process, an eerie tingle lifting all the hairs at her nape as code combinations slid smoothly into her mind. It was the first time she had actively tried to access those memories and she had been in no way certain that she would be successful.

She first deciphered, then decoded. The message was simple and declarative.

Someone important is going to die.

Eighteen

Helene Reichmann waited in the dim privacy of a sedan, which was parked a block away from a well-known chain motel. The darkly tinted windows blocked out the sporadic late-night foot traffic of tourists strolling to and from one of the several restaurants situated in the area and the occasional late-night jogger.

A cell phone vibrated. Cam Hendricks, who was seated in the front passenger seat, picked up the call, his voice barely audible. Hendricks was outwardly unremarkable, an ex-Army Ranger with the kind of tired, lined face and soft Minnesotan politeness that fooled most people. His impressive record, encompassing stints in Chechnya and Afghanistan, plus the utter lack of emotion in his eyes had been enough to convince her. Hendricks might look like a Minnesotan farmer, but he was smart, committed and brutally efficient at what he did.

He twisted around in his seat. "Larson's swept the room. It's clean. The two neighboring suites are empty. If you want to make the meeting, my recommendation is that we go now."

Minutes later, Helene exited the third-floor elevator, along with Hendricks and a third bodyguard, Marisa Sutton, a cold-eyed blonde who looked enough like Helene that they could be mother and daughter.

The inclusion of Marisa in the small, elite group Helene employed to protect her had been practical on more than one level. Part Russian, part Irish, Marisa was an ex-DEA agent with a formidable record in undercover work—notably, busting Colombian drug operations. She had "softened" the look of the security detail around Helene, making them appear more like a family group. The sleight of hand was subtle but useful, especially when they were in places they didn't want to be noticed. In the disparate worlds Helene moved between, superficial impressions were crucial.

Marisa had also been clear about what she wanted. The years she had spent in deep cover and comparative luxury, laundering money for drug lords, had resulted in a high arrest record, an intimate knowledge of Colombian cartels and a calculating ambition. At forty years of age, Marisa's ambition was clear-cut. She didn't want the gold watch and a service pension; she simply wanted the gold.

They paused outside the suite Hendricks had booked in response to the meeting that had been demanded. In all the years Helene had headed the remnants of her father's cabal, she had never given in to such a demand. She had made the rules and enforced compliance. That simple and effective strategy had changed the instant she had received a phone call advising her that the caller was aware of her identity.

The shock—the blunt statement of her real name, after almost an entire lifetime of operating under a number of different identities—had been considerable.

Blackmail was a bitch. She had little power in the arrangement, and only one card to play. Her blackmailer wouldn't expose her unless he was out of options, because the moment he did, he lost his power and his last chance at the powerful future he coveted.

Marisa knocked. Seconds later, Larson opened up and let them in.

The drapes were pulled tight, cutting down on the risk of any directional listening systems that depended on the vibration of sound on hard surfaces to pick up what was being said. The television was on, the drone of a sports commentator providing background noise and vibration that would mask the conversation in the event that Larson had missed a listening device.

Helene set her briefcase down on the dining table and extracted a newspaper. She dropped the paper onto the table. A story about two linked homicides occupied a single, narrow column. Needless to say, the story hadn't made the front page. Shreveport, Louisiana, barely registered in D.C. and it flat-out didn't exist on the international stage—her usual area of interest—but for the past twenty-four hours it had become her focus.

The man who had requested the meeting skimmed the story, although Helene had no doubt that he had been fully briefed. Rear Admiral Saunders was noted for his brilliance in the area of undercover operations.

A second fact registered.

He had cursorily acknowledged both Hendricks and Larson, whom he had met on one other occasion, but he had barely glanced at Marisa, who, to her knowledge he *hadn't* met. And, Marisa was ignoring him.

Interesting. Normally, Marisa was cool and unrelenting about her work. Larson had searched him for weapons and wires, but Marisa should still be watching him like a hawk. Added to that, any man with red blood running in his veins usually looked Marisa over, even if the perusal was purely automatic.

She was almost certain they knew each other.

Helene glanced at Hendricks. His icy gaze connected with hers, his message clear. He had noticed the slight oddness of the byplay; she could leave it with him.

She relaxed. "What do you know about the situation in Shreveport?"

"Delgado was Lopez's man."

She had known who Delgado was. It was the fact that he had been killed in Shreveport and in conjunction with Sara Fischer that caused her concern. "Who killed him?"

"Not one of ours."

A tingling started at her nape. If a federal agent hadn't been responsible for shooting Delgado, that opened up a raft of unpalatable options. "Was the killing cartel related?"

"The hit was internal."

A small shock of adrenaline went through her. *Lopez.*

He had killed his own man.

Not that murder was unusual for Lopez. He had been responsible for a string of cold-blooded killings over the years, including his father, Marco Chavez, and a number of her own people. But the location of the killing and the fact that he made no attempt to conceal the body was…disturbing.

A wisp of emotion caught at her, threaded with a raw undercurrent of fear. She should have ordered his death when she'd had the chance and buried her last, unpalatable link to Marco. Over the years there had been any number of opportunities to kill him. She hadn't taken them. He had been her one weak spot, a weakness he was now using to bring her down.

She picked up the newspaper, folded it and slipped it under her arm. There had to be more to justify a meeting that was, quite frankly, so high risk she had been tempted not to show. "What else?"

His expression didn't change. "Edward Dennison was in Shreveport."

Her gaze sharpened. Dennison was a complication she hadn't foreseen. The last she'd heard he was dead, killed by Lopez in a botched CIA operation. The fact that Dennison had also been in Shreveport pointed up the fact that Sara Fischer either knew something, or had something of importance.

The tension at her nape increasing, she studied her opponent. He was building to something—no doubt a further demand. "What, exactly, did Sara Fischer find?"

"The information Hartley handed to Todd Fischer, a copy of a Berlin warehouse manifest. It makes interesting reading."

It was also a link back to Berlin, to theft and murder—a link to her.

Her jaw tightened. She had made two major mistakes that she knew of in this lifetime. She had lost Reichmann's Ledger, the book containing identity information for the upper echelon of the cabal, and she had failed to kill Alex Lopez when she'd had numerous chances.

Now it seemed she had made a third mistake. Over twenty years ago she had arranged for George Hartley, a former cabal member and a traitor to their cause, to be executed. She had searched his house and put pressure on Hartley's son to turn over anything that might link Hartley to the cabal. They had found very little. A few WWII mementoes, a folder of old black-and-white photographs.

She had checked the negatives. Several of the photos had been missing, including a shot of George, herself and two others sitting on a river-bank in Colombia. The photo was distant and a little blurred, and she had been a child when it had been taken, but the fact remained that it had been a photo of her. To her knowledge it was the only one in existence that linked her to the *Nordika* debacle.

She had failed to find the photo. At the time the risk had seemed minimal. George had been dead and the *Nordika* tragedy had been covered up. The fact that somewhere, someone could possibly have in their possession a faded 1940s snapshot of an unnamed group of children sitting on a riverbank had ceased to be important.

Hartley had also dealt with the gold bullion and the other items looted from Berlin. He and a handful of others had worked with Dengler to shift and secure the crates. Hartley had been executed, then Admiral Monteith, who had proved elusive, eighteen months later. To her knowledge, she had been the only living person left who had known exactly what had been in the crates.

Or that there was a cache of diamonds.

Lopez had known about the gold bullion since he was a child. As part of the price for sheltering them when they had first landed in Colombia, Marco had taken more than half. Given that both Dennison and Lopez were chasing the information that Hartley had handed to Todd Fischer, she also had to assume that somehow, perhaps again through Hartley, they had found out about the diamonds.

And it was now possible that Saunders had, also. "What is it, exactly, that you want?"

"Lopez."

The sheer arrogance of the demand took her breath, but she had expected and planned for it. Capturing Lopez would be a very public coup, and would make up for Saunders's equally public disgrace as the prime mover behind the cover-up of the *Nordika* affair.

He produced another paper from his briefcase.

When she saw the page folded open to display the ACE advertisement, she went cold inside. Lopez wasn't the only one who liked to play games; Saunders wasn't averse to them, either. And even after all this time it was interesting to note that he still thought he could win.

His colorless gaze was icy. "You're corresponding with Lopez. Arrange a meeting."

"I can't guarantee he'll show."

"I've already taken the liberty of inserting the ad. Given his eagerness to make contact, he'll take the bait. All you have to do is arrange the time and place, I'll take care of the rest."

Minutes later, Helene allowed Hendricks to help her into the rear of the car. As they accelerated away from the immediate danger of the motel, she glanced at Marisa's controlled profile. Satisfaction eased the cold anger that flowed through her.

Saunders was playing the part of the gamester to the hilt. No doubt he assumed he held all the cards.

Too bad he wasn't playing with the full deck.

Nineteen

At one in the morning, Sara flicked off Bayard's wide-screen TV, walked out to the kitchen and made herself a hot drink. Winding her fingers around the mug and slowly sipping hot chocolate, she strolled around Bayard's lounge, studying the books on his shelves, a series of watercolors done by his grandfather of the Shreveport countryside and the odd piece of football memorabilia scattered around the room.

She felt alert and unsettled, and not just because she had deciphered another coded message.

Bayard had been gone for more than *three* hours.

The thought had passed through her mind that he wasn't working, that he was simply with Lissa, then she dismissed it. She had known Bayard for most of her life. In some ways she knew him as well as she knew Steve. He was as ruthless in his personal relationships as he was in his career, but he operated to a rigid code. He had dated a long list of beautiful women, but according to Steve, the ground rules had always been clear-cut. Bayard only ever dated one at a time, and when it was over, it was over.

The fact that he had openly declared his interest was subtly reassuring. Bayard was close to family. He wouldn't touch her if all he wanted was a short-term fling.

Nothing had been said, but at a primitive level the first and most basic foundation of a relationship had been laid. He'd claimed her in front of Rousseau and his men, and she had capitulated.

Ever since that frantic kiss in the kitchen, she had been on edge, sharply aware that she wanted him, that the logical conclusion to the kiss was lovemaking.

The thought that Bayard could, conceivably, date her for a time, sleep with her, then end the relationship, wasn't an option. She didn't love easily and, since he had never committed to marriage, she was willing to bet that neither did Bayard. But that didn't change the fact that falling for him was tantamount to stepping off a cliff. She was acutely aware of huge blank spaces in his life she knew little or nothing about.

Bayard was an alpha male and a self-professed overachiever. He had walked out on a promising law career to become an FBI agent. In the space of little more than a decade, he had made division head. Not satisfied with the FBI fast track, he had switched to National Intelligence. She didn't know exactly what he did there, and that was the scariest thing of all; when she'd asked him on the flight, his job description had sounded like a mission statement. Instead of controlling agents and operations, he appeared to control entire networks.

She rinsed her cup, placed it in the dishwasher and walked through to the sitting room. She picked up the remote and flicked through a number of channels. Unable to settle, she turned the set off. She was on the point of going to bed when Bayard stepped through the front door and dropped his briefcase on the floor. He walked toward her, and perversely she wished she had gone to bed. Waiting up for him suddenly seemed too needy.

Awareness flashed in his gaze. Seconds later, his mouth was on hers, his fingers digging into the soft flesh of her bottom, jerking her close.

Lifting up on her toes she wound her arms around his neck. The passion was white-hot and instant, the relief of her breasts flattened against his chest, the jut of his penis digging into her belly, burning away the gnawing insecurities.

Wrenching his mouth free, he dragged her sweatshirt and the soft, sheer tank she was wearing up and over her head and discarded it, baring her breasts. Dipping his head, he took one nipple in his mouth.

Sensation jerked through her in hot, dizzying waves. She tore at his shirt and found naked skin. Seconds later, she was on her back on the carpet, Bayard's mouth on hers. Impatiently, he shrugged out of the shirt and tossed it to one side. His fingers hooked in the waistband of her sweats and hauled them down, taking her panties with them. Cold air circulated around her bottom and thighs. The carpet was rough and prickly against her bare skin, but the discomfort barely registered as he came down between her legs. She fumbled at the fastening of his trousers, dragging the zipper down, and felt him, blunt and engorged, nudging between her legs. His gaze locked with hers. A second later he shoved deep and the room dissolved.

She had a moment to consider that he hadn't

used a condom, that he was naked inside her, then the driving rhythm shoved her over the edge.

Long minutes later, she stirred. Bayard had rolled over and pulled her with him so that she was lying half across him. At some point he had dispensed with his pants, socks and shoes and was now fully naked. One big hand was locked lazily over her bottom, keeping her leg draped over his hip and her pelvis angled so that he was still lodged inside her.

Just feet away, rain was pounding on the windows, the faint chill reaching through the glass, but she wasn't cold. Heat poured from Bayard. Wherever they touched their skin was glued together with perspiration.

She shifted slightly, adjusting her hips and felt him firm and extend inside her. One lazy hand swept up, cupping her breast and the low level throb in her belly sharpened. She lifted up on her elbows, her hair falling in a dark curtain around them and delicately, deliberately, clenched around him. "Shall we go to bed?"

He rolled her onto her back, lifted his hips and slid back into her with one gliding stroke.

"Not yet."

* * *

At four in the morning, Bayard pulled her to her feet and they finally made it to his bed.

He jerked back the covers, waited for her to climb in, then flicked on the lamp and slid in beside her.

She snuggled in closer and let her eyes drift closed.

Bayard propped himself on an elbow, one hand cupped lazily around her breast. "Are you likely to get pregnant?"

Her eyes popped open. The question, after what had happened, was incredibly mundane, but pertinent. She didn't need to count. Her period was due in a few days. "It's possible. I ovulated last week."

"Then there's no point in using a condom until after your period. If you get one."

"Why do I get the idea that won't bother you?"

His hand slipped down over her rib cage and spanned her abdomen. "If you're pregnant, you're pregnant. There's nothing we can do about it now."

"I could take a morning-after pill."

He looked briefly incensed. "Have you ever had to do that before?"

"No." She had never had wild, unplanned, un-protected sex in her life. Bayard was a first in a number of respects.

"Good," he said with evident satisfaction. "Don't do it this time. If you're pregnant, we'll deal with it. Thank God you didn't ever get married."

An odd note in his voice caught her attention. "What would happen if I had?"

"You wouldn't have."

"I had boyfriends."

"Like that guy you dated about three years back. What was his name? Oh, yeah, Les Culver. A councilor."

The fact that Bayard not only knew Les's name, but knew *when* she had dated him, rang alarm bells. "How did you know I dated Les?" She had dated a number of men over the years. Les was significant only because he had been the last one.

"Jay Guidry."

Now she was wide-awake. Jay Guidry was a detective working for the Bossier PD. "You had me *surveilled?*"

He looked impatient. "I wouldn't call it that, exactly."

"What then?"

"Calm down. I just got Jay to check on you every now and then."

"Why?"

His expression was unrepentant. "Steve was gone. You were alone except for your Dad, and he was sick."

A small piece of an almost forgotten puzzle dropped into place. When she had been dating Les, *he* had ended it, not her, which had been unusual. The relationship hadn't exactly been hot and heavy, which had been precisely the reason it had lasted so long. At the time she had been certain that Les had been warned off.

Her father, who hadn't liked Les, had denied it. Steve had been overseas at the time, so she hadn't been able to blame Les's default on him. "It was you. You warned Les off. I thought it could have been Steve, even though he was away, but he never admitted to it. *Why?*"

He bent and kissed her, the kiss oddly sweet. "Why do you think?"

At seven in the morning, Bayard took the message Sara had decoded through to his office while she pulled on one of his shirts and walked through to the kitchen to make coffee.

When he took the cup she handed him, he pulled her close for a leisurely kiss before starting on the coffee. "There's only one thing happening in town this week and that's a water conference. Nasser Riyad. He's the leader of a small, independent Arab territory, with huge oil reserves and a U.S. strategic air base. He styles himself as above politics but the reality is that he has a foot in each camp, cutting deals with the West while doing business with terrorist factions on the side."

"So now what? Check Nasser's Washington connections?"

"And his investment base. In 1984, when Hartley betrayed Reichmann, threatening the cabal with exposure, she liquidated assets and moved substantial sums of money. The problem has been finding where she moved it. If we can tie Nasser's oil shares to Helene, or any other member of the cabal, we can freeze the assets and impound them."

Bayard picked up his phone and began making calls. Thirty minutes later, Lissa called back. They had tracked down two major buys of Riyad's shares in 1984, by two separate companies. After checking with Inland Revenue, who had searched their database, they had established that both companies were owned by the same parent company. They were still fighting their way through a labyrinth of offshore shell companies, but they were finally getting somewhere.

Sara took one look at his complete focus and quietly left his office. It was Sunday, but evidently Bayard's people worked 24-7, and he was expected in at the office. She had a shower, changed into sweats and a tank top and tied her hair back in a ponytail, then padded out to the kitchen to see if Bayard had the makings of breakfast in his fridge.

Half an hour later she slid a large cheese omelet onto a warmed plate, cut off one-third for herself, transferred it to another plate, then divided bacon and a salsa she'd cobbled together from avocadoes, tomatoes and lime juice between the two plates. She checked the oven and noted that the biscuits she'd made from the unopened pack of mix she'd found in Bayard's pantry were almost done.

She knocked on the door of the study and opened it. Bayard swiveled around in his chair. His gaze shifted to her breasts and she logged the moment that his focus changed.

A small shiver went through her as he pushed

out of his chair and walked toward her. Sometime in the last hour he had rolled up his shirtsleeves and undone the top buttons of his shirt, baring a slice of tanned chest and dark, curling hair. "We have to eat first."

"That's what I had in mind."

She opened the door wider, so the smell of fried bacon could waft through.

His expression changed. "You cooked?"

She walked back to the kitchen, her cheeks burning because she could feel his gaze locked on her butt. "It's an old Southern tradition."

"My mother didn't cook. If there's food, don't let me touch you until we've eaten."

Grabbing a kitchen towel, she pulled the oven door open, slid the pan of biscuits out and deposited it on a heatproof pad she'd placed on the counter.

The expression on Bayard's face got even stranger. "You made biscuits."

She found butter. There weren't any jams or preserves, which strengthened the theory that Bayard had probably bought the biscuit mix so one of his girlfriends could make them for him, and in the process had neglected to buy jam.

When she set the butter down on the counter,

he grabbed her, lifted her clear off her feet and kissed her hard on the mouth. Setting her down, he took a seat at the counter, picked up his fork and began to eat, that same glazed look in his eyes. Finally she got it. The food was basic, down-home cooking, but for Bayard it was pure magic. His enjoyment of such a simple thing as a hot biscuit told her something else she needed to know about him. As high-flying as Bayard was in the intelligence world, his needs and his instincts were the same as most other men.

Twenty minutes later, when the security detail Marc had requested were in place around the apartment, he left for the office. He didn't want to leave. After waiting this long for Sara, all he wanted was to be with her. Drinking coffee, making love, watching TV or fighting, he didn't care.

He was thirty-six and he had wanted Sara for most of his life. He had tried to get her when he was twenty and failed. He wasn't about to let her slip away this time.

Satisfaction curled through him at the thought that he might have made her pregnant. It wasn't a guarantee, but close enough.

As he climbed into his car, he slipped back into work mode. The last piece in the cabal puzzle settled into place. Over the past few months he had unraveled the network, using information gleaned from investigations into the senior cabal members who had been murdered by Lopez and Helene. The scenario had unfolded in a predictable way. Helene and her aging court had been using money and political influence to play the war game, mostly in innocuous, low-risk ways. The result had been budgetary allocations that benefited certain arms corporations in which the cabal held a large number of shares.

Those had since been frozen, the sales history tracked, but at no point had any of the transactions led them to Helene, because she'd been clever enough to keep herself separate from the upper echelon. Two names had consistently surfaced with the multinationals: Seaton and Ritter. Both of those men were now dead, cutting off that avenue of investigation.

Helene had operated as a separate entity within the cabal, controlling the major assets and the accounts, making it easy to detach herself from it once it had gone belly up. But, as politically savvy as she was, she had made one major mistake. She had thrown in with Nasser, and from the coded threats, he was almost certain Lopez knew about it.

His cell phone rang as he pulled out into traffic. It was Bridges.

"Guess what?"

"Dennison?"

"Uh-huh. He just got into town."

"Keep the tail on him."

Dennison had an intimate knowledge of both Lopez and the cabal. When he had exited the country the previous year, after escaping CIA custody, Marc had made the decision not to have him arrested on the basis that Dennison was more use to him freelancing than kept under wraps in a cell.

So far, he hadn't pointed the way to any leads they hadn't already generated for themselves, but the possibility was there. If Lopez and Helene sank from sight, Dennison could conceivably be useful.

"What about Juan and Benito Chavez?" The two men in the four-wheel drive who had been Lopez's backup at the Fischer farm.

"They're heading for El Paso."

"Pull them in before they get to the border."

They'd hung off long enough. Benito would

never be anything more than muscle, but his older brother, Juan, was Lopez's right-hand man. He was also smart enough to pick up the pieces of the Chavez cartel and put them back in business once Lopez was out of the equation. It was time to close the net.

Twenty

Sara cleaned up in the kitchen, found the laundry, which turned out to be a high-tech cupboard in the kitchen and put on a load of washing. At loose ends, she checked the fridge and the pantry and made a list of groceries they needed. If she wanted to go out, one of the agents Bayard had assigned to protect her, Hudson or Glover, would accompany her. If she needed to drive anywhere, they had a car and could take her. With the day stretching ahead, she had nothing better to do than shop. Besides, apart from grocery shopping, she needed to buy a few personal items.

She nuked what was left of the coffee, added milk and sugar and leaned against the counter, slowly sipping as she surveyed Bayard's apartment.

In Sara's opinion, the way a person decorated their home revealed a lot about who they were. The Bayard family was well-heeled. A combination of old cotton money and the wealth provided by the law firm Bayard's great-grandfather had founded in the early 1900s meant Bayard could probably have afforded an inner-city penthouse if he'd wanted it. Instead he had chosen an older-style apartment building with romantic balconies, window boxes planted with geraniums, situated cheek by jowl to a bakery and a small collection of cafés. The view from his windows, aside from the park, was a jumble of narrow streets jammed with redbrick Federation-style houses and Victorian villas swamped by leafy oaks and maples. The atmosphere was intimate, almost neighborly.

His choice of furniture was also a surprise. She recognized some of the pieces: the matching mahogany bookcases in his sitting room, an armoire that held his stereo and CD collection, the chest of drawers in his bedroom. She had seen those particular pieces of furniture before. They had originally belonged to his grandparents and had once resided in the manager's cottage on the Bayard estate. The furniture was antique, expensive, but large. Most of the pieces were too big to fit easily into a conventional apartment; they needed a house.

The LSU photos on the wall, and the football occupying one corner of the bookshelf added to the picture. Bayard had left Shreveport behind, but in the heart of a city populated by politicians and government employees, he had created his own small slice of Louisiana.

After watching TV then trying, unsuccessfully, to nap, she walked down to the lobby and met the janitor, an older guy called Harry Claremont. Harry occupied a small unit on the ground floor and also doubled as the building's security guard. He showed her into his small office, where Hudson was busy watching security tapes of the last twenty-four hours and taking notes.

She arranged to go shopping. Hudson, who looked more like an accountant than an agent, drove her to the nearest mall and accompanied her. Glover, who was older and sturdier, with a locked-down manner, stayed behind to keep an eye on the apartment.

She stocked up on underwear and bought a light sweater, another pair of sweatpants and a pair of jeans, because the D.C. weather, while not cold, was several degrees cooler than Shreveport. After buying a few groceries, Glover delivered her back to the apartment.

She spent the rest of the afternoon doing odd chores around the apartment and cooking a pot roast, mostly to fill in time until Bayard got home. After the intense emotion of the last few hours, and the complete U-turn her life had taken, performing the simple, everyday tasks was a relief. She needed time to adjust.

As it turned out, the pot roast—an all-in-one meal which could stay in the pot for hours without spoiling—was a brilliant idea. Bayard got home before five, but they didn't get around to eating until after eight.

Bayard offered to wash up while she took a bath. When she got out of the bath, Bayard was already in bed and asleep, so she simply switched off the lights and climbed in with him.

The derelict farmhouse, situated on the edge of the dark forest that curved around Vassigny, was icy cold and gutted of anything that could provide comfort except for the wooden chair Sara was tied to.

Stein looked eerily perfect in his uniform.

After the scuffle in the forest, he had actually taken the time to change his jacket and wipe the mud from his boots.

Stein consulted his watch. "How long have you known Reichmann?"

She repeated the answer she had already given him several times. "I met him when I applied for the job in Vassigny."

"But that's not the case with Gerhardt."

She frowned, feeling punchy. Stein had cut her in a dozen different places. None of the cuts were deep enough to be life threatening, but they stung, and the smell of fresh and dried blood was making her nauseous. "I met Gerhardt for the first time today."

"What do you know about Reichmann's activities?"

Her jaw tightened. Stein had been trying to catch her out and make her admit she was involved with Reichmann, that she was his accomplice. She had refused to give him an opening. Whether she provided him with information or not, she was dead.

Closing her eyes, she thought about her parents. They had endured; she would, also. If she had to die, so be it. She wouldn't give away one piece of information that would hurt either the Maquis or the Allies. "I did the job I was paid to do, nothing else."

He gripped her hair and jerked her head back, the sudden movement shocking. "Most women would be screaming by now. Not such a mouse, after all."

She sucked in air and stared through him.

Sharp pain on the third finger of her left hand wrenched a cry from her throat.

He had ripped the diamond ring off, almost dislocating her finger in the process. She had forgotten the ring was there.

He held the ring in front of her face. Cold moonlight slanted through a window, making the diamond look like a chip of ice. Outside, a shadow moved; one of Stein's men, patrolling the overgrown fields that surrounded the house.

"Do you like diamonds, Madame de Thierry?"

"No."

"Are you sure?"

The sting of the knife made her gasp.

"What about Cavanaugh?"

Her gaze flickered, she couldn't help it.

A cold smile curved his mouth. "The British aren't the only ones who have spies. I know he's here, that he's working with de Vallois. Six months ago Cavanaugh was in Lyon. Before that, Toulouse. I missed him in Toulouse, but I destroyed the cell he was working with. This time I will kill him."

Another shadow moved past the window. Cold light glinted off the barrel of a gun. For a fraction of a second her gaze locked with Cavanaugh's.

A sharp detonation made her whole body jerk. At first she thought that she had been shot, that Cavanaugh had done what she had asked, then Stein's grip slackened and she realized that Cavanaugh had shot him instead.

A barrage of gunfire filled the night. Outside, Stein's men dropped. A window shattered. Simultaneously, the door slammed against the wall. Stein, who had staggerd against a wall, clutching his side, produced a Luger. A corner of the door exploded. Cavanaugh was already moving. A second shot showered stone chips and dust. With a guttural roar, Stein charged and both men engaged. Stein's Luger skittered across the floor. Cavanaugh had already discarded the Sten. Both men went down, rolling in the dust and dirt and the blood that was pouring from Stein's side. Cavanaugh was taller and easily stronger, but

Stein had a lean, feral build and she saw with a leap of fear that sometime during the struggle he had recovered the knife, which he had dropped when he was shot.

Cavanaugh clamped his wrist, stopping the blade short of his throat. Veins bulged in Stein's face. Cavanaugh pressed harder. There was a brittle snapping sound as the bone broke and Stein snarled as the knife clattered to the floor. Cavanaugh released him and rolled in one smooth, flowing motion, retrieved the Sten, shoved it against Stein's chest and pulled the trigger.

After the roar of detonation there was a moment of eerie silence as Stein's face finally went slack.

Cavanaugh sliced the cords that bound her and ripped off the gag. Face grim, he carried Sara into the cover of the trees, set her on her feet, and when he was certain she could stand, made her drink brandy. The liquor burned Sara's throat, making her gasp. He handed her a flask of water. She gulped it down, her thirst ferocious.

De Vallois's men encircled them. Some loped, catlike, after the soldiers who had escaped into the forest. They wouldn't get far; they were in the Maquis's territory now.

The potent liquor made her head spin, distracting her as Cavanaugh wiped off the cuts and bound up the worst of them with strips of cloth. His shirt, she realized.

His gaze locked with hers. *"Peut-tu marcher?"*

His voice was soft, the question serious. *Can you walk?*

"Bien sûr."

Of course.

He smiled, the first time she had ever glimpsed that phenomenon and her heart swelled with the sweetness of the moment.

She walked a few paces to demonstrate. The cuts were on her arms and her torso, not her legs. "Get me out of these trees and I'll fly."

Vallois's men closed in around them and they were moving through the forest.

Just seconds ago she had felt weak and drained but now adrenaline flowed and for the minutes, hours, that they walked, despite the sting of the cuts, she felt invincible.

They stopped and rested. Someone passed around chunks of hard cheese and dried figs. The food tasted like ambrosia. Cavanaugh bandaged the deepest cuts more securely, then they were moving again, flitting like ghosts through the trees, skirting tracts of open land that glowed, stark and bare beneath the moon.

Exhaustion dragged at her. Cavanaugh babied her along, his arm around her waist, taking her weight. The sky turned gray and a thin drizzle set in as they walked into a hay barn. One of de Vallois's men lifted a hatch, indicating that they descend into the cellar below.

Jacques lit a lantern, illuminating the rough walls. "The border is two miles away. We need to wait until dark to cross. Rest, *mes amies.* There's nothing more we can do until tonight."

Sara sat with her back against a wall and didn't protest when Cavanaugh sat beside her, slipped an arm around her and pulled her head down on his shoulder. She adjusted her position against bone and hard muscle, finding the most comfortable resting place for her head.

They were safe.

She hardly dared believe it.

The moon shone through the trees, dappling the ground as Sara walked through the silent forest. The air was thin and dry, burning her chest, slicing at exposed skin. Her cuts throbbed. Blood seeped, turning the wool that clung to her skin sodden, but despite the physical discomfort, her whole being was centered on moving forward. Escape.

The few feet in front of her—the compass of Cavanaugh's broad back—drew her on as they wove in single file behind de Vallois.

Cavanaugh turned. His gaze locked on hers. Emotion pierced her, followed by a powerful moment of connection.

Impossible. She had no room in her mind or her heart for any other drive but survival.

Up ahead, de Vallois had stopped.

Cavanaugh steadied her. "He's checking on the transport."

They were supposed to meet a truck, filled with Armand's cheeses and destined for an outpost situated in a tiny hillside village that straddled the border. The truck had a false bottom built into it. The space was narrow and claustrophobic. They would be black-and-blue by the time they arrived at the border, and choked by diesel fumes, but they would be in Switzerland.

Now that they weren't moving, the cold seemed to intensify. Steam drifted off Cavanaugh's shoulders, vapor billowed from their mouths.

His arms wrapped around her. She winced.

He touched a damp spot in her coat. "Damn, that's seeping again. You need stitching."

"It's all right." Once they were across the border she could get medical attention. Just a few more minutes, an hour at the most.

The sound of an engine cut the air. Headlights scythed through the trees. They crouched low.

De Vallois motioned them forward. As they stepped out onto the road, the driver of the truck pitched forward, a gaping hole in his forehead. Soldiers poured from the back of the truck. De Vallois was cut down in the first hail of bullets.

Reichmann.

Stein had said there was a spy. Someone had betrayed the escape route.

Cavanaugh dragged her through the trees. Her chest burned, her legs felt like lead. Her boot caught on a root and the ground came up to meet her with sickening force.

Warmth spread down her side. She was bleeding again. Her head spun as she pushed to her feet. The blood loss was catching up with her. She couldn't continue and she wouldn't allow Cavanaugh to carry her. Reichmann's soldiers were fresh. If Cavanaugh tried to carry her, they would both be caught.

Footsteps. Crashing through the forest.

Cavanaugh's arm around her waist, the pressure warm; his voice urgent.

A gunshot. Cavanaugh faltered. Fear rocketed through her; he was wounded. Shots sliced past her, shredding leaves. The forest was filled with the thud of boots.

With icy resolve, she turned away from Cavanaugh and lunged toward the soldiers, calling out in German. A soldier in a greatcoat loomed out of the shadows and she fell, suddenly terrified.

She couldn't see Cavanaugh. Rough hands jerked her to her feet. Pain from the wound in her side sliced through her. Abruptly the dim green of the forest spun into blackness.

When she came to, she was surrounded by German uniforms. From the orders being snapped out, Cavanaugh and most of the Maquis had escaped.

Reichmann stepped forward and gestured with his gun. Two of his men hauled her between them, her feet trailing on the rough ground.

When they reached the road, Reichmann stripped the small pack off her back and extracted his ledger, his gaze cold. He reached for his pistol, a Mauser. For a second Sara's mind went utterly blank, then comprehension dawned. There would be no time, no second chances. No rescue.

Cavanaugh didn't know what she'd had in the pack. She deliberately hadn't told him; the risk was hers. Reichmann had no interest in interrogating her. He wanted her dead and all knowledge of his crimes wiped out.

Something flashed in the trees. A message in Morse.

Courage.

Cavanaugh. Still here, and impossibly close.

The dreadful sense of isolation eased. The moment of connection she had experienced in the forest grew stronger, swelling her heart, followed by sheer unadulterated panic.

Reichmann's men had seen him. They were already running, shouting orders.

Cavanaugh. You shouldn't have stayed.

She stared at Reichmann, and the solution to preserving Cavanaugh's life. She knew Cavanaugh; he wouldn't leave until she was gone. "Traitor," she said succinctly.

Reichmann levelled the Mauser at her chest.

"Thief."

Twenty-One

Bright light catapulted Sara out of the dream.

Bayard was looming over her, pushing on her chest. The room swam, her vision dimmed.

"Dammit," he roared. *"Breathe."*

His head dipped, his mouth pressed on hers, the pressure urgent. Air forced past the tight rigor knotting her chest.

She gasped; oxygen flooded her lungs.

He continued to breathe with her, as if he couldn't fully believe that she could do it on her own.

Her fingers threaded in his hair, framed his face. She stared into his fierce, dark gaze. Emotion welled, sharp, urgent, and for a brief second time dissolved. Her hands tightened around his neck, pulled his mouth to hers. The first kiss was deep, the second wrenching.

Her fingers dug into his shoulders.

She was literally shaking with cold. Heat blazed from him, burning her chilled skin. She slipped her fingers down across his taut abdomen and found his erection.

"Now?"

Her mind was still reeling, her body icy. The recall had been too stark, too perfect. She needed warmth, life.

Positioning him between her legs, she pushed down, shoving herself onto him. He began to move, his mouth on hers, his body tight against her, as if *he* couldn't bear the separation. Her fingers bit into his hips. Heat and a piercing pleasure rolled through her, so intense that for an endless moment she thought she might faint.

When it was over they lay together, still and silent. Eventually Bayard moved, but only to flick on the lamp and retrieve the duvet, which had ended up on the floor.

When he got back into bed, he leaned back against the headboard, his arms folded across his chest. "Okay," he said grimly. "Now you tell me exactly what was going on. You stopped breathing."

"I dreamed I was dying."

When she didn't continue, his jaw tightened. "Tell me about it."

"Trust me, you don't want to hear."

"Isn't that what your father used to do? Talk you through the dreams? I was there, staying over with Steve one night when you had one."

Her stomach tensed. "What did I do?"

"Not much, but enough that I could see how real it was. I told you that I'd done some reading on the subject. Your father gave me a couple of books."

"When?"

His mouth thinned, his dark gaze was distinctly irritable. "A few years ago. The day after your eighteenth birthday."

"After the kiss." That made sense. He had wanted to know why she had rejected him, and somehow he had figured out that it had something to do with the dreams.

In short, clipped sentences she explained what she knew about that previous life. Stark images resurfaced as she told the story in cold sequence, but with the blunt retelling they lacked the clarity and punch they'd had in dreams. When she was finished she felt exhausted and wrung out, but oddly emotionless, as if whatever part of her had held on so fiercely to those memories had finally let go.

She studied Bayard, abruptly curious. He was Cavanaugh, and yet not. "Do you want to know what really happens to me? *You do.* You trigger the dreams. They started when you moved next door then stopped when you went away to boarding school. The night you kissed me, I had a flashback."

"I don't see the connection."

Now for the bit that was going to get her checked into a nice little "hospital" somewhere. "Because you were there. In 1943. Only your name wasn't Bayard, it was Cavanaugh. You were an American agent working for the British Special Operations Executive, and you parachuted into France to get me out."

Rain was pounding on the windows when she woke. Bayard was already dressed for work.

Her face burned when she remembered just how much she'd told him the night before. "You must think I'm crazy."

He pulled her out of bed and kissed her. "I've

been hanging around since I was nine. Figure it out."

"Then maybe you should consider that you're the crazy one."

He gripped her chin and turned her head so she could see the way they looked together in the full-length mirror affixed to his wall. With Bayard fully dressed and her naked, her hair trailing, the picture was decadent. "Not crazy. Fully sane."

He checked his watch. "I have to go. I've got a meeting to make. And I'll be late home. There's a private party tomorrow night. Nasser Riyad's on the guest list, and it's possible that Helene Reichmann and Lopez will be there."

She shrugged into the shirt she'd started using as a robe. "If that's the case, I need to go."

"No."

"I can identify them both."

His expression was cold. "If those messages are correct, Lopez is planning on shooting Riyad."

"In that case, the place will be crawling with security." She gripped the lapels of his suit. She couldn't explain her urgency to him. He couldn't remember being hunted by Stein and Reichmann, or that he'd been shot, but she could. "I can ID him. It's possible I can ID them both. How many people have you got who have seen Lopez in the flesh, who know how he walks, the way he moves his head. Marc, I know—"

"You called me Marc."

She stared at his expression. "I can do it more often if you'd like."

"Damn." He bent his head and kissed her neck. "You are so wasted in that library."

"If you let me come to the party, I'll do whatever you say. I'll stay out of trouble."

"I'll think about it, but I'm not making any promises."

After breakfast, she made space for herself at Bayard's desk, set up her laptop and dialed up a library search engine. The system gave her access to a large number of city and university libraries and a huge base of online research material. An hour later, after wading through repetitive sites detailing the history of the Special Operations Executive and the French Resistance, and without finding the specific, personal information she was searching for, she logged off and picked up the phone.

She hadn't really expected to find the names

and details of SOE agents. The information would have been classified, and only available to military personnel or the government officials of the countries involved—with the appropriate security clearance.

Searching the library database had been a stab in the dark. She had been counting on the fact that, like the Enigma information, after so many decades had passed, details of operations might have seeped into the public forum.

It hadn't, which meant that the only way she was going to find the information she wanted was to gain access to classified military and government records.

She dialed Bayard's office. He was in a meeting, but Lissa made it clear that she had been instructed to help her in any way she could.

"I need to get into personnel files that were generated in the 1940s."

"That will require a security clearance, but I think I can wangle it. Can I call you back?"

Half an hour later, Sara got Hudson to drop her off at Marc's work, and took a seat in a small interview room adjacent to Lissa's office, which was equipped with a desk, computer and two chairs.

Lissa pulled up a chair beside her and accessed

a military database using her security clearance. "And now for the magic carpet ride. Bayard's access code."

When the menu came up, Lissa left her to it. Heart pounding, Sara typed "Cavanaugh" into the search box. The name wasn't that common, but the list of hits was in the hundreds. Next she initiated a search on agents who had been seconded to the SOE. There were only two Cavanaughs listed.

She brought up the file on the first one then discounted it because this Cavanaugh had died in 1942. On the second try she hit gold.

Marc Cavanaugh.

The unexpectedness of Cavanaugh having the same first name as Bayard hit her like a punch in the chest, the sense of time shifting, dissolving, suddenly powerful.

She hit the print button and scrolled through his details as the pages printed out.

He had been seconded to the SOE in 1943. His hometown had been New Orleans, Louisiana. The information fitted with what she remembered. The fact that he had been from Louisiana and still had the same first name sent a cold tingle through her. It was as if, even though he had died, his identity had, essentially, remained the same.

He had died.

Grief hit her like a wave, even though she knew that, logically, Cavanaugh was no longer alive.

She scrolled down the file. The place of death was listed as France. The date, 1944.

There had to be a mistake. He had gotten away. He had been *safe.*

It didn't make sense. Unless he had been sent back. But after the exposure of the fight with Reichmann and Stein, he should have been removed from the roster of agents.

Bayard, Bridges and an older man with iron-gray hair and a military bearing, strolled into the office as she was leaving.

Bayard introduced the older man as Rear Admiral Saunders, his boss. When the introductions were completed, Saunders politely excused himself. Bayard directed her into his office, flipped open his briefcase and handed her a printed invitation.

She was coming to the party, but on a limited basis. She would have an assigned bodyguard. If she didn't see anyone within the first hour, she was gone. If there was going to be an attempt on

Nasser Riyad's life, they expected it to take place at a small official ceremony later on in the evening. Riyad would be briefly exposed while he received an award. If she wanted, after she left the party, she could join the surveillance team in a van off the premises. That was the offer, take it or leave it.

"I'm going." Bayard was worried about her, but she was worried about *him.*

Lissa stepped into his office, followed by Bridges.

Bayard pulled out his wallet and handed her a credit card. "You're going to need an evening dress."

Sara tried to push it back at him. "I've got money. I can pay for my own things."

"Use the card. We'll fight about it later." He pulled her close. The kiss was short, but thorough. Seconds later, he followed Bridges out into the hall.

"Wow." Lissa fanned herself. "Sorry, Marc's my boss. I'm not used to seeing him…like that."

Sara touched her lips. They felt swollen and a little chafed. Like the rest of her body, they weren't used to physical intimacy. Every step reminded her of exactly what they had been doing for the past two nights.

Sara slipped the credit card in her bag. She wasn't using it. It wasn't a departmental credit card; it was Bayard's personal account. "He's lived in D.C. for years. He has to date."

Lissa shrugged. "Not that I've ever heard, although I'm sure he has. He's the consummate professional. He *never* mixes business with pleasure… Sorry, I'm putting my foot in it."

Sara hooked the strap of her purse over her shoulder. "It's okay, I shouldn't have asked."

But she was glad she had. She had needed to know that Bayard wasn't a playboy. In some respects she had to wonder if it wouldn't be better if he had been. Women, she could compete with. His job was another problem entirely.

Twenty-Two

Sara showered and dressed in the black silk underwear she'd bought, then pulled on the stockings and fastened them to the garter belt. She didn't need to wonder if Bayard would like the underwear. She knew he would go nuts the instant he saw her in it.

A light tap at the door made her jump.

"Bridges is downstairs with the car. We need to leave."

"Just one minute." Sara slipped the black dress on, the thin silk sending a small shiver down her spine as it settled and warmed against her skin. She wound her hair into a smooth French twist, then checked her makeup. When she was finished, she slipped on the small set of fake diamond studs Bayard had given her to wear. One of the studs was a simple piece of jewelry, the other was a state-of-the-art transmitter and global positioning device. Wearing it, she would be able to pick up transmissions and if there was a problem, Bayard could find her fast. She would also be wired with a mike, but that wouldn't be fitted until just before they went into the party.

With the makeup she'd bought, her eyes looked smoky and exotic. The jersey silk dress, simple as it was, clung to her figure. The neckline dipped low, the draped line emphasizing the curve of her breasts.

Bayard appeared in the mirror behind her just before his hands curved around her upper arms. He looked large and imposing in a formal black tux, his hair still damp from his shower, his jaw freshly shaven.

His mouth brushed the curve of her neck and shoulder. He released her and produced a flat case. "You need to wear these."

The diamond necklace settled around her neck, a waterfall of cold fire.

She touched a finger to one of the gems. "Are they real?"

"They belonged to my grandmother. A courting gift from my grandfather."

"He had taste."

His mouth twitched. "*Grandmère* was a beautiful woman and wealthy in her own right. She had suitors lining up."

Sara had seen the Bayard family portraits. Jean Bayard had been tall and dark, but he hadn't been the most handsome of men. He would have had to pull out all the stops to get Heloise.

Bayard's phone buzzed. He released her and answered the call, his answers brief and monosyllabic.

When he hung up, his gaze was remote. "Time to go."

She picked up the gauzy silk wrap that went with the dress, draped it around her shoulders and collected her evening purse. Bayard's measured gaze tracked her as she strolled toward the door, making her heart pound.

She was in love with Bayard and the emotional risk was huge. As close as she'd been to her family, no one had gotten as intimate with her as Bayard. He had gotten under her skin. His taste, his touch, his scent were indelibly imprinted on her memory not through one lifetime, but two.

When they had made love the first time something inside her had clicked into place. She had been attracted to other men and had dated, but she hadn't been able to fall in love, or even in lust with any of them. She had made love, but she had never been able to climax during lovemaking. She had thought the lack was some internal quirk of her own, that she was frigid, but now the reason was clear. She hadn't been able to climax because at some powerful, underlying level she had remembered Marc.

If she couldn't have him, she knew suddenly that she would never marry or have children. She wouldn't grow old with a husband and her family around her. Life would go on. She would continue to work, take occasional holidays, maybe once in a while she would even get to be part of Steve's and Taylor's and their children's lives, but essentially, she would be alone.

Bayard locked the apartment door behind them. His arm automatically curled around her waist as they strolled toward the elevator.

The elevator doors slid open. She stepped into the warmly lit interior. The mirrored rear of the compartment threw their reflections back at them: Bayard, tall, broad-shouldered and remote. Herself, sophisticated and unexpectedly voluptuous in the clinging dress, like an expensive courtesan with diamonds at her throat.

His arm tightened. "What's wrong? If you want out, just say the word. I don't want you near either Lopez or Reichmann."

"Nothing's wrong. I'm fine."

Just a little shaky because there was too much at stake.

Bayard was worried about her safety, but he was the one walking into the front line.

Marisa Sutton strolled through the crush, snagging a champagne flute as she walked, although she had no intention of drinking it.

She didn't pause to make conversation as she headed for the hall, although she knew some of the faces in the room. Knowing the intimate details of people's private lives, including an endlessly surprising amount of scandal and dirt, didn't make for easy conversation. In the years she had worked as an agent, she had seldom, if ever, socialized.

She paused by an elegant fireplace filled with an arrangement of pale silk flowers and pretended to sip champagne as she skimmed the crowded room. Wintry eyes met hers. Setting the flute down on the sideboard, she slipped from the room.

The hall was filled with security personnel, both male and female. She acknowledged a White House agent. The president wasn't here, but thanks to the presence of Nasser Riyad, a large contingent of his people were.

She waited impatiently in the garden. When a figure separated itself from an archway covered with a fragrant white climbing rose, she moved out of the shadows. "Are we running to schedule?"

"Calm down, everything's covered."

"What do you mean, *everything?* The room's wide-open. I don't know who most of those people are and that scares me."

"Trust me."

Marisa studied Saunders's controlled expression, suppressing her instinctive dislike and distrust of a man who had uncovered her secrets then used them remorselessly to maneuver her. The only thing that made their partnership bearable was the simple fact that she could destroy him just as easily as he could destroy her. "I want out of this alive."

"Then do as you're told."

Sara studied faces. In 1943 Helene Reichmann had been a child, which put her in her early seventies. The room was filled with older women, and the predominant hair color was blond. Identifying Helene, a woman who had successfully blended for years, wasn't going to be easy.

To make things more difficult, silent black-and-white movies were being projected onto one wall, and the flicker from the old film was distracting.

Her gaze lingered on an elegant blonde with high cheekbones and light eyes as she strolled in out of the garden. The woman was in her late thirties, maybe early forties. Her head turned as if she had logged and noted Sara's scrutiny. Sara adjusted her focus past the woman. She couldn't be Helene—too young—but the resemblance was striking.

Bayard, who had been systematically working the floor, slid an arm around her waist. "See anyone you know?"

"Not yet." The only people she had recognized so far had been Lissa and Rear Admiral Saunders.

"Keep looking. Bridges is going to keep an eye on you while I check the perimeter security." He moved away from her into the crowd.

Bridges was wearing glasses, but the lenses weren't prescription ones. The disguise, at first glance, was effective, but it didn't hide the fact that he was lean, muscled and more likely to be security than ambassadorial staff.

"Have you worked for Bayard long?"

Bridges cupped her elbow and moved her out of the path of a waiter carrying a tray laden with empty champagne glasses, then instantly resumed his respectful distance. "Six months, give or take, but I've known him for longer." His mouth curved at one corner, and suddenly he looked boyish rather than dangerous. "I'm from Shreveport. I don't know your parents, but I used to work with Steve."

"You know that we're cousins?"

"Yes, ma'am."

"You don't have to call me ma'am. Sara will do."

She circulated with Bridges, doing a slow tour of two reception rooms and a chilly garden. She hadn't seen anyone who looked remotely like Lopez, however, she was almost certain she had spotted Dennison. She mentioned it to Bridges.

He shrugged. "We've already got him under surveillance."

She checked her watch. She had fifteen minutes before Bayard would have her removed from the party. On a large blank wall Charlie Chaplin twirled his cane, drawing a small round of applause from a group of exquisitely dressed Japanese guests. Sara stopped, concentrating only on facial features and let her gaze go loose. The blond woman with icy-blue eyes she had noticed before refused a glass of champagne, the action drawing her attention.

An older woman moved into her line of sight, her features instantly familiar. Ambassador Cohen was currently based in D.C. with a regular seat at the United Nations and an advisory role to the president. Cohen's rise to power had been quiet, but steady. A prominent magazine had tipped her to be the next Secretary of State.

Her gaze moved onto the next knot of guests. The flash of diamonds jerked her gaze back. Cohen had diamonds at her throat, the lobes of her ears and her wrist. The settings were discreet, but the diamonds were impressive.

Frowning, she studied the ambassador. She didn't look seventy—midfifties at most—which was why she had automatically crossed her off her list of possible suspects.

Mistake. A lot of older women had cosmetic surgery or procedures of some sort. As long as money wasn't a problem, neither was looking ten years younger. Looking twenty years younger was more difficult, but with enough wealth and discipline, it was doable.

The ambassador was average height, her hair tinted honey blond with elegant streaks of gray. She turned, the tilt of her head imperious, and for a millisecond the room wavered as Sara looked directly into Heinrich Reichmann's eyes.

She jerked her gaze away almost immediately and stared blankly at Bridges. "That's her over there, in the gray silk."

"Cohen. Shit." He turned away and talked rapidly into a microphone.

The younger blond woman with the ambassador turned. Sara caught the discreet bulge of a shoulder-holstered weapon beneath the woman's satin jacket, and her sharp watchfulness registered. Not Cohen's daughter, despite the resemblance: she was security.

Bayard appeared. When Sara checked on Cohen, the area that she and the younger blond woman had occupied was empty. She caught the gleam of light off blond hair and gray silk. "She's leaving."

Bayard spoke into the microphone on his collar. His fingers closed over her arm. "So are you. Now."

She gripped her skirt, holding it to one side as Bayard hurried her toward a side exit. "What about Cohen?"

"Bridges is following."

A split second later the room dissolved and Sara was knocked to the floor. When she came to, her nose was bleeding, her ears were ringing, and she was having difficulty breathing.

Strong fingers wrapped around her arm, hauling her to her feet. "Can you walk?"

The room was blotted out with thick smoke and dust. "Yes." Not Bayard.

Panic gripped her as she searched for Bayard. They had been in the middle of the reception room when the bomb, if that was what it had been, had exploded. A gaping hole had been ripped in the ceiling, and the entire landing and a wall had collapsed.

The man who was helping her, a security guard, kept her moving as they threaded past injured people and mounds of debris. He left her on the front portico, which was jammed with agents checking IDs and people talking on phones, trying to get their cars.

Rear Admiral Saunders materialized out of the crowd, waves of security parting automatically for him. "Sara, thank God you're all right." He handed her a pristine white handkerchief which she used to blot the blood from her nose. "Lissa's just getting the car. I think we're next in the queue."

Saunders's icy calm was almost incomprehensible, when all she wanted to do was plunge back into the building and find Bayard. "Marc's still *in* there."

A limousine pulled out and another pulled in. The window rolled down and Saunders took her arm. "He checked in with the command post about a minute ago. He's fine. That's our ride."

"What do you mean, *fine?*"

Saunders's phone rang. He lifted it to his ear, spoke briefly and slipped the phone back in his pocket. "I told him I'd take you home. He'll meet you back at his apartment."

He opened the passenger door. Sara stepped into the rear of the limousine. Saunders joined her and told the driver to move on.

As the car accelerated into traffic, she fastened her seat belt. "Where's Lissa?"

Saunders produced a gun. "I'm afraid she's not coming on this trip."

Twenty-Three

Saunders's men moved like dark shadows around her, taking up positions, two on a mezzanine floor of a warehouse, the other four fanned out on the ground floor, covering both doors and her.

Sara was pushed into the center of the dusty space. The entry door was directly in front of her. If anyone busted in, she would be in the line of fire.

"Sit down. There."

"You're working for Reichmann?"

"With her, not for."

"Oil?"

Saunders looked briefly amused. "The oil angle did work until Marc found the shares."

A blond woman Sara recognized as one of Helene's security detail strolled across the floor, wearing dark jeans and a black shirt, a large black handgun held loosely in one hand. A sharp sting at her throat and the diamond necklace dangled from the blond woman's fingers. "Guess again."

"The de Vernay diamonds."

Her gaze was icy. "What do you know about de Vernay?"

"Reichmann stole from de Vernay in France, then sent him and his family to Auschwitz."

"Now tell me *how* you knew that?" she demanded softly. "No one, except a handful of the upper echelon, even knew the diamonds existed. Since Hartley died, only Helene—and my father."

Sara studied Marisa's face. For her father to share any knowledge with Helene, he had to be part of the upper echelon. Four members had died last year: Onslow, Parker, Seaton and Ritter. All four stories, complete with photos, had made the front pages of the national tabloids. "Stephen Ritter?"

Marisa glanced at Saunders. "I thought you said she was just a librarian."

Sara recalled a news report on Ritter's death. "Ritter never married."

Marisa's expression was remote. "My father was a clever man. He kept us a secret."

Sara glanced at Saunders. "So that's how you found out Helene's identity." When Ritter had died Saunders would have had access to her private papers. He had discovered the existence of Marisa then cut a deal with her.

Ritter, a mathematical and financial genius, had been the most brilliant of all of the exposed cabal members, and the one most likely to take leadership from Helene. Helene was supposed to have murdered him. It made a twisted kind of sense that Ritter would leave behind a daughter who had the potential to destroy Helene and take control of the cabal's assets.

Sara glanced at Saunders. "So, who are we waiting for? Helene?"

His mouth curved with cold amusement. "Lopez."

She briefly closed her eyes. "This is the meeting Reichmann arranged."

"At my behest."

Saunders's motives were as clear as an icy pool. His reputation—and his career prospects—had been damaged by the discovery of the mass grave at Juarez, but bringing in Lopez would provide an instant career fix. "You want Lopez." And, at a guess, the director's job.

He checked his wristwatch. "Lopez should be here sometime in the next half hour."

Her stomach tightened. "And when he gets here, let me guess—I have a nasty accident."

"Correct again. With your family's connection to Lopez and the cabal, no one will question Lopez's motive for shooting you, or the fact that—" he bent down and brushed the transmitter earring in her lobe, which he had turned off at the same time he had removed her microphone "—I was able to find you and shoot Lopez."

"It's too late to keep a lid on Helene's identity. It was radioed in just before the explosion."

He shrugged. "Helene will have to take care of that little problem herself."

And now that Helene was exposed as Ambassador Cohen and on the run, her face would be splashed over newspapers and television screens. That would suit Saunders. With his power, he could easily arrange safe passage out of the country and name his price. With the death of Lopez and his public profile taken care of, that price would be the de Vernay diamonds.

"What makes you think Lopez will show?"

The answer came from Marisa. "He needs the diamonds to survive. Helene has promised him a share."

Saunders produced a handful of cotton wadding and a roll of tape, signaling that the conversation was over, and expertly gagged her.

Time crawled by. Her shoulders and back ached from holding herself in a sitting position and she was shivering convulsively. Her wrists and hands were numb. Her head periodically dipped forward on her chest as she slipped in and out of a dozing state, although she never quite lost consciousness.

The vibration of a cell phone jerked her fully awake. The toneless conversation, followed by a flurry of movement as Saunders's men shifted position, sent adrenaline pumping through her veins.

Glass shattered. Simultaneously, light flashed, temporarily blinding her, and an explosion made her ears ring for the second time that night. The door burst open, the sound of gunfire deafening. Saunders jerked her in front of him, using her as a human shield, one arm locked across her throat.

Her head swam. Acrid smoke burned her nostrils and throat as Saunders dragged her backward. Something whined close to her ear, the sound uncannily like a kitten mewling. A bullet.

A second shot and Saunders's grip loosened and she was rolling. Then Bayard was leaning over her, his eyes like chips of black ice. His hands swept over her stomach, her rib cage.

"I'm not hurt. You got Saunders." She sucked in air, adjusting to the fact that it was over and that Bayard was all right. "You *know* you got Saunders."

Aside from bruising and a stitched cut over one cheekbone where a piece of debris had sliced him, Bayard was none the worse for wear after the explosion. As soon as the area was secure, he bundled her out onto the street and into the back of a van with tinted windows. Bridges watched over her, his face grim, while Bayard dealt with the mop-up.

Thirty minutes later, a "caretaker" team of Bayard's people was in place, the jurisdictions sorted, and the paperwork in process. Bayard moved her from the van into a company car.

In grim silence he peeled out of his body armor and thigh holster, dropped both on the backseat, then shrugged into a shoulder rig and transferred the gun. He slid behind the wheel, dug in his pocket and handed her the diamond necklace Marisa had taken.

Her fingers closed around the stones. She was glad he had retrieved a family heirloom, but in that moment the diamonds and their value was utterly unimportant. Bayard was alive and so was she; that was all that mattered.

She had seen Marisa cuffed and pushed into the back of another van, along with two of Saunders's men. The rest had been loaded into ambulances on stretchers or in body bags.

Bayard stopped for lights. He checked the rearview mirror and Sara realized the reason he had been driving slowly was that Bridges and another agent were following them in the van.

Bayard parked outside the apartment. Bridges pulled in behind. The second agent, Hudson, she realized, got out and took the car keys from Bayard.

Bridges saw them to the door of Bayard's apartment, his eyes watchful. When the door closed behind them, Sara stared at the warm lamp-lit room. They had only left hours before, but it felt like weeks. "What about Helene and Lopez?"

Bayard shrugged out of his shoulder rig, and dropped it on a couch. "Marisa's talking. According to her, Saunders was too late making his play. Helene and Lopez have cut a deal."

"You knew it was going to happen."

"It was a safe bet. A few weeks ago, one of my researchers uncovered an interesting fact. On the day Alex Lopez was born in Bogotá, his mother, Maria Chavez, a hemophiliac, was admitted to a hospital for a blood transfusion. But not in Bogotá. She was in San Jose del Guaviare, a tiny clinic in the interior of Colombia."

"So there's no way she could be Lopez's mother."

Bayard collected a first aid kit from the kitchen. He made her sit on one of the stools at the kitchen counter while he cleaned the myriad nicks and abrasions she'd sustained at the embassy party, mostly on the back of her neck and arms.

"As far as we can ascertain, Maria Chavez had a number of miscarriages, but she never gave birth to a live child. There's no way to prove it, but given that Marco was desperate for a son, and Helene needed his backing to retain control of the cabal after her father died, it seems clear that they struck a bargain."

The puzzling, volatile relationship between Lopez and Helene Reichmann suddenly made crazy sense.

Alex Lopez was Helene's son.

"So Helene set Saunders and Marisa up?"

Bayard unscrewed a tube of antiseptic cream. "Saunders made the mistake of believing that he had the sole tools required to manipulate her. As soon as his demands became too great, she was always going to cut a deal with Lopez."

"But if you had informed him about the relationship, he would never have made that mistake."

Bayard smeared a thin layer of cream over the cuts. "Like I said, you're wasted on that library."

"How long have you known about Saunders?"

"Not long. I transferred to National Intelligence at the request of the director. He suspected he had a leak, and he wanted someone from out of department coordinating the investigations into Lopez and the cabal. I've had Saunders under surveillance for months, although, with the amount of traveling he does, it wasn't possible to watch him all the time. A few weeks ago he had a series of after-hours visits with Marisa. We had it logged as an affair."

"So you restricted information to him and watched—"

"And still made mistakes." He pulled her to her feet.

Her arms closed around his waist and he winced. Not so invulnerable, then. "So who set the bomb?"

"An explosives team is checking out the site. They think it was set by Reichmann's head of security, Hendricks, which means she was two steps ahead. The bomb was inserted into the floor cavity upstairs. She planned her exit—and Saunders's death."

Twenty-Four

Two days later, Portland, Maine

Midnight. An empty stretch of beach.

Helene Reichmann checked the luminous dial of her wristwatch as she studied the blank canvas of damp sand left by a retreating tide. The cold drift of the breeze raised gooseflesh on her arms as she tried to penetrate the thick darkness.

The cold, ceaseless rhythm of the Atlantic Ocean sweeping the coast spun her back. Lubek, 1944. Juarez, just a few weeks later. Costa Rica, 1984.

A dim shadow was briefly silhouetted by moonlight. Not Lopez; he was too elusive to show himself like that. But it was most certainly one of his men.

Concealed in the rocks behind her, Hendricks talked tonelessly into a radio, repositioning his men.

Silence, broken by the ceaseless rush of waves. More memories.

Marco Chavez hadn't wanted marriage—he'd already had the blue-blooded wife he'd ordered from Spain. All he had wanted from her was a son. She had agreed to give him the child in exchange for his backing. And the backing had been imperative. Despite the fact that she had held power by virtue of holding the money, without the brutal tactics of Marco's enforcers, the network her father had built would have disintegrated. She would have ended up exposed, imprisoned—more than likely dead.

She had slept with Marco because he had insisted on it. She had stayed in Bogotá, isolated from everyone but Marco and an old crone of a nurse, who had looked after her and made sure no other man came near her for almost a *year*. Long enough for her to get pregnant, bear the child—which, to her relief, was male—and hand him over to Marco.

When she'd handed the baby over, she hadn't expected to feel anything more than revulsion and relief. In her mind he had been a part of Marco, not her—the seal to a bargain.

A whisper of sound, shifting shadows. A hand clamped around her throat. A dark, flat gaze locked with hers, and any idea that there was a bond dissolved. Gunfire sounded, to the left, then another shot, higher up.

The choking pressure on her throat eased.

The cold gleam of a gun in Lopez's hand was outlined by moonlight. "That's Larson and Hendricks down."

She stared down the barrel of the gun. He could shoot, but he wouldn't. Not until he had gotten what he wanted. "You didn't need to shoot them, they were holding fire."

His list of demands was succinct and predictable. She could keep her shares and business interests; thanks to Bayard they were traceable, and the alliance with Riyad was now useless. What was left of the gold bullion and the artwork was too bulky; he would never get them out of the country.

He would take the Cayman Island accounts.

His mouth curved in a smile, and for the first time she saw herself in his features. "And the diamonds."

"You knew that I was your mother. Knew and used it."

"Are we dealing, or do I kill you now?"

"You won't kill me, so don't bother with the bluff. You can have twenty-five percent now, the rest when we reach the Caymans. Who told you about the diamonds?"

Over the years she had added to the original cache of diamonds, but always in secret, steadily converting cash reserves into cut and polished stones. They were small, portable and, thanks to the tight grip the South Africans had on the diamond market, more than held their value.

Abruptly, she was free. Something chill swirled at her back. Choking fear held her immobile for long seconds.

She whirled and stared at…blankness.

Hendricks stepped out of the shadows, his eyes empty. One arm hung limp and bloodied at his side. His Kevlar vest was punctured where he had taken multiple hits across the chest. A handgun was held loosely in his good hand. "Where did he go?"

She suppressed a shiver. "He's in the rocks somewhere. Be careful."

Hendricks edged between the rocks, staying

flat. Something dark flickered at the edge of her vision. The detonation of a handgun split the air. Hendricks grunted and stumbled back. He was dead before he hit the sand.

The cold breeze continued to flow across Helene's face, tugging at her hair and making her feel every one of her seventy-two years. But her mind was clearer and sharper than it had ever been. Lopez and the sniper he had up in the hills, could see her, probably as plain as day, but neither would shoot.

Not until Lopez had what he wanted.

Bayard took the call at one in the morning. Hendricks and Larson had been found on a beach in Portland, Maine. They also had a lead on Helene. Courtesy of information from Marisa, they had been monitoring a shipping firm. The trucks had just rolled up to a warehouse in an industrial area just outside of Baltimore. According to their source, there was a ship on standby.

Sara climbed out of bed and made coffee while he made calls and dressed. Bayard added milk to cool it down, then drank the coffee in steady gulps.

When he kissed her, she clung, briefly. He had

to go; it was his job. She discovered that she hated his job. "Be careful. I want you back."

When he was gone, she sipped coffee and turned on the TV, then, too restless to watch anything, turned it off. She walked through to the laundry, pulled clothes from the dryer and began folding them into piles. The T-shirt and pants Bayard had worn when he had rescued her for a moment brought back the darkness and confusion of the warehouse and Saunders's prone body.

She put the clothes away. The fake diamond studs she had worn to the reception were still sitting in a small dish on Bayard's dresser. Another reminder of how badly things had gone wrong at the reception, because they simply weren't dealing with people who had the usual criminal agendas.

Something was wrong.

She walked back to the sitting room and found her phone.

The warehouse had to be a setup, a diversion. With all the publicity, and Reichmann/Cohen's photograph being circulated amongst security and border agencies—not to mention the fact that the press were having a field day with the story— neither Helene nor Lopez would touch it. If they hadn't already left the country, they should be solely concerned with getting out.

If they had a normal, criminal agenda.

She remembered the conversation in Rousseau's office. Bayard had said Lopez was working on two levels; two of his men had been shot, his phone had been tapped.

Just days ago Bayard had been an acknowledged target—and the warehouse was a location that guaranteed his attendance.

Her heart slammed hard in her chest. She picked up her cell phone and speed dialed Bayard. When he didn't answer, probably because he was using the phone, she tried Lissa's number. Lissa picked up on the second ring. When Sara explained that she needed to get a message to Bayard and why, Lissa offered to try. "I'll call you back in a few minutes."

Lissa hung up and Sara dialed Bayard again. When she was shunted through to his answering service, she left a message. "The warehouse is a setup, and so is the beach."

A whisper of sound made her stiffen. Cold metal gouged into the side of her neck.

"Clever girl."

She stared into Stein's—Lopez's—eyes. There

was no recognition. Nothing personal. For him she was a complication, nothing more. Killing her would just be business as usual.

"You're not frightened. Now that surprises me."

"If you were going to shoot, you would have done it by now."

Something changed in his gaze, although she didn't make the mistake of assuming Lopez harbored any kind of human emotion. He was a coldly brilliant, clinically organized, psychopathic killer. When she had fulfilled whatever role he had assigned to her, he would execute her. "You're right, I'm not going to kill you…yet. You're my passport out of this country."

"He won't stop until he finds you."

Lopez jerked his head in the direction of the door. At that second her cell phone rang.

Bayard.

The preprogrammed number of rings completed and the phone lapsed into silence. A message appeared on the screen. She had voice mail.

"Put the phone down on the table."

He gestured with the gun and she moved back a step and watched as he listened to the message, then pocketed the phone.

"Time to leave. Hold your hands out."

He produced a pair of cuffs.

"You won't get me out of the building wearing those."

He snapped the cuffs on, then slid a flat black case out of his coat pocket.

A ripple of unease slid through her as he extracted a syringe and a small vial of colorless fluid from the case. "What is *that?*"

His expression was peculiarly absorbed as he broke the seal on the vial and filled the syringe.

When his gaze fixed on hers she realized he had heard her question, he just hadn't bothered to respond. She was cuffed and under his control. He had neutralized the threat of the phone and now he was proceeding with the next step in his plan. If she registered at all, it was as a logistical problem, not a human being.

She watched as he tested the syringe, the moment surreal. Within a short time she would be unconscious. When it suited him, he would kill her.

She took a deep breath and waited. When his gloved fingers closed over her arm, she jerked her cuffed hands up in a two-handed punch. As a blow, it wasn't that effective. She was too close, and she couldn't get much swing, but it was enough to throw him off balance and release his hold. Shoving a chair in his path, she lunged for the hall and the front door. One step away from the door, he caught her arm and swung her in a short arc. She slammed into the wall hard enough that she saw stars. His weight pinned her and she felt the sting of the needle.

He stepped back and she stumbled. Her head was throbbing and her mouth tasted of blood. Whatever it was he'd injected her with, it was already working. "You won't get out of the building. Bayard has his people in place."

Lopez tossed Hudson's and Glover's IDs on the hall table. "Had. Past tense."

"You won't get out of the country. The borders are being watched."

"Even Bayard can't watch every part of every border."

Her stomach sank. He wouldn't risk sea or air travel; he would be a sitting duck. A land crossing meant Mexico or, more likely… "Canada."

He said something in Spanish. She didn't understand every word, but she understood enough. She was female, barely human. Of no importance.

Which meant they were going to Canada.

It made sense. The border was huge and difficult to control. People crossed back and forth on
day trips and not every road had a checkpoint.
There were plenty of wilderness places where
anyone could simply walk across without being
either seen or stopped. Added to that, the places
that were checked were often flooded with tourists.

"If we're driving and you want to get me over
the border, I'm going to need clothes."

The logic was unassailable. She was dressed
for bed in a camisole and cotton drawstring pants.
If he tried to haul her outside, they could get
noticed. En route, the fact that she was dressed
for bed *would* make her noticeable, which Lopez
wouldn't want.

He jerked his head in the direction of the
bedrooms. "Two minutes, no more."

He followed her through to Bayard's bedroom,
where most of her things were now stored. She
collected socks, sneakers and track pants and
quickly pulled them on. She no longer had Todd's
gun. Bayard had taken it along with all the other
items she had retrieved from the attic. She
glanced at the earring with the transmitter and
GPS device on the dresser and gauged her

chances of getting it. Opening Bayard's drawer, she took out one of his sweatshirts, then feigned a dizzy spell and dropped it over the earring. Sliding her hand beneath the sweatshirt, she palmed both earrings as she straightened.

Lopez muttered a hard, flat phrase in Spanish. Her two minutes were up.

She turned to face Lopez, supporting herself with one hand on the chest because already she was beginning to feel woozy. "You'll need to take the cuffs off so I can pull the clothes on."

Lopez unlocked the cuffs and replaced them in his pocket, keeping the gun trained on her the entire time.

Her fingers clumsy, and keeping the hand with the earrings closed, she dragged the sweatshirt over her head and shoved her arms through the sleeves. The faint scents of laundry powder and Bayard registered, and fierce emotion swamped her. The sweatshirt was large. Thick folds fell to just below her bottom, and the sleeves were long enough that they sagged down over her wrists, hiding the fact that she was holding something.

While she'd pulled on the clothing, Lopez had found her handbag, upended it onto the bed, and pocketed her passport. He jerked the gun in the direction of the door, indicating that it was time to leave. When he didn't make any comment about the fact that she was wearing a garment that was obviously too large for her, relief made her head swim. He had been focused on finding her passport, and hadn't noticed anything suspicious about the clothing she had chosen. Even if Lopez suspected the sweater had originally belonged to Bayard, he probably thought she was frightened enough to need the comfort of her boyfriend's clothing.

Fighting waves of dizziness, she preceded him out of the apartment and into the corridor. As they waited for the lift, it registered that this time he hadn't bothered with the cuffs, but that made sense. He had needed them to keep her under control while he had injected her, but she was now in no condition to fight him and they would be a liability while trying to move her out of the apartment and into a vehicle. With the drug taking effect, he could project the fiction that she was drunk and no one would take much notice.

The elevator doors slid open. Lopez, gun held against one thigh so that it was almost invisible, gripped her arm and shoved her inside.

The downward motion of the elevator made her stomach heave, and for a moment she thought she was going to be sick. The doors slid open and the much cooler air of the foyer flowed over her.

Lopez jerked her into motion again. Jaw clamped, she fought to stay upright and mobile. She had no idea what he had injected her with, but she would fight it. She wasn't experiencing any kind of euphoria; the predominant feeling was drowsiness and an increasing clumsiness. The probability that he had given her some kind of sleep-inducing drug was high.

Fight the drug by making a conscious effort to stay alert. Hyperventilate to increase the amount of oxygen in the bloodstream. If you can get to water, drink as much as you can to flush the drug out of your system.

She didn't know where the information came from, it was possible she had read it, but she didn't think so. The knowledge was simply *there,* a part of that new awareness.

Sucking in a deep breath, she shuffled forward, delaying Lopez, although with Hudson and Glover both dead, the likelihood of rescue was slim. The harsh lighting in the foyer hurt her eyes, which had become ultrasensitive. Taking another deep breath, she lifted her head and looked directly into the security camera bolted above the front doors. That way Bayard would pay attention and get a good look at what she was holding in the palm of her hand.

Seconds later they were out on the street. The breathing wasn't working; her head felt thick, she was having trouble keeping her lids open, and her coordination was going.

Light and shadow striped a van parked beside the curb. She lifted her head and tried to fix on details, but in the dim lighting she couldn't make out the license plate. She hadn't seen any sign of either Hudson or Glover, which meant Lopez must have concealed their bodies, probably in the janitor's room. The thought that Harry Claremont, the janitor, was also probably dead made her feel sick to her stomach.

Lopez slid the side door of the van open. For the short time that his attention was diverted, it occurred to her that she could make a break for it, but the thought was fleeting and distant. Her breathing was shallow and she was having trouble staying upright.

Lopez half dragged, half carried her into the interior of the van. While he cuffed her to the steel frame of the seat, she kept her fingers closed grimly around the earrings.

The side door slammed. Seconds later, Lopez slid into the driver's seat and started the van. As they pulled out into traffic Sara noticed that someone was sitting in the passenger seat.

A small shudder went down her spine when she recognized the back of Helene Reichmann's head.

Turning her attention to the earrings, she isolated the transmitterized one. Fighting lethargy, and a dangerous clumsiness in her fingers, she turned the bezel, switching the transmitter and the GPS on, then slipped the earring into her mouth and swallowed.

Twenty-Five

Bayard's phone rang as he pulled in at the curb outside his apartment. Bridges had beat him by two minutes. He had found Hudson and Glover—both dead. Harry was okay, although still dazed. He had been knocked out and locked in the basement. Sara was gone, the apartment left wide-open.

Bayard walked through the apartment, his jaw tight. Bridges hadn't touched a thing. The two IDs Lopez must have taken off Hudson and Glover were still sitting on the dining table.

Bridges poked his head through the door. "I've rewound the security tape."

Bayard secured the apartment and took the elevator down to Harry's office.

Bridges pressed a button on the VCR.

Bayard watched the surprisingly crisp footage. When he saw Lopez herding Sara toward the front door, fear and raw panic briefly paralyzed him.

Profilers had written endless papers on Lopez. He was a vicious and inventive killer, juggling modus operandi in a way that confused the purists. But there was one common theme—that Lopez was escalating in his behavior, becoming less and less able to hold to any kind of pattern.

Given that he had spent years altering his appearance and remaining anonymous, he had taken a huge risk snatching Sara. His reasons in taking a hostage were clear enough, but the act itself bordered on insanity. He had exposed himself to security cameras and left a raft of DNA evidence.

Although, as with everything he did, Lopez had achieved his purpose. In one stroke he had obtained a hostage and delivered a message. He had Bayard's woman. If Bayard tried to stop him, he would kill her.

Lopez also knew that he would follow.

Bayard watched the footage as Bridges ran it through again. Lopez walking to the elevator then, approximately twenty minutes later, leaving with Sara. Sara lifting her head, her face bruised on one side, her eyes blank as she stared directly into the security camera.

He frowned. Bridges replayed the last section of the tape. This time, instead of watching Sara's face, he studied what she was wearing. An over-size sweatshirt shrouded her upper body, hanging down low enough that it skimmed her upper thighs. The sweatshirt was familiar—it was his—but that wasn't what grabbed his attention. Something glinted in her palm.

Bridges ran the tape again.

His heart pounded once, hard, at the risk she had taken. "She's got a GPS with her."

Bayard made a call. Minutes later, Lissa rang back. They had a signal.

When Sara woke it was light and they were still driving, but with a difference. Skin crawling, she examined her immediate surroundings. At some point, Lopez had ditched the van and trans-ferred her to the backseat of an SUV with darkly tinted windows. One wrist was shackled to a door handle and a blanket had been thrown over her, concealing her from anyone who might see into the car if a window was wound down or a door opened.

She lay quietly for long seconds, systematically flexing muscles and gauging her condition. Aside from a few bruises and the headache, she felt surprisingly alert.

Moving slowly, and keeping her expression slack, as if she were still fighting the drug, she eased into a sitting position and stared out of the window. The light was bright enough to hurt her eyes. She had no idea what the time was. At a guess, from the heavy traffic it wasn't early, maybe nine or ten in the morning. They were in a sizable town. A sign flashed past. Rochester.

The traffic slowed to a crawl—morning gridlock. Adrenaline surged, burning away the last remnants of lethargy.

They were stopped in traffic now, with cars hemming them in from behind. The SUV inched ahead a few feet.

Helene craned around, almost unrecognizable in a fluffy gray wig that made her look like everyone's favorite grandmother. "She's awake. You should have injected her the last time we stopped."

Lopez glanced in the rearview mirror. The chill that just looking at him gave her deepened.

Wearing a fake salt-and-pepper beard, a pair of aviator sunglasses and a ball cap, she could have walked past him in the street and not recognized him.

"The syringe is in the glove compartment," he said flatly.

The SUV moved forward, then came to a halt.

Sara heard the click of the glove compartment.

Helene leaned over the backseat with the syringe in her hand, her eyes cold. "If you give me any trouble I'll shoot you. He's the one who wants you along. I don't."

Leaning over the headrest of her seat, she grabbed at Sara's arm and peeled up her sleeve, but the angle was awkward. She leaned over farther. Sara kept her arm limp until all of Helene's attention was on inserting the needle. Sucking in a breath, she twisted free, caught Helene's wrist and jerked. She sprawled forward, her wig flying. The syringe dropped to the floor.

Sara lunged for the syringe, but at that moment Lopez, aware that the syringe was rolling loose, accelerated then braked so that it rolled under the driver's seat and out of her reach.

Helene was scrabbling at the glove compartment. Lopez, once again stopped in traffic, wrenched the gun out of her fingers. "If you lose that," he said coldly, "we're both dead. Get the syringe."

Lopez swung around. Keeping the gun low so it couldn't easily be seen by anyone in adjacent vehicles, he aimed the weapon at Sara. "Move while she's getting the syringe and I will shoot. I won't kill you. I'll just shoot your arm and shatter the bone."

Helene leaned down between the two front seats, reached around and beneath Lopez's seat and retrieved both the wig and the syringe. A car horn blasted. Ahead the traffic had moved, leaving a gap of about a car's length.

As Helene slid back into her seat, Sara glimpsed a uniformed officer walking down the stationary line of cars.

Helene pulled the wig on as Lopez moved forward, closing the gap. "Something's wrong. It's Bayard up ahead. He knows where we're going."

Lopez swore. The SUV reversed with a sickening jolt, hitting the car behind. The car ahead crawled forward, creating more space and he spun the wheel, cut across the median strip and accelerated back the way they had come.

Somewhere in the distance a siren wailed. Sara

fumbled for the seat belt and eventually got it locked in place as Lopez accelerated, driving in silence.

Ten minutes out, the sirens, plural, were now distant. Lopez took a right turn, cutting away from a light flashing at a distant intersection. He turned again, this time onto a dirt road. For long minutes they drove through rolling farmland dotted with houses and barns, the road empty, the countryside peaceful and silent.

Helene had a road map out on her knee and a cell phone to her ear. "Take the next left," she said tersely. "The airfield's just outside of Middleport."

Instead of turning, Lopez continued to barrel straight ahead.

"What are you doing?"

"Stop talking and listen."

The faint pulse of a chopper registered over the sound of the car engine.

"So what's the solution?" Helene demanded coldly. "Drive until we hit a blockade?"

"We forget about the airfield and walk across the border."

Lopez's flat gaze, checking on her in the rear-view mirror, sent a ripple of unease through Sara. Even if that was Bayard and his men chasing them, there was no easy way out for her. Shackled to the rear passenger door, she was out of options.

Helene whipped around in her seat, the gun back in her hand, the sound of a round being chambered was almost drowned out by the rotors of the chopper, now almost directly overhead. "It's her. She's got a tracking device."

The car swerved. Helene was flung sideways. A shot discharged, shattering the side passenger window directly behind Lopez's head. His hand snaked out, wrapped around her wrist and wrenched her hand back at a painful angle, aiming the barrel of the weapon at the roof of the car. "Shoot her and I'll shoot you. This is where she becomes useful."

Helene's face contorted. The gun discharged again, blowing a hole in the roof. The detonation was punctuated by the squeal of locked tires as the car fishtailed. Sara jackknifed, bracing her legs against the back of the seat as the car careered out of control. Seconds later the side of the SUV bounced off a bank, spun almost three hundred and sixty degrees and plunged nose-first down a hill.

Twenty-Six

When Sara came to, Lopez, the cap and beard gone, and blood streaming from multiple cuts to his face, was hauling her out of the backseat. Sharp pain seared up her right arm. Seconds later, he unsnapped the cuff around her wrist and jerked her to her feet. She staggered and gripped the bent and twisted car door. Pain shot up her arm again. It wasn't broken, but she must have come close.

She checked inside the car and the immediate surrounds, but she couldn't see any sign of Helene. Either she was crushed beneath the vehicle, or she had gone out on her own.

Lopez jammed the barrel of a gun into the side of her neck. "Walk, or I'll shoot."

Pines towered, the canopy cutting out the sun as they climbed. The thick layer of needles muffled their footsteps. A chopper skimmed overhead, hidden by the thick branches. In the distance she could hear the slam of car doors.

Lopez continued to push her ahead of him. They stopped to rest on a ridge. Disoriented, she tried to get her bearings. The sun was almost directly overhead, which didn't help, and there were pines on all sides, flowing in ranked formation, which indicated that they were in a managed plantation, not a wilderness area.

Lopez produced a GPS then slipped a cell phone out of his pocket. In the distance a second helicopter hung in the air, and she realized what was happening. They were close to the border, possibly in Canada already, walking toward a prearranged rendezvous.

He crouched down, put the GPS on the ground and dialed a number. Taking a deep breath, she threw herself down a bank, rolled to her feet and hit the ground running. She could hear Lopez behind her, the thud of footfalls, the whipping sound as branches rasped against his clothing.

Fingers caught in her hair and bunched in the material of her sweatshirt. Her feet slid from under her. As she fell, she twisted and rolled. Something punched into the small of her back. Lopez's knee.

Panic, raw and visceral exploded. She twisted, using the downslope of the hill to knock him off balance. The hand in her hair released, the gun went flying. Something snapped beneath her weight, a small sapling. Then she was in midair, falling.

Iron-hard ground punched all the breath from her lungs and for a stunned moment she stared blankly at the sky, unable to breathe. Lopez appeared, looming over her.

There was a deep sting in her arm. Then he was gone, withdrawing silently into the trees.

Oxygen shoved into her lungs. She doubled up, rolling onto her side, gasping at the painful rip of air. She pushed to her knees, and rubbed at the numb tingling area where Lopez had injected her, as she took stock.

Lopez was nowhere in sight, although that didn't mean he was gone. If he had simply wanted to cross the border and disappear, he would have left her. Instead, he had taken the time to inject her.

Sucking in a deep breath, she began to climb

back up the bank she'd fallen down. Aside from the sound of the helicopters, the forest was utterly silent.

Gripping the trunk of a pine, she pulled herself up and over the lip of the bank. He had dropped the gun. Unless he had retrieved it, it had to be here somewhere. She could see the disturbed patch of pine needles where they had fought, the smashed sapling at the edge of the drop-off.

Something flickered at the edge of her vision. Her head jerked around. Adrenaline pumped. Lopez, melting into the trees. A split second later her gaze locked with Bayard's.

Shock held her immobile for long seconds. He was standing amongst the trees, almost invisible in a dull green T-shirt and camouflage trousers. She shook her head, indicating she didn't want him coming to help her, then stared directly at the last place she had seen Lopez. When she looked back, Bayard was gone.

Head feeling progressively heavier as the drug took effect, her limbs already clumsy, Sara searched the small clearing, but she couldn't find the gun, which meant Lopez must have come back to collect it.

With the gun no longer a viable objective, she

moved a few paces to her left. Lopez was using her as bait, therefore he would want to keep her in sight and would have to move with her. When he shifted position, Bayard would have an opportunity to pinpoint him.

She continued to scan the forest as she sat down, propping her back against a tree so she would stay upright and awake. A shadow materialized, more forest than man, but the cold prickling at her nape told her it was Lopez. The way he had disappeared into the trees after he had injected her replayed itself. He hadn't run, he had *withdrawn*.

The shadow disappeared and she blinked, fighting drowsiness, abruptly caught between two worlds, one warm with dappled sunshine filtering through the trees, the other, icy-cold and filled with shadows. Stein.

A flicker of movement snapped her back to sunlight.

Not Stein. Lopez. And it was Bayard he wanted—his focus intent, malicious.

The breeze lifted slightly, a branch shivered.

Something moved off to one side. *Lopez.*

On the opposite side of the glade, a figure Sara hadn't noticed before, also dressed in camouflage, was briefly visible. Lopez took a half step to make his shot. Simultaneously, Bayard, who until that point had been standing absolutely silent and still, stepped out of the shadows, a rifle nestled in the crook of his shoulder, and fired two shots at Lopez in quick succession. In contrast to the popping sound of the pistol, the sharp crack of rifle fire echoed in the valley below. Lopez toppled forward.

Bayard walked through the trees and stood over Lopez for a few seconds, the rifle still in the ready-to-fire position. The second man, now recognizable as Bridges, joined him.

Sara blinked at the textbook simplicity of the action. A decoy to draw Lopez out. No messing around with handguns—just two businesslike shots from a weapon that had guaranteed accuracy over long range. Clinical and effective.

Seconds later, Bayard dropped down beside her and gripped her arms. "What's he given you?"

"He injected me with a sedative. It's the second shot. I slept for several hours before. I don't think it's fatal, but I don't know how much he gave me."

Bayard's face went bone-white. "You are not going to die." He made her lie down, spoke briefly into his lip mike then reached for his cell phone and stabbed the speed dial.

When he couldn't get service, he stood upright, moving to a slightly higher position, standing almost exactly where Lopez had when he had made his call.

Lopez. A stark shudder went through her.

The low timbre of Bayard's voice indicated that the call had finally connected.

Her lids slid closed.

Heart pounding at the paleness of her expression, Marc shook Sara awake. "Wake up, honey. We need to walk."

Her eyes flickered, fixed on him, and she smiled sleepily. *"Bien sûr." Of course.* And for an eerie moment something inside him shifted, refocused.

"Get me out of these trees and I'll fly."

The pulse of helicopter rotors snapped him back to hot sunlight and the warm scents of earth and pines.

Sara's eyes had closed again. He shook her slightly, until she was able to focus on him. "Try to stay awake. It'll take a few minutes to get down to the road, another few minutes flight time to Rochester."

It took twenty minutes to reach the road, fifteen to touch down in Buffalo—not Rochester—where a specialist medical team and a toxicologist were waiting.

Marc stayed close to Sara, using his clout to stonewall state and federal authorities and generally piss off the medics. He pulled rank, using the federal investigation and the fact that Sara was a federal witness to justify his presence in the emergency suite.

A suit from admin had balked at Bridges, who stood outside the door, still dressed in a faded green T-shirt and DPM trousers, a businesslike Glock holstered at his thigh. But when Bridges had politely produced his National Intelligence ID and referred the suit to him, the protest had dissolved.

Marc watched like a hawk as intravenous lines were put in, demanding to know what drugs were being used, and the precise quantities. He knew enough about the procedures to be damned irritating, but he didn't care. This was about Sara. And if anyone slipped up, he wanted to know about it before it happened.

An hour later, in a quiet private room Marc had demanded Sara be moved to rather than the much noisier recovery room, she came out of her unconscious state.

Her gaze fixed on his. His grip on her fingers tightened. And just like that, happiness surged, making him feel as giddy as a kid at Christmas. "How are you feeling?"

"Horrible."

"That's because you should still be out cold."

She blinked. "I need coffee."

"I'll get it."

He poked his head out the door. Bridges was still on guard, looking toned down now that he'd changed out of the camouflage gear and into street clothes, but still dangerous enough that the medical staff were giving him a wide berth.

Five minutes later, Bridges walked in with a foam cup of coffee. Two minutes later, he reappeared with a second cup. The reason he hadn't carried two at once was habit, pure and simple. He was on guard duty, which meant he needed to keep one hand free to go for his weapon if he needed to. The pedantic attention to detail was one of the things Marc liked most about Bridges.

He had to help Sara hold the cup, because she was still shaky. By the time she had sipped her way through the first coffee, she was steady enough to hold the second cup on her own.

A nurse, carrying a clipboard, stepped into the room. "I heard she's awake." When she saw the empty foam cups she frowned, but didn't say anything. Marc figured she thought he'd had the coffee.

She took Sara's pulse and fixed Marc with the kind of look he hadn't been on the receiving end of since his mother had swatted him for dragging his grandfather's air rifle out of the gun cupboard at age four. "She's not supposed to have anything but water. According to the toxicologist, she was injected with a cocktail of drugs. So far he's identified the constituents for Temazepam and Rohypnol. There are even traces of some kind of antihistamine. I heard she also swallowed some kind of transmittor. The last thing she needed was a dose of caffeine."

"I feel fine," Sara said flatly. "I'd like to go home."

The nurse shook her head, checked Sara's blood pressure, asked her a few questions and made some notes then walked to the door. "The doctor will be along in a few minutes."

Thirty minutes later, the doctor was convinced

that Sara was well enough to leave. If they didn't let her go, having Marc and Bridges on the premises was going to be an even worse pain in the ass than it already had been.

Bridges produced the keys for an SUV he'd had delivered to the hospital parking lot. He had also arranged a flight to D.C., complete with an attending doctor. The private jet was waiting, fueled and ready at the airport.

Marc opened the back door of the SUV and helped Sara in before walking around to the other side to join her. Bridges climbed behind the wheel.

Now that Sara was away from the prying eyes of the doctor and nurses, her energy had evaporated in a rush. She was having trouble holding her head up, and staying awake.

He had expected it, which was why he had arranged for a doctor to attend her on the flight. He had wanted her away from Buffalo and into a safer environment, but he hadn't wanted to take any unnecessary risks.

Sara smothered a yawn. "Did you find Helene?"

He buckled them both in and pulled her head down on his shoulder. "Helene got away. She had a plane waiting at a private airfield. She's free. For now."

Twenty-Seven

Two weeks later, Grand Cayman Island

Dawn limned the sleek lines of a luxury yacht as two men, dressed in chinos, polo shirts and deck shoes, stepped onto the dock. A few minutes later an older woman, casually but elegantly dressed in white drawstring pants and a white shirt, her face obscured by a wide-brimmed straw hat and dark glasses, emerged from the sleek yacht, assisted by a third man, this one wearing a business suit.

Helene Reichmann walked briskly to the waiting car. They had docked just after midnight; it was five-thirty now. They would be gone before seven. Just minutes ago, she had rung the bank manager who oversaw her affairs at his home and set up an appointment—before the bank officially opened for business. Harold Aubrey, a man she had dealt with on several occasions, and whom she paid well to accommodate her unusual needs, had assured complete discretion.

Although, this time, things were a little different. Over the past few weeks her face had been plastered across newspapers, television screens and the Internet. Unfortunately, now Aubrey knew exactly who she was and where her money came from. A cool one million pounds sterling, with the promise of a further two million on safe completion of the funds transfer, was the incentive she had offered. The threat that she would expose his links to South American drug cartels and provide Interpol with details of the enormous amount of money he had accepted in bribes over the last twenty years was her guarantee that he would behave with his usual discreet greed.

Aubrey was waiting at the rear entrance of the bank. A quick reconnaissance by the security expert she had brought with her ascertained that for the time she would be in the bank—little more than fifteen minutes—the night watchman had been dismissed and the security cameras disengaged.

Minutes later, Helene took a seat in Aubrey's elegant office, with its panoramic view of the harbor. Two of her bodyguards remained with her. The third was downstairs, watching the entrances to the bank. The lure of the cash aside, she didn't trust Aubrey any more than she would a rattlesnake.

She checked her watch again as Aubrey accessed the bank's computer and brought up her account. When he was finished, he left his chair, indicating that she take his place in order to enter the access codes.

Helene extracted a slip of paper from her bag. The days when she could remember the codes, which were regularly changed, were long gone. Instead she used a simple, easily remembered transposition code as a security measure. And even if someone managed to get hold of the slip of paper and decode it, it wouldn't do them any good. The one unalterable condition of this particular account was that money couldn't be moved unless she was personally here.

She entered the series of codes, submitted to both a retinal and a thumbprint scan, then handed Aubrey the transfer instructions and waited for him to clear the transaction.

Cold satisfaction wound through her as Aubrey initiated the transfer. Bayard had frozen her accounts in the USA. He had even reached offshore, using reciprocal security agreements with a number of European and Middle East countries to close her out of a number of those accounts, but he had only affected a percentage of her operating capital.

She was her father's daughter, and he had taught her well. Money was power. The equation was simple. To maintain power, she had to control the money, and for over fifty years she had. Despite Bayard's intervention, nothing had changed. The cabal was dismantled, a great many valuable assets frozen, but she, and approximately one billion pounds sterling, remained. It was a pittance compared to what she had once possessed, but it was enough to guarantee a new, improved future in a different country, with a new identity. Her father had achieved the transition sixty-five years ago; she would achieve it now.

Aubrey adjusted his spectacles. Helene checked her wristwatch. The transfer was taking longer than expected.

A small, inane fact registered. Aubrey was sweating, despite the fact that the air-conditioning kept the entire bank cool to the point of chilliness.

Alarm feathered her spine.

She lunged for the computer and encountered unexpected resistance from Aubrey. Simultaneously, the door burst open. Her fingers clawed at the Walther she kept in her handbag. Aubrey was on the floor, clutching the laptop. A sharp burst of gunfire registered. Something hard hit her in the back—the hand of one of her bodyguards, she realized, as he shoved her to the floor.

Gunfire exploded. Within the space of seconds, the room was filled with men dressed in dark clothing, holding gleaming black weapons, balaclavas pulled over their heads.

Using the desk as cover, she scrambled toward Aubrey, who was cowering in the corner, and fired two rounds at point-blank range into his chest. He slumped over the laptop and she panicked, grabbing at the machine. The screen glowed, riveting her attention. The transaction hadn't been completed.

Something hard and cold was shoved against her throat. Dazed, she stared at Bayard, cool and urbane in a suit.

"Touch that keyboard," he said softly, "and I will shoot."

* * *

Helene Reichmann, alias Elizabeth Cohen and Elizabeth Richmond, was finally in custody, along with a cache of diamonds which had been recovered from her yacht and a staggering amount of money. But the morning's work wasn't over.

Marc lifted his phone to his ear. "Where's Dennison now?"

Bridges answered. "The sneaky bastard was searching the yacht. He's just swum to shore."

"Bring him in."

Dennison agreed to talk, for a price. Marc had created the fiction that Dennison was legally dead; he wanted to stay that way. He had no intention of returning to the States. All he wanted was to remain in the islands and live out his last years in peace, yada, yada, yada…

Marc studied Dennison. He was a curious mixture of character traits and motivations. Neither black nor white, Dennison existed in a gray world. He had been both an FBI agent and a criminal. He had loved his wife and cared for her even after she had become a quadriplegic in a car accident, and yet he had committed murder. He had been Lopez's right-hand man for years, then had turned federal witness and supplied them with vital information. "If you step on U.S. soil, I'll put you in prison."

"Believe me, I don't want to go back."

Marc picked up his briefcase and shrugged into his jacket. "I'm going out for five minutes."

Dennison's gaze darted to the desk where the cuff keys were prominently displayed. The previous year he had escaped from CIA custody by knocking out an agent with a ketchup bottle, unlocking his cuffs, then cuffing the agent before he had come around. Marc was well aware of the details.

This time he had made it easy for Dennison, but not too easy. He would have to climb out the window, then he would have to make it through the bank's security and the local police.

Dennison's optimism flickered. "You know where I live."

Marc paused at the door. "That's right."

"I figured."

Dennison climbed out of the window, scuttled into the nearby shrubs and belly crawled. It took thirty minutes. During that time he must have twisted in a weird way, because he pinched a nerve in his back. He spent ten minutes in fiery agony, too frightened to move until the pain started to ebb, then an armed guard almost stepped on him, and that galvanized him into action. When he was free and clear, he hobbled in the direction of the beachfront. He stopped beneath the pilings of a pier to retrieve a spare weapon, duplicate passport and a bulging wallet he'd stored there after swimming to shore—just in case he'd had to make a run for it—then headed for the launch he'd hired.

Once he was on board, he cast off, started the motor and headed out to sea. He found some anti-inflammatory pills, gulped them down with a glass of tepid water and waited for the pain to ease.

He had enough food and fuel to last him a few days, and a radio if the weather turned bad and he got into trouble. When he was feeling better and he judged the coast to be clear, he would come back in at night, abandon the boat, call a contact he had and charter a flight out.

Costa Rica, or Belize, maybe. Anywhere but Colombia.

Once he was out of the Caribbean and away

from Bayard's influence, he would decide where he went from there. Damned if he would touch Africa or the Middle East—too dangerous. He was thinking the South Seas, Australia, maybe even New Zealand—if he could weasel his way past their security.

When the searing pain in his back was blunted and he judged that he was far enough offshore, he dropped anchor and made himself a cup of coffee.

Moving gingerly, in case he aggravated his back, he pulled out his wallet and emptied the contents onto the table. The glitter of the diamonds didn't take away any pain, but they made him feel ten years younger.

There wasn't enough to make him rich, just enough to ensure his retirement.

Always cover your ass.

Twenty-Eight

She *was* pregnant.

Sara walked out of the medical clinic in Georgetown feeling light-headed and decidedly different. She had tried a test kit that morning. Then, to confirm, she'd made an appointment and had a second, more conclusive test. At four weeks, it was too early to guarantee that she would stay pregnant, but the doctor was optimistic. Lots of women her age were having first babies, she was in good health and her blood pressure was fine. As long as she took it easy, he couldn't foresee any problems.

She caught a cab at a taxi rank, slipped into the backseat and gave the driver Marc's address. Her address now.

The changes were dizzying.

For days now she'd had to hide her mounting anticipation when she'd missed her usual period date. There had been nothing weird or psychic about it, just a normal, hyped-up, burning hope.

Marc rang as she reached the apartment. He had just landed at Dulles and he would be home in forty minutes, give or take the usual rush hour hell.

An hour later, Sara opened the door, slid her arms around Bayard's neck and kissed her man.

He dropped his briefcase on the floor, walked her backward into the room and kicked the door closed.

Long, drugging minutes later, Marc lifted his head and jerked at his tie. "I need a shower before we go any further."

And, from the look of the dark circles under his eyes, a good night's sleep. "You found Helene?"

He shrugged out of his jacket and tossed it over the back of a chair then pulled her back into his arms. "Uh-huh."

The guarded remoteness of his gaze sent a faint chill down her spine. "How?"

"You're not going to like it."

"Dennison?"

"He followed the diamonds."

So predictable.

She studied Marc's movements, more concerned with his well-being than Dennison's. His clinical approach to his job no longer worried her. She had made the mistake of assuming that an essential hardness—a lack of emotion—went with the job, and had made him the way he was, but she knew now that had never been the case. Behind the cool control there was plenty of emotion. Marc was, quite simply, a committed perfectionist. Whatever he did, he did one hundred percent. The reason he had been so successful was because he never let a detail slip. He followed every lead, no matter how insignificant, and he didn't flinch from being a hard-ass.

Marc was also committed to his country and to justice. He had taken an oath and he lived by it—a fact Saunders had failed to understand. "Where's Dennison now?"

His gaze was wary. "He was last seen catching a flight to Mexico."

"You didn't arrest him?"

"Not exactly. Dennison knows more about the running of the Chavez cartel than anyone else

alive. Names, addresses, operational procedures…
We've got enough now to close them down completely."

Sara went still inside. There it was again: the emotion. He had let Dennison go.

She wrapped her arms around his neck. "You are not cut out for this work."

His grin was slow, his hands even slower as they took a leisurely tour of the curve of her butt, and the sensitive line of her back before pulling her close. "Which is why I've resigned, effective immediately. The case is wrapped up. From here on in, the paper pushers can take it."

Sara tried not to show her delight. She loved Marc; hated the job. "If you hadn't done that, I would have made trouble."

Marc pulled her down into his lap. "I know it. Intelligence work is something I never intended to do. Don't forget, I started out studying law."

"Then got sidetracked when Steve became obsessed about Uncle Todd."

He shrugged. "It ticked me off. Todd Fischer was like a father to me. Some of the best times I had as a kid were either at his place, or your folks'. When Todd disappeared, your father stepped in.

I've always had a vested interest in the Fischer family."

"More than a vested interest." She pulled his hand to her abdomen. "You know that wedding you mentioned? Let's make it sooner, rather than later."

They were married two weeks later in the tiny chapel on the Bayard estate. The wedding, which would have caused a stir in either D.C. or Shreveport, was kept firmly under wraps. Lopez was dead, and Helene Reichmann was in prison, finally making it safe for a number of federal witnesses on the Witness Security Program, including Steve and Taylor, to resume their normal lives. But there was still the press to contend with. The guest list was tiny, but included Steve, Taylor and their new baby, a seven-pound bundle of joy they had named Faith. And Steve had insisted on giving her away.

Marc's mother, Mariel, flew in from Florida to take care of any of the wedding details Marc's ex-PA, Lissa, had missed. Bridges was the best man, and Sara had asked Lissa—who, after the hostage crisis, had put both herself and Bridges out of their misery by moving in with him—to be her bridesmaid. The small group filled the high, vaulted chapel, with its simple arched windows, heady with the scent of freshly picked roses. The vicar and Amalie's husband, George, an accountant with the city council, stood out like sore thumbs as being the only males present who weren't linked to either law enforcement or the military.

The reception was held on the terrace and catered entirely by Amalie and her daughters, who had also attended the ceremony. The food was simple and elegant; the champagne, French; the sunset clear and pure, with a golden afterglow.

Twenty-Nine

Vassigny, France, Two months later

The road to Vassigny was still narrow and precipitous, forced as it was to wind through the darkly wooded slopes and the stony plateaus of the Jura Mountains that marked the Franco Swiss border. To the east, Mont d'Or thrust up almost a kilometer and a half, its snowcapped peak piercing a brilliantly blue sky. Closer, to the south, vast tracts of forest known as the Parc Natural Regional du Haut-Jura dominated the landscape.

The sign for Vassigny loomed and the road became, if possible, even narrower. Stony pasture predominantly used for dairy farming and the production of the famous Comte cheeses gave way to lush vineyards. The landscape was familiar, and yet, not. Modern barns and houses had sprouted, along with a small airport. Signs were everywhere, indicating tourist attractions, cafés and accommodation. Marc slowed for a corner, seconds later the town appeared.

The trip to Vassigny had been a natural choice, both to put the past to rest and answer a number of questions. Sara needed to know what had happened to Armand and his family—and they both wanted to find out about Cavanaugh.

Now that she had the memories, they were a part of her, as valid and real as her memories of her parents and Eleanor and Todd Fischer. She had loved her present-day family and grieved for them; she kept their photos, remembered important dates and cherished their memories. As distant as those war years were now, it didn't change the fact that she needed to do the same for the people she had loved back then. She needed closure.

After several weeks of searching, Bayard had managed to locate Cavanaugh's file. The manila folder had been mottled and darkened with age. When she'd opened it, the paper was yellowed, the typescript old-fashioned, as if someone had thumped it out on a manual typewriter, which was exactly what had happened. At the bottom of one of the pages was a neatly scrawled signature.

All the hairs at the base of her neck had tightened as she'd studied the strong, slanting script.

Marc had traced the signature with his finger. He didn't have her memories, but he had recognized that the handwriting was eerily similar to his own.

She had checked the document. Of course, it was the official secrecy act.

Marc's expression had been wry. "Standard procedure. He was in Intelligence."

The contents of the file were sparse, just four photocopied pages. Marc Cavanaugh, originally from New Orleans, had been seconded to the SOE in Britain in 1942—on request, because his mother had been from Lyon. He had parachuted into France in 1943 on a high-priority mission to escort an English agent across the Swiss border. The last entry was a letter to Cavanaugh's parents advising them that their son was missing in action. The date was 1944.

Sara had read the letter through twice. It hadn't said what happened to him, or how he had died.

France had still been occupied. A lot of soldiers had gone missing in action and their bodies had never been recovered. Sometimes soldiers had been reported dead but had actually survived.

She needed to know.

A few days later, Bayard had produced another sheet of paper, this one covered in his own handwriting. It was a brief genealogy. "I thought the name was familiar. Turns out that Marc Cavanaugh's aunt was Heloise Louviere."

The sense that a piece of a subtle, complex puzzle had just fallen into place had been strong. The coincidence was too powerful to be pure chance. Heloise Louviere had married Jean Bayard and had been Marc's grandmother.

Sara held her breath as she studied Vassigny's main street, and the cluster of hostels, cafés and sports shops catering to tourists and cross-country skiers.

The familiar frontage of a bakery registered. "Pull over. There."

Inside, the shop was small and dark, the plain rolls and baguettes still in evidence, but accompanied by a mouthwatering array of both savory and sweet pastries.

Gaspar Autin was behind the counter. He was

barely recognizable, thinner than she remembered, his thick dark hair, gray, his eyes rheumy. Her heart swelled. She felt like flinging herself into his arms, but it couldn't be Gaspar.

It was his son, Louis.

Her throat closed up. "When did Gaspar pass away?"

Louis's gaze was curious. "My father has been dead for more than twenty years. When did you meet him?"

"It was a long time ago. But maybe you can help me. I'm looking for Pascal Dutetre, the grandson of Armand de Thierry. Does he live in his grandfather's house?"

"The de Thierry place. *Oui.*" He cocked his head to one side. "Are you sure I don't know you, madame. You seem familiar to me."

Sara shook her head. "*Non, je regrette.* I've never met you before. And the Château? Does Pascal own that?"

Louis shook his head. "Armand let that go, gladly, you understand? After the SS had it…" He made an expressive face. "No one wanted to sleep there. The Château is now a hotel, with a four-star restaurant. They get a lot of German tourists." He shook his head. "Who could know?"

* * *

Marc drove to the house. As they walked up the path to the front door, shivers ran up and down her spine.

After a phone call explaining that they were distant relations of Marc Cavanaugh, a meeting had been arranged.

Armand's grandson was waiting for them at the front door of the house. Pascal, a far cry from the skinny child she remembered, had filled out and now had grandchildren of his own. He looked remarkably like his grandfather.

Goose bumps feathered her skin as they stepped into the dim hallway. For a moment the déjà vu was so strong she almost expected to see Armand. Instead, a cheerful, elegant woman with iron-gray hair—Pascal's wife, Marceline—appeared to usher them into the study.

Pascal made introductions and Marceline brought coffee and what looked like pastries from Louis's bakery. Sunlight slanted through the windows as cups and plates were handed out, and the initial awkwardness evaporated as they settled on the subject of the Second World War and the role the Special Operations Executive had played in Vassigny's Maquis.

"I never met Cavanaugh, unfortunately." Pascal's gaze settled on Sara. "But I did meet Sara Weiss. One moment."

He rummaged in a heavy armoire and produced an ancient photograph album filled with small, old-fashioned, black-and-white snaps and a few sepia-toned ones.

He pointed to a wedding photograph. His gaze connected with Sara's. "It's a remarkable coincidence, but you look very like my stepgrandmother. I still remember her clearly. She tried to teach me mathematics."

Sara studied the photograph. Unlike the living, breathing reality of Louis and Pascal, the photograph failed to evoke heart-pounding emotion. She remembered dressing for the photo, the charade of a wedding ceremony that had never actually taken place, because neither Armand nor Sara had been prepared to make a promise before God that would not be carried out. They had settled on the legal paperwork, signed by the priest and left it at that. "And you weren't a good pupil?"

He grimaced. "Not when it came to calculus."

Bayard leaned forward on the couch, his thigh brushing hers, drawing her back to the present.

He directed the conversation back to the events following Sara's shooting.

Pascal closed the album and placed it on the desk. "Reichmann and his SS officers went back to Berlin. De Vallois was killed, but his Maquis continued to operate. Grandpère was incarcerated for a short time, but they released him. With Stein and Reichmann gone, there were no charges to answer and the prisons were already full. Besides, the Germans needed him to run the farms." His expression was wry. "Food! They could not function without his cheese."

An image of the truck loaded with cheeses and fresh milk, the false bottom containing its most precious cargo, headed for the Swiss border was suddenly vivid in her mind. With resources stretched thin, and starvation common, Armand had cleverly gauged the value of his products. Even the Germans had to eat. When they had seen his truck, the last thing they had wanted to think about was the possibility that Armand's food delivery was a cover for the activities of the Maquis.

Her fingers closed around her cup. "When did Armand die?"

Pascal's gaze grew intent, and for a moment

she wondered if he had guessed. Although, that wasn't possible.

He pushed to his feet. "Come with me."

A short walk later, through fields that skirted the village, they arrived at the church and a small cemetery. Pascal gestured at a headstone and the faded date, 1973.

Relief made her feel light-headed and a little weepy. Not only had Armand survived the war, he had lived to the ripe old age of eighty-three.

Pascal laid a hand on the stone, his affection clear. "He used to say that his *vin jaune* preserved him. I'm not so sure he was wrong."

"What about the American agent, Cavanaugh? Did he leave?"

"The Americaine? *Non.* He stayed with De Vallois's men. He ran the Maquis after de Vallois's death."

Her hand tightened on Marc's. "But he didn't survive the war."

Pascal's face tightened with regret. *"Non,"* he said softly. "Marc Cavanaugh was killed in action."

"When?"

"Sixth of June, 1944."

The date of the Normandy Invasion.

Her chest felt as though it was being squeezed by a vise. "Why did he stay? Why didn't he leave? He was with the SOE—"

"He could not," Pascal said simply. "He was in love with the Anglaise. When she was shot by Reichmann, he chose to stay and fight."

Bayard's arms came around her.

He was safe…*here, now*…and suddenly she knew him with absolute clarity. He had loved her. He had never given up on her and he had never left her, not even when she had died.

Bayard's voice broke the silence. "Why didn't Armand bury Sara in the de Thierry family plot?"

Pascal shook his head. "That could never happen. They were married, but it was only a paper marriage to fool the Germans. It was not…appropriate."

He walked farther on and gestured at a small private plot, set a little apart. "You see? He knew they were in love."

Two simple, lichen-encrusted headstones sprouted side by side, one with an American eagle carved into the stone, the other with a fleur-de-lis, the national symbol of France. The in-

scriptions were simple—names, dates and a brief
phrase on both:

Jusqu'à ce que nous réunissions encore.
Until we meet again.

New York Times bestselling author

MAGGIE SHAYNE

Before she joined Reaper in hunting Gregor's gang of
rogue bloodsuckers, Topaz was gunning for just one vamp:
Jack Heart. The gorgeous con man had charmed his way
into her bed, her heart and her bank account.

Now she and Jack are supposedly on the same side.
As Reaper's ragtag outfit scatters, Topaz sets out to solve
her mystery: what really happened to her mother, who
died when Topaz was a baby? And what stake does
Jack have in discovering the truth about her past?
Topaz is sure he's up to something—but her suspicions
are at war with her desires....

LOVER'S BITE

**Available the first week of May 2008
wherever books are sold!**

MIRA®

FIONA BRAND

32563 KILLER FOCUS	___ $6.99 U.S.	___ $8.50 CAN.
32546 DOUBLE VISION	___ $6.99 U.S.	___ $8.50 CAN.
32289 BODY WORK	___ $6.99 U.S.	___ $8.50 CAN.

(limited quantities available)

TOTAL AMOUNT	$ _____
POSTAGE & HANDLING	$ _____
($1.00 FOR 1 BOOK, 50¢ for each additional)	
APPLICABLE TAXES*	$ _____
TOTAL PAYABLE	$ _____

(check or money order—please do not send cash)

To order, complete this form and send it, along with a check or money order for the total above, payable to MIRA Books, to: **In the U.S.:** 3010 Walden Avenue, P.O. Box 9077, Buffalo, NY 14269-9077; **In Canada:** P.O. Box 636, Fort Erie, Ontario, L2A 5X3.

Name: _____
Address: _____ City: _____
State/Prov.: _____ Zip/Postal Code: _____
Account Number (if applicable): _____

075 CSAS

*New York residents remit applicable sales taxes.
*Canadian residents remit applicable GST and provincial taxes.

MIRA®

www.MIRABooks.com

MFB0508BL